The Bike Messenger

Ruth Foster

Front Cover Photograph © Jon Foster
Back Cover Photograph © John Logoyda

ISBN-13: 978-0-9891435-3-0

To family, as always.

Ruth Foster

Prologue

"A toast to your most recent acquisition!"

Loch Douglas Daziel acknowledged his friend Robert's words by a slight downward nod of the head. Despite his normal reserve, Loch could not keep a broad grin from spreading across his face.

"It's truly a magnificent work of art," Robert said, refilling his champagne glass and taking a step closer to the canvas.

Loch moved alongside his friend and studied the painting anew. "It takes my breath away," he said slowly. "I could never tire of looking at it."

"And yet you told me you're going to lend it to the Scottish Trust Museum for the next 80 years," Robert said dryly. "Explain that to me."

"By loaning it, I'm preventing the Trust from selling it. As long as the painting is exhibited, the loan will be renewed in perpetuity. And, as the agreement is ironclad, if something happens to me, no greedy relative can come out of the woodwork and claim it."

"Very clever." Robert was silent for a moment, and then he spoke again. "But why the Scottish Trust Museum? Why not here in New York? If you gave it to the Guggenheim, you could see it anytime you wanted. You wouldn't have to cross an ocean first!"

"It just seemed right. After all, modern golf was developed in Scotland. This might be the oldest painting in existence to depict the game as well as the last commissioned piece of work of Matea Raphael."

"Matea Raphael – the Italian painter known for his more natural portraits? Could it be?" Robert couldn't keep the excitement from his voice.

"Well, as you know, letters were found in the MacDonald estate discussing a portrait Lord MacDonald had ordered painted of his two sons. MacDonald was quite proud of the fact that Raphael had consented to the task, though in the same letter he complained about the length of time it would take Raphael to travel from Italy to his estate.

"There is Raphael's signature, of course, on the painting that has been authenticated. In addition, three independent experts have studied the painting's form and content. Each one came back saying they believed it to be between 1400 and 1420 because of the dress and golf clubs. Then, when paint and canvas samples were sent to three different labs – two of them anonymously – the date was confirmed as being early 15th century."

"And as for it going to Scotland," Loch continued, "I'm not really sure. Maybe it's a gesture to my grandmother."

"The one who wanted you named Loch?"

"Insisted is more like it."

"Did she ever tell you why?"

"No. When I was about ten, I found out that in Scotland lakes are called lochs. I asked her if she knew."

"Did she?"

"She snorted and said she of course she did. That's why she insisted on my name. Said she didn't care if my mother liked it or not."

"Your mother never came across as weak. What made her give in to her mother-in-law?"

"One million dollars."

Robert gasped audibly, and then there was a moment of incredulous silence.

"You never told me that," Robert said slowly, once he had regained his voice. "Doesn't that make you even more curious as to why your grandmother insisted on you being name *Loch*?"

"Not just *Loch*, but *Loch Douglas*. As to being made more curious, no, not really."

Loch's tone was casual, but Robert insisted. "You must have been curious! She paid half a million dollars for each name!"

"If I had shown curiosity, it would have shown she had power over me."

As Loch said these words, Robert recognized the tone. It was calm but blandly emotionless. It gave nothing away. It was one of Loch's most valuable weapons when it came to business negotiations. It belied the ruthlessness with which he could so suddenly strike.

Robert gave a sideways glance at his friend. "You said giving the painting to the Scotland Trust Museum was a gesture to your grandmother. A kind gesture or a middle finger kind of gesture?"

An impertinent grin spread across Loch's face. "My grandmother came to this country when she was fifteen years old. She has traveled the world several times, but she has never returned to Scotland."

Loch's grin became cheekier as he continued. "As you know, she is an avid golf player. I told her I would give her this painting if she told me the origins of my name."

"And what did she say?"

"What do you think?" Loch asked rhetorically. "This is my grandmother we are talking about. All she did was snort. Then she said it would behoove me not to hang the painting in my bedroom, as she would be over daily to look at it. She suggested the far wall of the living room, as then my bedroom dalliances could remain private, and she could see it while sitting in her favorite chair."

"Bedroom dalliances?"

"Her choice of words, not mine!"

Robert started to laugh. "I get it, I get it," he said. "You wanted to show her she couldn't control you like she did your mother."

"Perhaps I just didn't want her to have a reason to visit me daily."

Robert shook his head. "Not buying that," he said. "If you didn't want her in your house, you could have just as easily donated it to the Guggenheim. Come on, admit it! You just wanted to infuriate her."

Loch was careful not to say anything out loud, but the corners of his mouth spread upward into an impudent smirk while he nodded affirmatively.

Robert let out a low whistle. "When you decide to show someone up, there's no stopping you. Still, 36 million is an awful lot to pay just to irritate someone."

One

There was a blaze of horns from cars and trucks at all four ends of the intersection. Each noisy assault was directed at a bike rider who seemed oblivious to the stir she was creating. Ignoring the traffic light, she wove between cars and trucks as if she were performing steps on point in a choreographed ballet.

A large parcel truck passed her, and the rider momentarily disappeared from sight. It wasn't until the vehicle had cleared the intersection that she was spotted again, nonchalantly holding onto a side door handle of the parcel truck and taking a break from pedaling.

The truck driver opened his window and shook his fist at her. The bike rider nodded, but she didn't let go until the truck had to slow because of traffic. Then, and only then, did she release her grip and start to pedal. When she came up to the driver's side window, she matched her speed to the truck's.

Smiling broadly, she called, "I thank you dear Mr. Truck Driver! You helped make everything come up roses!"

Then, with a wave of her hand, she sped off, her legs a flurry of motion. The truck driver could only stare at her receding figure in astonishment. He felt he should be upset. In fact, he knew he should be upset, but for some inexplicable reason, all the anger he had felt when he first discovered his errant hitchhiker had evaporated.

Was it her smile? Was it her sheer joy? Was it her blithe gratitude? And what was it she said to him?

You helped make everything come up roses!

"No, thought the truck driver as he maneuvered through the crush of cars, "I didn't help everything come up roses. You did!"

Ivy Marie Washington's bicycle, like most bike messenger's bikes, was nothing fancy. It was fixed gear, chosen for its simplicity and low weight. There were no derailleurs, shifters, cables, cable carriers, multiple chain rings, freewheel hubs, or mounting lugs that could break or require maintenance.

Though many bike messengers chose to have a good set of brakes on their bikes, Ivy had foregone that option. Every piece of gear she could remove from her frame meant less weight as well as one less thing to malfunction. If Ivy wanted to brake or abruptly decrease her speed, there was only one way to do it. She had to stop the motion of her pedals in mid-rotation, forcing the rear wheel to lock in place. This in turn would cause the tire to skid.

Although Ivy had suffered a few falls when she first started riding brakeless, she had perfected her technique when it came to controlling the skid. She knew the exact moment when to shift her weight slightly forward and when to pull up on the pedals.

Of course, there were many who were appalled at Ivy's choice to go brakeless. They would speak of danger and risk, but there was nothing they could say that Ivy didn't already know. In fact, she could cite statistics back to them. She could tell them about the

Harvard Medical School study that showed that injury rates amongst Boston bicycle messengers required time off work more than thirteen times the U.S. average. She could tell them that injury rate of that same sample group was more than three times higher than the next highest group – workers in the meat-packing industry.

What Ivy could do and what Ivy would choose to do were two very different things. Ivy would not waste time talking about risk and dire consequences. Instead, if asked about her job, Ivy would talk about the thrill, the excitement, and the adrenaline rush. She would talk about how free she felt being out in the elements, no matter the season or inclement weather. She would mention the wonderful feeling of exhaustion and how sleep comes so effortlessly after a day of physical exertion.

She would also talk about the cognitive stimulation that comes from one needing to hold a mental map of the city in one's head and the necessity of overlaying on that map, one's knowledge of normal traffic patterns, changing construction zones, and abruptly closed passageways due to unexpected blockages.

If she so chose, she could mention, too, the anthropological and psychological aspect of her job. How important it was to quickly access a situation and decide who or when a pedestrian might step off a curve, a driver might switch lanes without looking or signaling, run a stop sign, or even, in a fit of road rage, use their vehicle as a weapon, swerving suddenly so as to crush her into a parked car.

"An easy delivery," Ivy thought to herself as she pulled up in front of the Chrysler Building. "17 minutes ahead of schedule!"

With practiced ease and economy of motion, Ivy took the chain from around her waist and locked her bicycle to a small rack on the side of the building facing 42nd street. Swinging her messenger bag from her back side to the front so she could access its contents more easily, she had the slim package out and in hand before even entering the building.

"Daziel Traders ..." she thought as she punched the elevator button for the 61st floor.

Ivy had delivered a lot of packages to the Chrysler Building, but she wasn't familiar with the name Daziel Traders. "Must be yet another one of those commodity trading businesses," she thought, "with just a bunch of drones working there in white shirts and tailored suits. Boring, boring, boring."

Ivy shot out of the elevator when the doors opened and made her way to the suite number that matched the package. When she opened the door, she expected to see men and women, all dressed basically in the same black suit, sitting in rows of desks staring intently at computer screens. Instead, there were only two long wooden tables. The tables were mostly clear, with a few neat piles of documents arranged on them. A single woman was sitting at one of the tables. She was talking to a man who was standing next to her and pointing at her computer screen. At the far end of the room, by the window, two men were standing at what appeared to be a large multi-colored board.

Her eyes not leaving the screen, the woman made a motion with her hand for Ivy to come to her. Ivy strode quickly to the table and said, "I have a package for ..."

Before she could finish, the woman interrupted her brusquely. Her hand outstretched, palm open, she said, "I'll take it."

"It has to be signed by ..."

"I'll sign for it," the woman said, once again cutting off Ivy before she could finish her sentence.

Ivy stood her ground. "It has to be signed by a Mr. Loch Daziel. Although your cashmere dress is elegant and disarmingly soft, your strength still shines through. I admire you for that. Nevertheless, the fact remains that your beauty or your strength is not enough. I need a Mr. Loch Daziel."

The woman looked up from the computer screen for the first time, her eyes narrowed. Then, when she saw Ivy's huge grin, the woman burst out laughing.

Ivy didn't notice, but it was the sound of the woman's gleeful mirth that made the two men at the end of the room look up and stare in their direction. It wasn't a sound often, if ever, heard.

"Okay, then," said the woman, shaking her head humorously, "Your needs will have to be met! You can take it to him."

"And he is …"

"By the window, the taller one with the brown hair."

Ivy nodded, showing that it was now clear to her whom she needed the signature from, before beginning to purposefully walk across the room. She had not gone more than a step or two when she realized the men were staring at her.

Ivy was used to being stared at. Her best friends Nora and Wes told her it was because of her looks, but Ivy scoffed at that.

"It's my clothes," she told them firmly. "Bike messengers have to wear bright clothes. It makes us more visible."

Today she was wearing baggy turquoise shorts that had faded a bit due to being laundered numerous times over black Capri-length leggings. Her top, long-sleeved and close fitting, was a bright scarlet red.

As Ivy drew closer to the men, she began to feel her ire mount, especially toward the one the woman had pointed out as Loch Daziel. Okay, her clothes were eye-catching, she knew, but his staring went beyond rude. It was as if he wasn't just scrutinizing her. He was assessing her, sizing her up.

Ivy tossed her head contemptuously. She had no worries about coming up short!

"Mr. Daziel," she said, her voice melodious.

Ivy was not aware that she did not pronounce his name with an upward lilt at the end, as many women did unconsciously, making it seem as if they were questioning themselves. Rather, she had spoken his name with surety, as if merely stating the obvious.

Loch noticed though. In fact, he couldn't stop noticing everything about her, let alone take his eyes off of her. He had noted the fit of her shirt on her rounded breasts and the way it clung to the curve of her slender waist. He had seen how even with her legs partially covered by baggy shorts and leggings, she could not hide their length or shapeliness.

He had seen immediately that her hair was blond, almost white, and that the simple ponytail she had it pulled back in was thick and fell almost a third of the way down her back. He had found himself impatient as she came closer, wanting to know immediately the color of her eyes. He had suspected blue, but much to his surprise, they were a dark, shimmery brown. They were surrounded by a thick fringe of dark lashes, and the total contrasting effect of light hair to dark eyes he found enchanting.

He even sensed her disdain for him! He saw it when she had tossed her head. It had been a long time – if ever – that he had been so casually dismissed by a woman!

"I need you to sign for this …"

Ivy broke off mid-sentence. Without a glance at the two men, she focused all her attention on what she had seen them previously looking at. It wasn't a board – it was a painting, and oh, what a painting!

The background and much of the foreground was a palette of greens that gave the viewer an overall sense of serenity. The right side of the canvas was dominated by two boys dressed in old-fashioned clothing playing a game with sticks and a ball. On the left side, much smaller, but in exquisite balance, one could see a man and a woman, most probably the boys' parents, picnicking.

The couple's lunch, spread over a tartan blanket, could have been a complete still-life in itself. Breads and meats were in copious quantities around a basket turned up on its side. Spilling out of the basket were an assortment of fruits, including apples, pears, grapes, and even a pineapple. The fruit was drawn with such delicacy and lightness of brush that if one didn't know better, one would be tempted to try and pluck it off the canvas.

Without a word, Ivy slowly moved closer.

"You should be impressed," Ivy was told by the shorter man she only knew as "not Mr. Loch Daziel." "You are looking at an extraordinarily rare piece of early 15th century art. It may well be the earliest surviving painting of someone playing golf as well as the last piece of work by Mateo Raphael."

Clearly, the man wanted Ivy to show some bit of admiration or even awe toward him for his knowledge or for the painting. How Ivy reacted was a complete shock.

"I don't think so," Ivy said, a broad smile spreading across her face. "Now if you could sign this, Mr. Daziel," she said, backing up from the painting so she could hand the necessary form to the taller man.

"Why don't you think so?" the man asked, his gaze intent.

Ivy didn't answer, but she tapped the form on the signature line. Loch quickly scrawled his name, took the offered envelope, and then said in a seemingly casual tone, "You know that this painting has been authenticated by …"

"And you say it is by Mateo Raphael? The Italian painter Mateo Raphael?" Ivy asked, cutting him off.

Loch wasn't sure, but was there a hint of humor in this woman's voice? Loch was used to picking up and understanding all nuances that went behind someone's words, but he found himself perplexed. Had he misread her tone? And if he was correct, what could she possibly be finding humorous?

"Mateo Raphael," he said, his voice calm and giving no hint of his bafflement. "Born 1378 in Florence, Italy and died in the year 1421 or 1422. He was on his way back to Italy after his sojourn to Scotland. He had traveled there at the expense of Lord MacDonald."

"All that may be true," Ivy said, shrugging, "but he didn't paint it."

"Don't be ridiculous!" Robert, the man standing next to Loch, took a step forward. Speaking in an angry, contemptuous tone, he said, "You expect us to believe you – a simple little messenger girl?"

Seemingly unperturbed by Robert's outburst, Ivy turned once more to look at the painting.

"Just when you think everything is coming up roses," she said, once again shaking her head. Then, without a backward glance, she began to walk away.

Loch did something he had never done before in his life. He chased after a woman. His action was as surprising and as unheard of as the woman's laughter.

"Wait!" he said.

Ivy didn't slow her step until Loch moved quickly in front of her. "Wait!" he said again, "Please wait!"

Everyone in the office was staring, open-mouthed at the commotion.

"You're eating into my lunch hour," Ivy said, stepping to the side so she could continue.

"We'll eat together, then," Loch said, hastening to catch up with her.

"No thank-you."

Loch was not so easily deterred. "It will be my treat!"

Ivy didn't stop walking, but she found herself laughing at the man's audacity. "It's a kind offer, and I thank-you, but no."

"I won't take no as an answer."

Ivy stopped laughing at the same time she stopped walking.

"Mr. Daziel, you may …"

"Loch."

Ivy tried again. "Mr. Daziel …"

Once again, she was interrupted.

"Loch. You may call me Loch."

Ivy kept her body still, but her eyes flashed. "Mr. Daziel," she said in a firm voice, "this simple little messenger girl will not be having lunch with you."

Ivy heard an audible gasp, and she guessed that it came from the man who had been standing next to the woman in the woolen dress. Then, there was only silence. Everyone seemed to be waiting, but Ivy wasn't sure for what. The passing seconds seemed interminable, and Ivy felt her skin begin to prickle uneasily. She realized that everyone was looking at Loch. Following their lead, Ivy did, too.

Loch was staring at her intently. He didn't appear angry at all. Rather, he appeared amused!

Ivy felt her spine stiffen. How dare this man think she was there to entertain him! Bracing herself for a sexist barb, she looked at the man with narrowed eyes.

When the man spoke, his question was so far off the mark of what Ivy expected that it took her a moment to comprehend what it was he asked.

"Why isn't everything coming up roses?"

Ivy stood motionless for a few seconds before beginning to take the final steps to the door. The silence in the room wasn't broken until she had opened the door. She didn't turn around until she was half-way out, one foot already in the hall, a broad grin spread across her face.

"That pineapple," she said. "It's that pineapple in the painting. It keeps getting in the way."

Two

There was complete silence as the door clicked shut behind Ivy. The people at the table looked at each other with puzzled expressions. Unsure of what to say or do, they remained quiet and looked at Loch. Robert's reaction was not as subdued. He snorted derisively.

"Now we know why she's a bike messenger," he said. "That girl is too spacey for any other kind of job."

Loch didn't respond. Instead, he walked across the room and stood in front of the painting.

"It's just a pineapple," Robert said, joining him.

"There was something in her expression and her tone," Loch said slowly. "She knew something. Something she found amusing."

"I doubt she knows anything about pineapples except how they taste in piña coladas."

Loch didn't answer. He remained motionless, staring at the painting. The scene was dominated by the two boys playing golf. Why did she focus in on the pineapple?

"World to Loch," Robert said, giving his friend a gentle nudge in the back. "Time to get back to making money."

When Loch didn't respond, Robert grew impatient. "If you're not going to open what she brought you, then I will!"

It was only when Robert tried to grab the envelope from Loch's hand that Loch paid attention to what Ivy had delivered.

"It will be the latest demand from the Salvador case. We're only going to be able to stall them another week."

"Before they kill her?"

"They may already have."

"Then we won't get paid!"

Loch said, "We've been friends long enough that I'm going to pretend I didn't hear you express dismay at not getting paid rather than at the possible murder of an eight-year old girl."

Robert retorted, "We've been friends long enough that I'm going to tell you that someone here has to be pragmatic. That's why you hired me as your financial manager.

"You've got an amazing business. You're the best kidnapping negotiator I know. Your retrieval rate is higher than anyone else's. No other contractor – government or independent – comes close. Not only that, you're cheap. Your fee is only 50% of the ransom demand!"

"Which you always make them put on retainer before I even start …"

"Can't make me feel bad about that," Robert said. "And I'll take this opportunity to say it again. I don't care how many times I have to repeat myself. You should not be refunding the money if the victim is killed before retrieval.

"You put yourself in incredible danger from start to finish. You meet with some of the most despicable people in the world. I don't know how you stay so cool about it. One wrong word or one misinterpreted act, and they would think nothing of beheading you or feeding you piece by piece to rabid dogs."

Loch shrugged. "I just tell them I'm a trader."

"Some trader," Robert said dryly.

"Their life for the victim's life," Loch said. "I make it simple."

"I suspect that is often many lives for a victim's life."

Loch shot a look at his friend's face. "I thought we agreed we would never talk about the details."

Robert sighed. "No details. Safer that way, I know. It's just that I'm worried your luck is going to run out."

"I told you. There is no luck. It's all in being prepared. It's in doing your research beforehand and being sure of your facts. Then, when it comes down to negotiations, it's reading your opponent and knowing when and how to act. If a surprise is expected, then it's not a surprise."

"Experience in special ops also helps …"

"That it does," Loch said, grinning.

"So, open the envelope," Robert said, his voice brusque. "If you're going to keep doing things like throwing away 36 million dollars on paintings that you're not even going to keep, then I need to be keeping track of every possible source of income …"

"Safe to go in, Coach!"

Nodding thanks, Ivy walked into the men's locker room and jumped up to the bench that ran in front of a row of lockers.

"Today I saw a piece of art …"

Ivy was interrupted by one of her players who rolled his wheelchair up the bench where she was standing and said loudly, "Art! Coach, have you forgotten that you're supposed to inspire us before we go out and kill? Who cares about art?"

"Art?!" all the other players laughed, rolling their chairs back and forth. "Art!" they hooted.

Furiously, Ivy blew her whistle. The sound was too loud to be ignored. She didn't stop until every wheelchair was still. Despite the age of her players (the youngest being 18, the oldest all of 32), Ivy's look was so indignant that they couldn't help but look sheepish.

"Today I saw a piece of art," Ivy continued, as if she had never been interrupted, "of what was claimed to be the earliest depiction of someone playing golf."

"Golf!" one of the men started to sneer derisively, "a game for sissies!"

Ivy brought the whistle up to her mouth, but she didn't have to blow, as the other players quickly shushed their teammate from uttering another word.

"Golf," Ivy continued, "was invented in Scotland. No one is sure as to the exact date, but back in 1457, King James the Second of Scotland issued an edict. This edict, an act of Scottish Parliament, prohibited the playing of the game of golf. Further bans were again imposed in 1471 and 1491.

"This is not a history lesson, so I'm not going to test you on dates. What I want you to do is think for a moment. Why would a king make it illegal to play golf?"

"You all know," and at this point Ivy's could not hide the twinkle from her eyes, "that golf does not come close to the level of danger and carnage intrinsic to the sport you have willingly chosen to engage in. Even though the name of your sport has been changed to Wheelchair Rugby, you and I all know that its original name is more apt. Murderball!"

At this, all the players let out a little cheer. Ivy quieted them by raising a single palm.

"Greatness does not come easy. It only comes from hard work and practice. King James knew this. Back in the 15th century, at the time of his reign, if you were to have a strong military, you had to have excellent archers."

Knowing looks spread across some of the players' faces.

"Golf had to be banned because people were spending too much time playing it! They weren't spending enough time practicing shooting arrows!"

"I mention this painting," Ivy said, "because the King knew what I know, and what I can't tell you enough. I've said it before, and I will say it again. Greatness does not come easy. It comes from hard work and practice."

"Practice," Ivy said. She paused for a moment, making sure that every eye was upon her.

"I've made you practice," she said. "I've made you hate the very sight of me, but men, you've never quit on me. You have practiced until the palms of your hands have bled. You've practiced until you can execute plays rolling backwards if need be. Men, others may see you only as paraplegics. As disabled victims with loss of function in at least three limbs.

"I don't look at you and see anything soft or worth pitying. I see men with hard bodies and muscles of steel."

"I see a team well trained. I see a team of …," and once again Ivy paused for emphasis, "… military might!"

Simultaneously, the men let out raucous cheers.

Ivy had to shout to be heard. "Now let's get out there! Let's play hard and win!"

"I was going to bring you roses, but …"

Ivy turned, and finding Loch only a foot away from her, her mouth fell open in surprise.

The game had ended; her team had won. Quiet had begun to settle in on the gym that just a few minutes earlier had been a din of exuberant players and fans. Spectators were making their way to the exits while the volunteer clean-up crews, large trash bags in hand, were beginning to work their ways through the aisles.

"You?" Ivy sputtered.

Loch continued as if she had never interrupted.

"I'm hoping these will do."

Loch didn't say anything more. He simply extended his arms out to Ivy so she felt obliged to take the green paper wrapped bundle.

"Daisies!" she said, moving the paper aside with one hand. "Daisies!"

"Not as romantic as roses," Loch said, conversationally. "But they're cheerful. And since someone told me something is getting in the way of roses, I thought these would do for now."

"For now?"

"For now." His tone was so certain that Ivy was momentarily at a loss. She was still getting over the shock of seeing him again.

"Aren't you going to ask me about the pineapple?" she said warily.

"No."

Ivy waited. Loch stood quietly, and Ivy found herself becoming irritated at his terseness. If he wasn't going to ask, then she wasn't going to reveal a thing!

"It's a brutal game. Relentlessly fast and uncompromisingly tough."

It took Ivy a moment to realize Loch had switched topics. He really wasn't going to ask her about the pineapple!

"A lot of people don't understand why they do it," Ivy responded slowly, her tone still reserved.

"Athletes are always willing to put themselves at risk. It's an adrenaline rush. Seeking it is part of their makeup."

"Yeah," Ivy said, dryly, "but these athletes are in reinforced wheelchairs. They're smashing into each other so hard that they're knocking themselves out onto the floor."

"Nora was kind enough to explain the rules to me."

For the second time, Ivy found her mouth dropping open in surprise. Nora! This man knew Nora!

"I got that points were scored when the ball was carried over the line. I saw that there were four players from each side on the court at any moment and 12 people to a squad.

"I needed Nora, though, to explain the fine points. How, for example, the substitutions worked. Players are classified from 0.5 to 3.5, depending on their disability. Players with the greatest level of restriction are classified as a 0.5. Substitutions are rolling, but you have to be careful, as you must have an overall total of eight points or fewer on the court at all times."

"How do you know Nora?"

"I just happened to be sitting next to her in the stands. We introduced ourselves. She's delightful. And wonderfully informative."

"And I wonder just who happened to decide sit next to whom." Ivy's tone was sarcastic.

"You already know," Loch said, his teeth flashing amusement. "I made sure to sit next to her after I saw her hug Wes."

Wes! Did this almost perfect stranger standing in front of her just say the name Wes! Nora and Wes were perhaps the two most important people in Ivy's life. The three of them shared all secrets. How could this man speak their names with such familiarity? How could he enter into her world with such casual insouciance?

Ivy put a hand to her head, trying to hide her bafflement. Forcing herself to breathe normally, she got right to the point.

"Why are you here?"

"I came to bring you the daisies, of course, but I also wanted to tell you something."

"What?" Ivy asked warily.

"I'm going to be away for about a week. Business. Phoning and texting might be difficult so I wanted to tell you that I wasn't ignoring you. That I'd notify you as soon as I got back so we could have dinner. I didn't want you to think I had forgotten our date."

"What are you talking about?" Ivy sputtered. "What date?"

"You said you wouldn't be having lunch with me, so we'll have dinner."

"That's not what I meant!"

"Nora assures me you will."

Ivy wasn't sure what to do. Her initial instinct was to bristle in indignation, but she didn't understand Nora's involvement. Nora and she always looked out for each other. Why would Nora think she would have dinner with Loch?

How Ivy would ultimately decide how to respond became moot, as Loch spoke again.

"I know you have a lot of questions, but I have a plane to catch. Nora can give you the details. After all, she was the one who chose the restaurant."

A look of sheer astonishment passed over Ivy's face as Loch nodded at her, as if a bargain had been sealed. Then, without a backward glance, he turned and made his way across the court. Ivy couldn't stop staring. Part of her expected him to stop, or at least look back and wave.

He didn't.

Three

"He couldn't take his eyes off of you!"

"Who?"

Nora shook her head knowingly. "Don't play the innocent with me Ivy Washington! You know exactly who I'm talking about. It's the reason you raced over here after the game. Loch Daziel!"

"Is Loch as handsome as Nora says?" Wes asked, wheeling his chair up to the kitchen table where the two women were sitting.

Ivy tried hard to mask the astonishment she felt. Nora and Wes spoke Loch's name with a familiarity she wasn't comfortable with. Nora and Wes were her best friends. Together, the three of them formed a close knit and tight circle. No one had the right to try and enter it without her approval! What had Loch done to so quickly gain Nora's confidence?

Ivy knew Wes first. She had met him when she first started her job as a bike messenger. He was several years older than she was, and he didn't mind showing the newbie some tricks of the trade. They began to spend time together after work, getting together for a movie or a meal. People at work had wondered if the two of them would get romantically involved, but there wasn't a spark of romantic chemistry between them.

"I love you like a baby sister," Wes said one night, clinking his beer bottle against hers.

"Love you, too, Big Brother," Ivy had toasted him back.

Nora entered the scene after Ivy was called to her apartment for a delivery pick up.

"It's a dead fish," Nora explained to Ivy as she handed her a rectangular box. "I want you to take it to this man at this address."

"I want him to know it's really over this time. Really. I'm done. I'm not going to ask him to take me back again. Ever."

Ivy didn't say a word, but Nora babbled on. "I read in a magazine that if you really want to get back at someone, you should send them a dead fish.

"Three times … three times I've caught him cheating on me! And I always take him back. Well, not this time! This time he's getting a dead fish! At his office! Oh, I wish I could see the shock on his face when he opens this! There's going to be no hiding what a jerk he is!"

Usually Ivy didn't make comments about deliveries, but this time she felt she had to. "Perhaps you should keep this fish and send another."

"Why would I want to do that?" Nora asked curiously. "This fish is dead. Very dead. I want my message to be very clear. He's a horrible, horrible man, and I'm not going to take him back. No, I'm not; I'm not," Nora repeated, wiping her eyes as a fresh tide of tears began to stream from her eyes.

"I think you're confusing a dead fish with a rotten fish," Ivy said gently. "This fish is dead, but it's not rotten. I recognize the name on the box. What you picked up at the store is a fresh salmon packed in dry ice. This fish is a special treat. It's not a break-up sign at all. If anything, the horrible, horrible man who receives it might think you're just sending him the main course of a very expensive dinner! A dinner he might expect you to grill for him."

There was a profound silence for a few seconds, and then Nora giggled. "Oh dear," she said, "I almost muddled that up! I was thinking it was an awful expensive way to break up with someone! Of course, a dead fish is very different from a rotten fish!"

Even though Nora cancelled the delivery, she had insisted on paying Ivy.

"The fish is yours, too," she said. "Come by after your shift and pick it up. I don't know what to do with it, so you can have it. It would be a shame for it to go to waste, as I've spent so much money on it."

Ivy had agreed, but she didn't go to pick up the fish. Instead, she had sent Wes. "I think she's your match," Ivy said when she gave Wes the address.

When Nora opened the door, all it took was one look. "I'm here to grill a fish for my future wife," Wes said.

Wes and Nora were married within the year. Wes wanted Ivy to act as his best man, but Nora wanted Ivy to be her maid of honor. Ivy told Nora that she had to go with Wes, as he didn't have any brothers and she had known him longer. Nora had told her that she would accept Ivy's decision but that one day Ivy would have to do something for her to make up for it. Laughing, Ivy had promised her she would.

That day had come just one short year later. Wes was on his last run for the day. He was wearing his helmet and obeying all safety rules.

It wasn't enough.

A 34-year-old private school teacher carelessly swung open his car door and knocked Wes into the path of an oncoming truck. Wes was caught and tossed beneath the truck's rear wheels.

Wes's injuries were so traumatic that at first no one believed he could survive. Nora was relentless in insisting to the doctors and nurses that he would. "His will is strong," she said repeatedly. "He wants to live."

Wes may have rallied at first, mentally willing himself to heal, but it all changed when he found out the extent of his injuries. "I cannot be a paraplegic," he said. "I would rather be dead."

When Wes had refused to eat for the fourth straight day, Nora had come weeping to Ivy. "It's time for you to do something," she said. "You have to make him eat. You promised. Ivy, you have to!"

Ivy had remained mute. She didn't know what to say because quite honestly, she understood Wes's desire. Everything to Wes was physical. He had often told her that he if was going to go, he wanted it to be fast and on his bike. Lingering in a paralytic state, with someone having to take care of your basic needs, would be equivalent to eternal damnation. She wouldn't wish it on her worst enemy.

Then, by sheer chance, while sitting by Wes's sleeping form, a movie came up on the television set attached to the wall. The movie was called *Murderball*. It was a documentary film about physically disabled athletes playing wheelchair rugby.

Ivy had never heard of the sport, but she found the movie riveting. Despite the late hour, she watched it until the very end. When she found out which team came out the winner at the Paralympic Games, she found herself weeping.

She was still tearing up while she starting googling and searching for information on her phone, but she didn't stop until she had all the information she needed. By the time Wes woke up, she had a plan of action in place.

"I have something for you to see," she said.

Despite Wes's protestations, Ivy had an aide help seat him in a wheelchair. She ignored his pleas to be left alone as she wheeled him down to a van.

"You're as good as dead, you said," she said, "so don't pitch a hissy fit on me now."

Wes had retreated into a sullen silence, but all changed when Ivy wheeled him into a gym. The noise was startling, as the crash of metal against metal made for a ferocious clanging. But it was the sight of the men in their Mad Max-like fortified wheelchairs, their faces intent, sweat dripping down their brows and soaking their shirts, which caught Wes's attention.

When one man was knocked to the floor and practice continued, with no one coming to help him up, Wes's lethargy was no longer an issue. As Ivy began to explain the rules, Wes began to watch the action with narrowed eyes.

"Brute force is the least of it," he said. "Strength is necessary, but it's all tactics. You've got to think moves ahead. It's like chess on crack!"

"I don't know if I would describe it that way," said Ivy. "Not exactly politically correct."

"Okay."

"Okay, what?"

"Okay, I'll play, but you have to be my coach."

It was like a chain of falling dominoes. At first Ivy worked only with Wes. Then, as other men watched her assigning him different exercises, pushing him to do more despite his saying he couldn't, other men asked if they could join the workouts. When Wes tried out for a team and was accepted, Ivy thought her work was through. To her surprise, Wes's team coach asked her to be his assistant. When he had to step down due to time constraints, Ivy was asked to take over.

Ivy spared no one. "Life is tough," she told her players. "Tough it out."

There were parents and social workers who took affront at Ivy's seemingly callous attitude. When Ivy was told that her workouts should be less rigorous and that she should be more considerate of the disabled, Ivy would point out that no one had to play. Players were competing so as to be chosen for *her* team.

At this point, many of these same well-meaning souls would tell Ivy that winning didn't matter. After all, everyone was out there just to have fun. Everyone who showed up was a winner. Ivy knew these were the people who made sure every child got a trophy. Ivy understood their sentiment, but why should the same size trophy go to a child who never practiced, tried, or improved?

"Winning isn't a right," Ivy would say. "It's earned."

Under Ivy's tutelage, Wes and his teammates had excelled. Ivy felt they had a strong bid for winning the Paralympics, and they were being asked to play games in leagues all over the country. They had even been extended an invitation to their first international competition!

The men had been excited when Ivy told them, but they all knew they would not be attending. The competition was taking place in Scotland. Even if Ivy's team could have afforded the tickets, there was still the cost of meals and hotel rooms. Perhaps one or two players might have been able to pay for a plane ticket, but for the majority of the players, the cost was prohibitive. As it was, players had to pay for their own game wheelchairs. For many, this cost came at a sacrifice from other family members. As much as they wanted it, not one of those proud athletes would ask their loved ones for a ticket to Scotland.

"I'll repeat the question Wes said. "Ivy, is this Loch man as handsome as Nora says he is?"

"He's a dream!" Nora said before Ivy could answer. "He makes me …"

"I'm sitting right here!" Wes protested warningly.

"Oh, darling," Nora said, blowing Wes a kiss from across the table. "You have nothing to worry about. I'm yours. You're the only one for me. But this man is something else! And to think our Ivy is going to have dinner with him next week!"

"No, I'm not!"

"Yes, you will," Nora said. "I promised him. I told him you would meet him at *La Scala's*. Seven o'clock. I'll text you what night, as he's not sure when he's getting back. He hoped it would be next week, Friday, but that's only if things go as planned."

"*La Scala?*" Wes gave a low whistle. "You're talking …"

"Yes," Nora said. "We're talking the *La Scala*. The one where one has to have reservations at least three months in advance."

"Somehow I don't see this working out," Wes said, shaking his head. "Three months reservations needed, and you're talking dinner next week Friday – maybe!"

"Loch told me not to worry. He assured me he would have a table." Nora said, primly.

"Well, if Loch says!" Wes said in a mocking but jesting tone.

"I'm not going. Nora, you can tell him that when he is done doing whatever it is he had to do."

"What does he do?" Wes asked, curiously. His eyes twinkling, he turned to Ivy. "What do you bet my darling wife didn't bother to ask!"

"I didn't have to!" Nora said, tossing her hair. "I know he's responsible and very successful at his job!"

"Which is?"

"Some type of trader," Ivy said. "Boring and stuffy. Probably never leaves his air-conditioned suite once he gets to wherever it is he's going."

The three friends were silent for a moment, and then Wes spoke. "Just tell me one thing," he said. "Why is he texting you, Nora? Why doesn't he just text Ivy the day and time? After all, he's having dinner with her – not you!"

"He asked for Ivy's number, but I wouldn't give it to him."

Nora turned to Ivy. "I know how you are, dear, about privacy."

"Still, you told him I'd be there! Why did you do that?"

"He offered me something. It was something I couldn't refuse."

"What?"

For the first time Nora looked uncomfortable. Shifting in her seat she said, "I'm not supposed to say."

Four

"You shouldn't be here! My God, Ivy, you're going to be late!"

Ivy stared at Wes in astonishment. "What are you talking about?" she asked. "It's Thursday night. Practice. I'm on a court; I see a team, and I *am* the coach. Why shouldn't I be here?"

"You're supposed to be at *La Scala*! Ivy, you've got to go! Now!"

"She told you!"

"Yes," Wes said impatiently. "Nora told me why. Ivy, go!"

"She wouldn't tell me!"

"It took me singing *Old MacDonald Had a Farm* for seven hours straight. She really didn't like my pig sounds, but it might have been the hippopotamus roar that did her in. She said if she heard it one more time she was going to scream. I was down to a whisper and couldn't talk for two days after, but it was all worth it."

Wes was silent for a moment and then he said, "Ivy, you really need to go."

"No."

A strange expression came over Wes's face. He put his hands to his chair's wheels, and he gave a huge push. With a start, Ivy realized he was going to run into her!

"What are you doing?" she sputtered angrily, as she jumped up on the first row of bleacher seats.

"I'm not letting you down until you promise you'll go. If you leave now and use every trick I ever taught you, you might just make it in time. Trust me Ivy; you don't want to make him wait!"

Ivy hesitated, and then she nodded. "Okay," she said. "Okay."

She looked at her watch and jumped off the bench. She didn't say a word to Wes until she got to the door. She turned around and saw him staring at her.

"Might just make it in time?" she scoffed. "I'll get there with time to spare!"

Leaving her bike and lock with a very surprised valet, Ivy strode purposely and with quick step into the restaurant. As heads turned to stare, Ivy did her best to hide her sudden feeling of self-doubt. Women in form-fitting sheaths literally glittered with diamonds. Men in tuxedos and tailored suits were in no less sartorial elegance.

"Ms. Washington?"

Ivy turned and saw a woman walking toward her who could have come straight from an English wedding – complete with high stiletto heels and feathery hat perched at an impossible tilt on her head!

"Ms. Washington?" the woman repeated. When Ivy nodded warily, the woman explained, "I'm the hostess. We've been expecting you. There's a bag waiting for you at the reservation stand."

"I'm not here to pick up a package," Ivy said. "I'm here to dine."

"I'm afraid that …"

The thought flashed through Ivy's mind that she was going to be thrown out of the restaurant! Her working clothes did not match their dress code! Ivy stiffened, ready to show that no one could make her feel uncomfortable or of less worth simply because of her apparel.

"… you need to pick up the package before you dine. Madame Nora insisted."

It took a second for the hostess's words to register, as Ivy had initially misunderstood her intention. In addition, she had never heard Nora referred to as a Madame before!

"And I so must do what Madame Nora directs," Ivy said, a mischievous glint in her eyes.

When the hostess handed Ivy her bag, the woman's cool composure finally broke. "And it just so happens that Madame has left directions on the bag," she said, giggling.

The hostess was a powerful woman. The movers and shakers who wanted to show their power or their wealth all depended on this receptionist to seat them. She was a gatekeeper they courted. At times, bribery, flattery, and outright begging had been tried. All had been deflected with steely courtesy.

Yet, now, while people waited and looked with covetous glances and those being seated, she was giggling! All eyes turned to the sound, everyone wanting to know what precipitated it.

They watched as the hostess, still uncharacteristically smiling, handed a bag to some shabbily mismatched dressed woman holding a bike helmet. When the woman took the bag, she, too, began to giggle. Then, to their utter disbelief, the hostess gave the woman a quick hug.

All eyes switched from the hostess to the woman with the bike helmet. She walked a few steps into the dining room, quickly scanned the room, and then smiled at someone. She held up one hand, palm out, fingers spread, and mouthed the words, "Five minutes!"

Loch, sitting at his table, nodded in silent understanding. Watching Ivy then turn her back and make her way back to the hostess, Loch found himself letting out a sigh of relief. He realized that he hadn't been at all sure that Ivy would show up. As the minutes had passed and the clock had ticked, he had found himself becoming increasingly nervous. He, whose mission had just ended in success — an eight-year old girl no one ever expected to be seen alive again reunited with her parents — had felt more anxiety in the last quarter hour than he had all week!

He didn't know what it was about Ivy. He remembered the first time he saw her. Marcella, his primary research assistant in his office, had laughed. The sound had caused him to look up. As Ivy had walked toward him, he had found himself unable to look away.

Tonight, just as before, he spotted her because she had made someone laugh. And it wasn't just anyone she made laugh. It was perhaps the most formidable hostess in the entire city, if not state! Somehow, Ivy, in a single moment, had enchanted her, just as Ivy had him!

He would deal with her like he did all of his cases. With precision and relentlessness. She would not get away until he released her.

There was a collective gasp. Several pieces of silverware were dropped. No one paid attention to the clatter.

Loch's face remained a mask, but his eyes were riveted on the woman coming so purposefully toward him.

Ivy had followed instructions. Pinned onto the bag, written in huge black block letters, were the words that had caused Ivy and the hostess such merriment.

TAKE OFF EVERYTHING YOU ARE WEARING! EVERYTHING!

Ivy only followed "Madam" Nora's command because of what was written underneath, though in much smaller letters.

PUT EVERYTHING IN THIS BAG ON!!! EVERYTHING!

"You can put the clothes you're wearing in the bag," the hostess had told Ivy. "I'll keep it for you while you dine."

Before Ivy followed Nora's instructions, she washed her hands and splashed cold water on her face. Releasing her hair from its elastic band, she brushed it out so that it fell like a soft curtain down her back. Quickly, then, she stripped off her clothes and opened the bag.

The first thing she took out was a matching black lacy bra and panty set. "Very different from my sports bra and wicking undershorts!" Ivy grinned to herself.

What followed was a fully lined black cocktail dress. Cut with simple elegance, it featured a cap sleeve bodice and a demure square neckline. The bust line, as well as the back, was detailed with exquisitely stitched darts that allowed for a contoured and flattering look.

"Not bad," Ivy thought as she smoothed her hands over the front of the dress. "Not bad at all."

Ivy wasn't so sure of what came next. The shoes were fine-grain black leather one-half inch platform pumps with four-inch heels. But the stockings! Sheer black silk. Fine. Yet when Ivy pulled them on, they ended just a bit above her knees! A two-inch gap of flesh showed between the top band of the stockings and the bottom of her dress!

Ivy was about to discard them and go without, but then she changed her mind. She didn't care what she looked like. She was only here for Wes and Nora. With the shoe style Nora had chosen, it would be more comfortable to don stockings than go without. Nora had told her to wear everything. She would!

"Madame Nora has selected quite an ensemble," the hostess told Ivy as Ivy handed over her bag.

Ivy couldn't tell if the hostess was aghast or amused. Deciding it didn't matter, she tucked and errant tendril of her hair behind her ear and made her way to the table where Loch was sitting.

The dress revealed less cleavage than any other in the room. It did not fit like a second skin. It was of modest length. There were no jewels or dangly pendants to catch the light. There was only two inches of bare flesh to break the single color.

No one, not one person – server, busboy, sommelier, and diner – could stop staring at the person who wore it and the narrow band of leg revealed.

It wasn't until Ivy reached his table that Loch realized he had stopped breathing.

"You're … you're … breathtaking," he said, finally able to get the words out.

Ivy stood, a faint smile on her face, waiting. It took a moment for Loch to realize what she was waiting for. He stood hastily so that he could pull her chair out for him. As he made sure she was comfortably seated, he felt a flush of embarrassment. She had made him forget his manners!

As Loch settled himself back in his own seat, Ivy looked at him, an amused expression on her face.

"*For the apparel oft proclaims the man*," she said. "But in this case, it's all Nora. She chose the outfit. It was here waiting for me."

"Does Nora know Shakespeare, too?"

"You're familiar with *Hamlet*!"

"You're having a hard time hiding your surprise."

Ivy bowed her head sheepishly. "I'm sorry," she said quickly. "That was rude. It's just that *Hamlet* is my favorite play of Shakespeare's. Most people are more familiar with his *To be, or not to be-that is the question* line."

"It is a worthy line."

Ivy nodded.

"If we're discussing favorite lines, then I'd have to give you: *Clothes make the man. Naked people have little or no influence on society.*"

"Mark Twain," Ivy said with a giggle. Daintily, she took a sip of water from her water glass before speaking again.

"I've seen a lot of naked people."

Loch was momentarily speechless. Would he ever know what to expect with this lady?

"Would you have preferred them dressed?" he asked slowly.

"Yes!" Ivy said, nodding emphatically. Then she explained. "You would not believe how some people come to the door when I ring the bell! If it were I, I would never open a door unless fully clothed."

"Perhaps it's intentional. They want you to see them."

"Maybe," Ivy agreed, "but a lot of them don't care. They don't see me. They just see a messenger. I'm not in their world long enough to matter."

"It's rude and wrong."

Loch's tone booked no equivocation. Ivy liked his certainty.

"So why am I here?"

The change of topic was so abrupt that once again Loch was startled with the direction of the conversation.

"You don't know?"

"Nora told me I had to come. I wasn't going to, but Wes," and here a playful smile hovered around Ivy's lips, "insisted."

"How did he do that?"

"Trapped me in the bleachers. I couldn't get past his wheelchair."

"Ah."

"You were testing me."

"Why would you think that?"

"You told Nora she couldn't tell me why I had to come. You wanted to see if I would come without being told. Nora didn't reveal anything. I came. So, tell me."

"Maybe I was testing Nora."

"No," Ivy said emphatically. "It's me you're interested in."

"Are you always this self-confident?"

"No."

Loch started to laugh. "Your honesty is like a breath of fresh air," he said.

"Tell me, please."

The words had no sooner left Ivy's lips when the waiter came to the table. Loch gave a little nod to Ivy, and even though he had not uttered a sound, Ivy knew that he was telling her to have patience. He would tell her as soon as they had ordered.

It was only when Ivy was back home replaying in her mind every bit of the evening that she remembered this detail. There were times she could communicate with Wes nonverbally, but they had known each other for years. How strange that this man – almost a perfect stranger – could, without a word and naught but a simple nod, relay his message to her with such surety and ease.

Ivy chose carefully, first asking the waiter several questions. After Loch ordered, he asked Ivy if she would trust him with the wine selection.

She said yes, but she also told him she would only imbibe one glass. "I'm riding home," she explained.

"I could take you."

"No."

Ivy's refusal was immediate. It was only in the strained pause that followed that Ivy realized how rude she might have sounded.

"Thank you," she added quickly. "No, thank you."

Loch wasn't perturbed by her answer at all. It only added to the challenge.

"I told Nora that if you had dinner with me, I would send your team, players and support staff included, to Scotland. Entrance fees, airfare, room and board, all taken care of."

The piece of bread Ivy had just bitten off and put in her mouth came flying out.

"Get out!" she cried, looking at Loch in disbelief. Her shock was so great that she couldn't even be embarrassed about spitting out her bread.

Loch didn't have to say a word. All he had to do was nod. Ivy could also tell, by the laughter lines that began to form around his eyes, that though he was trying not to show it, he was greatly amused at her involuntary loss of manners.

"But, the money," she said weakly. "It will be thousands of dollars."

"The final figures aren't in yet, but it's all under control. Wes has been working with one of my assistants, and everything is almost done. Tickets have been purchased, and the hotel has been booked and paid for. Wes is hoping that you don't have to play Germany first. He said better not to have to face them until the final round."

Ivy continued to sit, dumbfounded, a million thoughts racing through her head.

"This is the first time," Loch said, "That you haven't responded with immediacy. All in all, I think I won this round."

"But passports," Ivy said feebly. "I don't think anyone has one. We'll never get them in time."

"Taken care of. Expedited processing paid for. Didn't you wonder why Wes had everyone's photo taken last week?"

"He told me those pictures were taken so he could update the team's Facebook page!"

"No."

"Oh," Ivy gasped, suddenly growing very still.

"What now?"

"I didn't have to have dinner with you! You've already paid for everything!"

"True, but if I were you, I'd stay at least long enough to taste the food. You'll regret it later if you don't."

"So, I should stay only for the food?"

Loch hadn't been sure that Ivy would remain until he heard the playfulness in her voice as she asked her question. He hadn't even realized how worried he was about this until he felt the tightness in his abdominal muscles begin to relax! What was it about this woman that he should react so viscerally?

Perhaps to deal with his unfamiliar feeling, Loch spoke more brusquely that he had intended.

"I owed you a dinner."

"Why?" The puzzlement in Ivy's voice was apparent.

"The pineapple," Loch said. A broad smile spread across his face as he leaned back in his chair.

Ivy's eyes twinkled, but she didn't say a word.

"Pineapples," Loch said, "are a New World fruit. They are indigenous to South America and believed to have originated somewhere between Brazil and Paraguay. Christopher Columbus brought the first pineapple back to Europe. As he didn't see or taste one until he visited the Caribbean island of Guadeloupe in 1493, it would have been very difficult for Mateo Raphael to include one in a painting of a picnic lunch!"

"Especially since Raphael died in 1421 or 1422!" Ivy giggled.

"You turned the art world upside down."

"Please tell me you got your money back!"

"Every cent!"

"Don't you mean every million?"

"Which is why your team is flying first class instead of coach."

"Ah," laughed Ivy, leaning back in her chair. "Such a deal."

"It was an amazing forgery. The chemical paint composition matched the time period, and the canvas was just as old. The experts had noted that it had been scraped and reused, but that was a common practice back then."

There was a moment of silence and then Loch asked curiously, "How did you notice? It was such a small detail."

Ivy shrugged. "Luck, I suppose."

"I don't believe in luck. Why are you a bike messenger?"

This time it was Ivy who was startled at the abrupt change of conversation.

"Why do you ask?"

"You knew who Mateo Raphael was. Obviously, you're well read. You are used to noticing and assessing details, both static and changing. If you weren't, you wouldn't be any good at your job. You'd be too slow to merit employment, or worst-case scenario, maimed or even killed in some kind of accident.

"Someone so intelligent and highly attuned to what is going on could do anything. Why a bike messenger?"

"It's fun."

"That's it? That's all you're going to tell me?"

"It's amazingly fun."

Loch looked at Ivy with narrowed eyes. Most women couldn't stop talking about themselves. Would he have to beg to get her to open up?

"What about your family?" he asked. "Do your parents worry about what might happen to you?"

"I'm not interested in talking about my family."

Loch had thought family would be an innocuous topic. He could tell from the brittleness of Ivy's tone that he had touched on a sore point.

Wanting to avoid any further dangerous ground, he said, "You ask the questions then. But the deal is we both have to answer them." He was worried for a moment that Ivy wouldn't acquiesce, but then she smiled.

"Fair enough," she said. She took a sip from her wine glass, daintily wiped her lips, and asked, "Have you ever seen a pelican?"

"Brown or white?" Loch asked, letting out a whoop of laughter.

Five

Ivy had heard the phrase "Time flies," but it had done more than that. It had evaporated. When the *maître d'* had arrived and told them they had to leave because the restaurant was closing, Ivy had looked around in shock. They were the only two patrons remaining! She, who was usually so alert to movement, hadn't even noticed the egress of all the other customers!

"I'll drive you home," Loch said when they stepped outside and saw the valet waiting with her bike. "We can fit your bike in the trunk."

"I'll be fine," Ivy said, stepping out of her high-heeled shoes. With practiced ease, she slid the pair of long gym shorts she had been wearing previously up over her stockings and under her dress.

"I had a wonderful evening," she said as she put the dress shoes in her messenger bag and her well-worn sneakers on her feet. "Truly, I did."

Even as Ivy heard herself saying *Truly, I did*, she cringed inwardly. She sounded like a soppy teenager! But the truth was that she did indeed have a wonderful evening. Not once had conversation lagged. There was so much to talk about, and strange as it seemed, she felt they had barely scratched the surface. There was so much more she wanted to know!

Even more disturbing was the undeniable fact that she found herself wanting to kiss Loch! She knew that his lips would feel firm and soft. She wanted to breath in a bit of him, feel a hint of his soul.

Unsure of what to do or how to regain her dignity, she took a step back, buckled her helmet, and held out her hand. She wasn't going to risk looking foolish. Loch was attractive and rich. He was the type of man women threw themselves at. Just because he was paying for her team to go to Scotland didn't mean that she was his to toy with!

When Loch took Ivy's hand, she felt a warmth spread up her arm and straight to her heart. She pulled her hand back, looking at Loch with a strange expression.

"I'll follow you then."

"What?" Ivy said, feeling stupid and dense.

"If you don't want a ride, I'll accept that," Loch said, "but I need to see that you get home safely."

Ivy started to protest, but before she could even get a word out, Loch said firmly, "For my own peace of mind."

Ivy had been acutely aware of Loch's presence all the way home. As she pedaled, she kept wondering if he would ask if he could come in. She was in mental turmoil as to what her answer would be.

She never had to decide. When she pulled up at her door, Loch remained in his car. He never got out, nor did he roll down his window and say anything to her. Ivy could hear the engine purring as she unlocked her door. She waved, expecting Loch to leave immediately, but he remained where he was. It wasn't until she had pulled her bike inside, closed the door, and flipped on several lights that she heard the sound of the engine moving down the street.

Loch had told her that he needed to make sure she had gotten home safely. He had not left until he knew there was no question that she was.

Roses had followed. First there was the bouquet delivered the next morning to the messenger office when she went to sign in. Then there was the delivery that same day but in the early evening to the gym while she was holding practice. Then, as if that wasn't enough, there was yet a third bouquet delivered to her front door! The delivery man was waiting patiently, amusing himself by playing a game on his phone.

When Ivy apologized for his wait, the man had shrugged. "Trust me, I'm doing great. Largest tip I've gotten all year."

None of the bouquets had a note. Ivy knew that they had to have come from Loch, but she wasn't quite sure what to think about the lack of a card. Was it an oversight? Or did Loch so routinely send flowers to his dates that he didn't bother with cards anymore?

The flowers came again the next day, and the next. Each time they arrived without a note or message. Workmates and players began to make comments, but Ivy would only shrug at their good-natured teasing.

"Take them," she told Wes the second and third nights they had been delivered to the gym. "I don't have enough vases."

Ivy knew that Wes bringing home roses to Nora would elicit questions.

"I was expecting you after the first dozen!" Ivy told Nora when she showed up at her doorstep.

"Wes told me I should show restraint," Nora laughed. "That's the only reason I waited the extra day!" "Oh, Ivy," she continued, "it's so romantic!"

"There's never been a card."

"What do you mean there's never been a card?"

"Not one. Ever. There's not even a sender name."

"But they're from Loch!"

"You would think, but …"

"Of course, they're from Loch!" Nora's tone bunked no disagreement.

There was a moment of silence while the two friends looked at each other.

"I'm still going with it being romantic," Nora said. "He went to a lot of trouble. Three deliveries a day, each one to a different location!"

"Or one of his assistants went to a lot of trouble." Ivy said dryly.

"But roses are awfully expensive."

Ivy snorted. "Money means nothing to this man. He was going to spend 36 million on a single painting!"

"It's good that he's rich," Nora said with a giggle, "because he paid a lot of money to have dinner with you! First class travel to Scotland for the entire team! Think about that before you get so high and mighty about the lack of a simple little card!"

"I can't be bought," Ivy said stiffly.

Nora looked aghast. "Oh, Ivy," she cried. "You know I didn't mean that!"

Ivy nodded.

"This goes back to your family — or lack of it," Nora said softly.

Startled, Ivy looked at Nora warily.

Nora patted Ivy's arm. "It helps to have a reputation of always getting things mixed up and muddled," she said. "No one expects me to be especially perceptive. Despite my reputation, I do notice things.

"You're amazingly loyal. You're hardworking, kind, intelligent, and beautiful."

Ivy started to object, but Nora continued to speak. "You are all those things. I'm not the only one who has noticed that! You and Wes are so close. You could have seen me as an interloper. Instead, you took me in. That's the type of person you are. Giving. You're the daughter every mother dreams of. You're the sister we all want!

"But this too I know – if there is ever any mention of family, your body tenses. You hide it well, but it's there. A sudden stiffness in your face.

"That tone you had, when you said you couldn't be bought – that tone matched the stiffness in your face when anyone talks about family. Now why is that, I wonder?"

"You know what they say," Ivy said. "*Happy families are all alike; every unhappy family is unhappy in its own way.*"

"Now that's a perceptive comment."

"It's from *Anna Karenina*. It's the very first line of the book."

"*Anna Karenina*? Who wrote that?"

"Leo Tolstoy."

"You're not going to tell me in what way your family is unhappy, are you?"

"No."

Perhaps a lesser friend would have pushed for or felt they deserved more details, but Nora simply put her arms around Ivy and hugged her.

"Wes and I are your family," she said. "And we're happy."

On the fourth day, when Ivy found yet another dozen roses waiting for her when she went to check in for work, she decided it was time to put an end to it. She called Daziel Traders and asked to speak to Loch. Loch was busy, she was told, but he would be available for lunch.

"Tell him I'll bring it," Ivy said.

Ivy showed up with two large pizzas.

"That smell!" one of Loch's assistants said, "It makes me want some!"

"That's why I brought two pizzas," Ivy said, placing one of the boxes by the surprised but delighted assistant. Turning to Loch, she said, "Where shall we eat ours?"

"Come with me!"

Ivy followed, and Loch led her out to a small narrow hallway and a labyrinth of stairs. Ivy had no idea where they were going to end up until Loch pushed open a door that opened up onto a small terrace. Ivy gasped at the view.

"It's stunning," she said. "And it's time for the roses to stop."

"What roses?"

Ivy rolled her eyes. "You know perfectly well," she said while taking out two bottles of diet coke, two bottles of water, and a bundle of napkins from her messenger bag.

When Loch didn't respond, she said, "I'm here because I don't think it was arrogance."

"What in the world are you talking about?"

Ivy unscrewed the cap off of one of the diet cokes, took a sip, and said, "The no cards. No messages. Not even a name. Did it ever occur to you that you're not my only suitor? That I might not know the roses were from you?"

"Do you?" Loch's response was immediate and harsh. "Do you have other suitors?"

Ivy arched an eyebrow, giving him a saucy smile before taking a huge bite of pizza. Loch found himself irritated that she hadn't answered! It had never crossed his mind that she would even begin to think the flowers weren't from him! *She must have known!* he thought. *Otherwise she wouldn't be here!*

Loch spoke carefully, knowing instinctively that his answer would mean more to Ivy than all his money.

"At the restaurant, when you were leaving. I took your hand. You didn't let me hold it very long. The truth is that I've held a lot of women's hands …"

"And much, much more, I imagine!" Ivy said, eyes twinkling.

"But when I held your hand," Loch continued, as if Ivy had never interrupted. "It felt as if it was my first time."

A silence followed. Ivy swallowed, but she still didn't speak. She was remembering well the strange warmth that had spread up her arm and straight to her heart. Loch had felt it, too!

"It was easier not to write anything than to write that." Loch said. "It wasn't arrogance."

"No."

Ivy's one word of denial confused Loch, but he carefully kept his face devoid of all emotion. Would he ever be able to understand this woman? He should not have spoken the truth! He was scaring her away!

"No, I don't have any other suitors," Ivy said at last, a broad smile flashing across her face before she took another bite of pizza.

Six

When Ivy crawled into bed, she could not close her eyes. She lay there, reveling in the plushness of the luxurious cotton sheets and the soft downiness of the thick feather pillows. Loch had scrimped on nothing when it came to providing for the team. The way they had been coddled on the plane in first class was an experience in itself, but even Vinny, the brashest and wildest of her team, was brought to silence when the charter bus brought them to their hotel — The Balmoral Rocco Forte.

Anthony, the youngest and most tech-savvy of her players, had looked up the hotel beforehand. He had told everyone that they would be staying in one of the top five most expensive hotels in Edinburgh, but no one had believed him. Now, awed to silence by its 195-foot clock tower and its stone Victorian façade, they were like little children scared to enter the doors on their first day of school.

Connecting suites had been reserved for all the players, but Ivy was given a room to herself. When she and the others had been informed that complimentary benefits included packing and unpacking services, as well as free ironing to rid any clothes of unwanted wrinkles, they could only grin at each other in dumb amazement.

"You don't have time to unpack anyway," Ivy told the group as she handed out kcys. "We've got a sight-seeing bus that leaves in thirty minutes. We'll return here after the tour for an early dinner and bed. No arguments. I want you well-rested and ready to play your hearts out tomorrow. I don't want to hear about 'jet lag' either. I'm preemptively striking it as an excuse for not winning!"

The tour and dinner had been the right thing to do. The men had seen enough that they wouldn't be thinking about what they might be missing out on when they were playing. But it had also made them relax. Ivy had asked the bus driver to stop at the stadium where they would be playing. She had made everyone get off the bus and roll themselves onto the court. Then, she had made them get out of their chairs and lie on the floor.

"Feel it," she told the team as she made her way between the strewn bodies and chairs. "It's wood. Just as hard. Just as unforgiving. No different from the wood you play and practice on every day. That's what I want you to remember tomorrow when we come to play."

The men were silent, lost in their own thoughts, but then Mario spoke up. "Coach," he said, "I get around the city with a monthly bus pass that gives me unlimited rides for 116 dollars and fifty cents. All I know is – this floor may be just as hard, but it cost a lot more to get here!"

"No worries," Ivy said, as the men burst out laughing. "The return trip tickets have already been paid for!"

As Ivy pulled up the sheet, she forced herself to close her eyes. When she did, Mario's comment came to mind. Ivy could understand Mario's concerns about money. Loch had asked that his contribution be kept anonymous. Anyone who was unfamiliar with the source might worry that they were overspending, especially after seeing the opulence of the hotel.

The thought of Loch's largess reminded Ivy of one of their conversations. It had been on the day she had brought him pizza and they had eaten it up on the terrace of the Chrysler Building. It was immediately after she had told him she didn't have any other suiters.

"I wouldn't have rented an apartment for you."

"What in the world are you talking about?" Ivy asked, completely baffled.

"This Chrysler Building …"

"Yes, we're sitting on it! Perhaps the most iconic Art Deco skyscraper in the world," Ivy said. "Also, the tallest brick building in the world, though of course it has an internal steel skeleton."

"Margaret Bourke-White lived in an apartment on the 61st floor."

"The famous photographer Margaret Bourke-White? The one who invented the photo essay? The one who took the first cover photo for Life magazine?"

"That is she. The partition of Pakistan, Dust Bowl refugees, concentration camps, the Germans invading Moscow, she documented it all. There's even a photograph of her sitting perched on one of this building's gargoyles while she was taking a photograph!"

"The first selfie?" Ivy giggled.

"Selfies weren't possible, then," Loch said, "but you know that."

"What I don't know is how we came to be talking about her. What does she have to do with you not renting me an apartment?"

Loch explained. "Bourke-White was already rich and famous when she wanted to move in here. Still, she couldn't sign a lease because it was against building rules to rent to a woman."

"But she lived here anyway?"

"Time, Inc., the company she worked for — they signed the lease for her."

"That was good of them."

"Yes," Loch said, "but I wouldn't have rented an apartment for you."

"Why ever not?" Ivy asked, a mix of curiosity and indignation in her tone.

"I would have bought the building and allowed you to rent it yourself."

It was the perfect conversation to play over in her head while nodding off to sleep.

Seven

The crowd was screaming for blood. They got it.

It was the third day of the tournament, and they had advanced to the semi-finals. Vinny lay sprawled on the floor, his legs twisted uselessly beneath him. He saw the opposing player hurtling toward him, and Vinny knew he was going to be run over. Desperately, he grappled with what movement he had in his arms, but he could not slide across the floor fast enough. There was a collective groan as one of the wheels slashed across his right thigh.

At first it looked like a ribbon had been laid gently across Vinny's leg, but that vision soon changed as the blood spread into a puddle around him.

Even as Ivy ran across the floor, Vinny was shaking his head no.

"Cover it," he said to Ivy in a determined voice. "Press down hard. You can't take me out."

"Vin, I've got to," Ivy said once they were on the sidelines. The medic is coming over now. You're going to need stitches."

"You can't!" Vinny said. "You can't!"

Ivy had never seen Vinny so upset. She understood. She knew that he had worked hard for this. He, of all her players, deserved to be in this competition.

Vinny had been a soldier serving in the infantry in Iraq. An IED (improvised explosive device) had sent their Humvee up in the air. It had landed in flames, upside down. Vinny was thrown across the road. His spine was broken, along with both of his legs, one of which he found out later in 17 places. Without stopping to think about possible enemy fire or what an easy target he made, Vinny pulled himself across the road using just his arms. He was able to save the driver, cutting him free and pulling him from the twisted wreckage, even as the flames melted two of Vinny's fingers together. Vinny had received a Medal of Honor for his valor, but he never spoke about it.

Torrance, another veteran, had told Ivy why. Torrance was the team's mechanic. The other players considered him a genius. No matter how twisted or mashed a wheelchair, Torrance could look at it and instantly know how to keep it together using only what was on hand.

Torrance, too, had served in Iraq. His primary responsibility had been to maintain the transport fleets. There, he had devised ways to reinforce and protect all kinds of vehicles from IEDs. "An easy switch to wheelchairs!" he would say when he would show off another innovation he had welded on or applied.

Torrance had come back with sound body, but as he explained cheerfully, "Not in sound mind!" He drank liberally to deal with the memories and nightmares. Stateside for less than a year, he left a bar so drunk that he could barely stand. Two blocks from the bar, he crashed his pick-up truck into a tree and severed his spine.

"I'm just lucky I didn't kill anyone," he would say, shaking his head at his own past behavior. "Funny how luck is a different thing to different people."

"Some things can't be explained," Torrance told Ivy. "You just had to be there too. That's the only way you can really understand. Vinny … Vinny can't talk about it because he doesn't think he deserves a medal. You see, he was only able to save the driver. He had to leave someone to burn. He was dead, had to be, but Vinny doesn't know that. He keeps thinking that just maybe, just maybe, even though he wasn't moving and Vinny didn't feel a pulse, he was only unconscious. What if the pain of being burned alive was enough to wake him up? It will be in the back of Vinny's mind forever – what if he left a man to burn alive?"

"Duct tape."

The words were spoken with authority.

"What?" Ivy looked up at in complete bewilderment. What was Loch doing here? And what in the world was he talking about?

"Torrance, duct tape. ASAP! Before the medic gets here!"

Torrance hastily pulled a roll from his tool box and threw it to Loch.

As Loch pulled off a strip, he said, "It's just a flesh wound. The artery's intact. We can stem the bleeding for now. Push the skin together."

With the help of another player, Vinny quickly complied. Without hesitation and economy of movement, Loch taped the leg.

"You'll have to get that stitched," he said, sitting back on his heels. "And, you'll need a dose of antibiotics to stave off infection."

"After the game!" Vinny said. "Coach, put me back in!"

"Where's the injured player?"

The entire team was silent. There was no possible way Vinny could be cleared to play if the medic could see the extent of his injury.

"Over here!"

Heads turned in astonishment to Wes.

"Over here," Wes said again. He held up a bloody hand, and then placed it back down on his leg. "I'm the one with the injury."

"You're going to need stitches," the medic said, hurrying over.

"Oh my God, he cut his own leg!" Ivy murmured.

"Stitch me up, Doc!" Wes said cheerfully as he surreptitiously hid the Phillip's screwdriver he had taken from Torrance's bag.

The medic snapped on some rubber gloves and took out a syringe. When Wes asked what he needed a shot for, the medic answered, "It's a numbing agent. Don't worry. You'll only feel the needle stick for an instant."

Wes started to laugh. "Doc, save that for someone else! One of the few perks of being paralyzed – I won't feel a thing!"

Vinny was back on the floor before the medic had taken the first stitch.

Eight

"You need to sleep with me now."

The game had been won. The team had advanced to the final round. The next time they played – tomorrow – it would be for the championship. Ivy had finished speaking to her players. She had told them that the bus would take them back to the hotel, but then they were free for the rest of the day. There would be a nine p.m. curfew, and she would be there to check personally that it was made.

It was when the men were making their way to the bus that Ivy had turned to Loch and told him he needed to sleep with her. Her voice was so casual that at first he thought he had misheard or even imagined it. Then she repeated herself.

"You need to sleep with me now."

Now that he was sure of what he had heard, Loch stood stunned. She had done it again! Her words had taken him completely by surprise. Would he ever know what to expect from this woman?

"You have something else to do?" Ivy asked when Loch didn't answer immediately. She cocked her head and looked at him curiously.

"If I did, I wouldn't now."

"So, you will."

"Will what?"

"Are you being deliberately obtuse? Do you want to sleep with me or not?"

"Of course I do!"

"Okay then."

"Okay!"

Ivy caught sight of the clock next to the bed.

"It's six o'clock," she gasped in surprise. She turned and nestled her head against Loch's chest. He held her close with his arm.

"I can't believe we've been here so long," she said.

"I'm willing to stay longer," Loch said, bending down and kissing the top of Ivy's head. "Much longer."

"I still can't believe it," Ivy said, raising herself up and resting her head on one bent arm. She ran the fingers of her other hand across Loch's chest as she voiced her musings aloud.

"It's like the hours just disappeared. Truly, Loch, how is it possible?"

Loch grinned at the sight of the tangled sheets and discarded clothes strewn across the floor. "Do you want me to go into detail?"

"No need," Ivy giggled. "I'll remember well enough!"

There was a silence for a moment. Loch hadn't questioned Ivy's reasons for her physical consent before. Once she had leaned against him and he had felt her warmth, breathed in her clean scent, he could only think of what was going to come. He wanted her with a force he had never felt before.

Their first union reflected this. They were like two wild animals driven by primordial desire. Fierce in their giving and taking, they were oblivious to everything but the searing touch of their skin, the pounding of their hearts, and the overwhelming need for the other.

The second time was gentler, with each leisurely exploring and reveling in secret parts. At one point, Ivy tenderly whispered into Loch's ear, "It's like a conversation that needs no words. I don't want it to end."

Loch was experienced. He had slept with so many women, but the third time … the third time was different. Loch didn't know why exactly but he knew that he had never felt so sated or complete. He was as if he was where he was supposed to be. He had found home.

"Why now?" Loch asked, breaking the silence. "Why did I have to sleep with you now?"

Ivy continued to trail her fingers across his chest. She smiled seductively, but she didn't say anything.

Loch caught her hand, grasping her fingers in his own. "Answer me, please."

Starting to pull her fingers free, Ivy said, "It's past six, and I want to eat before going back to my hotel. I'll tell you at dinner."

Loch wouldn't let her fingers go. Holding them firmly, he said, "I can't wait till dinner."

"You're going to have to!"

The two stared at each other, each wondering if the other would back down. It was Loch who broke the stalemate. Letting out a laugh, he said, "We'll compromise!"

Before Ivy could ask how, Loch reached with his free hand for the phone. "I'm calling room service," he said. "What do you want?"

Ivy asked, "Do I get to see a menu?"

"You don't need one. They will make whatever you ask for."

"You and I really do live in different worlds! Are you always so sure you'll get what you ask for?"

Loch covered her tender lips with his own. It wasn't until several minutes later that he said softly, "When I'm lucky."

"I can't believe we're eating in bed!" Ivy giggled, licking her fingers and smoothing the top sheet over her folded legs.

"I can't believe that you're eating your dessert first!"

Ivy defended herself. "Cranachan is a traditional Scottish dessert. It's the first time I've had it. I wanted to make sure I had a clean palate before tasting it."

"Yummmm," she said, savoring the creamy froth. "Sure you don't want to try a bite?"

Loch looked doubtful, but he opened his mouth when Ivy spooned up some of the creamy mixture from her glass and held it out to him.

"Do I taste whisky?" he asked doubtfully.

"Yes! Cranachan is a mixture of whipped cream, whisky, honey, and fresh raspberries. The topping is made from oats that have been soaking in whisky overnight and then toasted."

"I hope you're not thinking there is an *e* in your whisky," Loch said as he kissed a speck of white cream on the corner of Ivy's mouth.

"What are you talking about?"

"Whisky can be spelled two ways — with an *e*, *whiskey*, or without *whisky*. Both are correct, but in Scotland, using *whiskey* to refer to Scotch *whisky* can get you in trouble."

"Why is that?"

"Country of origin. American and Irish liquor producers favor the spelling whiskey. Scottish, Canadian, and Japanese producers go with whisky."

"I've got it. If a country is spelled with an e – UnitEd StatEs and IrEland – whiskey has an e.

If there is no e, like in Canada, Japan, and our illustrious Scotland, it is spelled whisky!"

"Very good!" Loch said.

"How did you come by this bit of trivia?"

"A forgery."

"What are you talking about?"

"Someone tried to sell a case of Balvenie 50-year-old Scotch."

"So? What's the big deal? We're talking whisky, not Scotch."

"Scotch is whisky. It's whisky made in Scotland. And it is a big deal because of the money involved. One bottle of Balvenie 50-year-old Scotch goes for about 33,550 U.S. dollars. Some bottles have gone for over 47,000 dollars."

Ivy was silent for a moment, and then she said, "But the labels spelled whisky with an e, so you knew it couldn't really have been brewed in Scotland!"

"Exactly!"

"So," Ivy said, "The *e* on the label was the pineapple in the painting!"

"You could say that."

"Would you really spend that amount of money on a bottle of liquor?" Ivy asked curiously.

"No, I wouldn't. My grandmother was looking for a gift for my grandfather. He loves his Scotch, and she decided that he should have the best. She asked me to go with her when she went to the store. She wanted someone with her when she brought the bottle home. She said she was afraid she might drop it."

"She must have been really glad that you went with her."

"You would think," Loch said starting to laugh. "She certainly didn't say so."

"What did she say?"

"She was indignant. She told me that thanks to me, she would now have to think of another gift for my grandfather."

"But all she had to do was buy another bottle somewhere else!" Ivy said.

"Exactly. And that is what I told her."

"So, did she?"

"Yes."

"I think you enjoyed her indignation," Ivy said slowly.

"Oh, I did!"

"But you like her."

Ivy said it with such certainty, that once again Loch felt something in his chest. She was right, but how could she be so sure when they had said so little?

"We're in constant battle."

"Why?"

Ivy listened carefully as Loch revealed how he came to be named and what little he knew of his grandmother's history.

"Do you know what I'd do?" Ivy asked.

"Go to Castle Douglas and Castle Dalziel and find out for myself."

"No!"

Loch was surprised at Ivy's vehemence. He looked at her curiously.

"Let sleeping dogs lie. If you search, you may not like what you discover."

"I'd rather know the truth," Loch said slowly. Then he took a deep breath and said, "Does your reaction have something to do with your own family?"

"Yes."

"The curtness in your voice tells me not to query further. I won't. You can tell me on your time, but for now, you can help me. Come with me to Castle Douglas and Castle Dalziel! We can take our time, explore the countryside, sleep in lots of different hotels …"

Loch kept waiting for Ivy to agree. Most people did not need to be cajoled into a luxury vacation. Ivy was proving once again not to be like most women.

"At any point, if you're unhappy or just want to go home, we can cut it short. But you should come. It will be a grand adventure."

"A grand adventure? As opposed to just an adventure?"

"Yes, most definitely a grand adventure," Loch said pulling Ivy to him so he lick a small speck of cream that remained on her lip.

"Okay," Ivy said, nodding her head slowly. "Okay."

"One more thing."

"You haven't asked enough?"

"This was promised!"

Loch cleared the bed of dishes, setting them on the floor. "I want an answer. Why did I have to sleep with you now?"

Ivy tossed her head saucily. "Tomorrow's game – the one for the championship …"

"Yes."

"If we lost, I didn't want you to think that the only reason I slept with you was to make myself feel better."

Nine

They didn't win. They lost in a second overtime.

Ivy stood in front of her players. Some of them still had tears running down their faces. Family members and aides, some still sobbing, stood by to help the men shower and dress when they were ready, but for now, everyone waited on Ivy. Her voice was pure and strong.

"William Henley is an English poet. He is essentially known for a single poem. The poem is titled *Invictus*. Henley wrote it while in the hospital in 1875. Henley had already had one leg amputated. He was told the second had to go, but he refused. Instead, he suffered through multiple surgeries on his foot in an attempt to save it. I'm not going to recite the entire poem to you, but you can look it up later if you want. What I am going to do is recite to you two lines from the first stanza and the last two lines."

Taking a deep breath, Ivy spoke without falter.

I thank whatever gods may be
For my unconquerable soul.

I am the master of my fate:
I am the captain of my soul.

"Men," Ivy's voice was gentler but still clearly audible. "I did not know what unconquerable was until you allowed me into your lives."

"I ..." and here Ivy's voice caught and a few tears began to seep from the corners of her eyes. "I thank you."

In all the times that Ivy had been the men's coach, she had never betrayed such depth of emotion. The single break in her voice and the wetness of her cheeks were more moving to the men that if she had burst into sobs.

It was Vinnie who said just the right words to break the tension and bring levity back into the room.

"Coach," he called out, "We're thankful, too! For you and duct tape!"

"The duct tape. How did you know?"

Loch and Ivy were in a rented car headed in the direction of North Lanarkshire. Their first stop was Castle Dalziel. From there, they would head to Galloway and Castle Douglas.

"You didn't hesitate, and you were so calm, Ivy said slowly when Loch didn't reply immediately. "The blood, the gore. It didn't faze you at all. It makes me think ..."

"Think what?"

"You're not the typical Wall Street stock broker."

"Why do you think I'm a stock broker?"

Ivy said, "Are you forgetting that I've delivered things to your office? The name's right on the door – Dalziel Traders."

"I don't deal with stocks. I …"

"Oh my God!" Ivy said, cutting Loch off. "Look at that!"

The castle had come into view when they had gone over a little knoll. It was a massive stone edifice with towers, turrets, and rambling wings.

"It's breathtaking," Ivy said as Loch pulled into the parking lot.

"If you hurry," the lady sitting at a table in the main entrance hall and selling tickets said, "you can catch up with the tour that just started."

Ivy grabbed Loch's hand and pulled him behind her as she headed in the direction they were told to take. They came upon the group around the very first corner. Ivy stopped abruptly and stood at the back of the crowd. Loch seized the opportunity to hold her close, his arms around her, his chest pressing gently against her back. Breathing in the clean scent of her hair, he found himself hoping that the tour guide would speak for quite a while longer.

The guide, a young lady dressed in what she explained was a Dalziel tartan, or plaid, was still in the middle of regaling the crowd with how the clan motto had come about.

"During the reign of King Alexander II, one of his kinsmen was hanged by the King's enemies. The kinsmen's body was left danging. It wasn't cut down so it could serve as a warning to everyone who passed by. As the body hung in a public square, it was impossible for anyone to avoid the gruesome sight of the decaying corpse and the crows pecking out its eyes before feasting on softer tissues.

"The king offered a huge reward to any person who could rescue his kinsmen's body. Only one man stepped forward. As he did, he uttered two words: *Dal zell*, or, in English, 'I dare.'

"When this daring man successfully rescued the body, the King rewarded him with land. *I dare* became the Dalziel clan motto, and it remains so even today."

"Do you feel any link to any of this?" Ivy asked curiously. She could speak in a normal tone, as the guided part of the tour was over and they were free to wander through the rooms open to the general public.

"No, not really."

"And you've found out nothing that you couldn't have discovered on the internet. Do you really want to find out why your grandmother was so adamant about your naming and her refusal to talk about why she left Scotland?"

"Are you mocking my efforts?"

"I don't think you're putting any effort into it!"

"Maybe I'm distracted."

"Oh?"

"Yes, I'm definitely distracted," Loch said, pulling Ivy to him and putting his lips to hers.

It felt so right. Loch had wanted to kiss Ivy so many times while they were in their rental car making their way to Castle Dalziel that at times he thought he would go mad. She had seemed happy with their conversation, and in truth it had never lagged. There was so much to talk about with her! There was so much to learn! She made everything fresh and interesting — even the fact that, unlike driving in the United States, they were driving on the left-hand side of the road instead of the right.

"Do you think they will ever switch sides, join the majority and drive on the right side?" Loch had asked Ivy.

"Not any time soon. At least if we're going by men's underwear."

There was a moment of silence where Loch had to think about what Ivy had said.

"Did you say men's underwear?" he asked slowly.

"Yes," Ivy giggled. "Think Sweden."

"I'm thinking Sweden," Loch said slowly, "but I'm not seeing the connection to men's underwear or driving on the right-hand side."

"Sweden switched in 1967 on September 3, a Sunday. At 4:50, all traffic had to come to a complete stop. Everyone had to move over to the right lane. No one could start driving again until 5:00. The government already had street signs in place, but they were covered in black plastic until switchover."

"And I'm waiting to see how this ties into men's underwear."

Ivy giggled. "The switch over just didn't happen. They had four years to prepare. Besides doing the physical act of moving bus stops and getting buses with doors on the right side, they wanted to prepare people psychologically."

"Now I'm not sure I want to know how this ties into men's underwear! Are we talking boxers or briefs?"

"So, they had this logo for the switchover," Ivy said, playfully jabbing Loch in the arm. "In order to get people more comfortable with the change, they put the logo up all over. They even put it on milk cartons and on men's underwear!"

"Are you kidding me?"

"No," Ivy laughed.

"So, are you saying part of the reason Scots drive on the left-hand side is because they wear kilts?"

Now it was Ivy's turn to not know where the conversation was going.

"I'm completely lost!" she said, laughing. "You're going to have to tell me how wearing kilts has anything to do with what side of the road one drives on!"

"You said the logo on underwear helped people accept the change. Underwear isn't worn under kilts."

"Ugh." Ivy's face wrinkled up in disgust. "Are you sure?"

"I haven't looked under any kilts, if that's what you're asking," Loch answered, but I've heard that people don't. Do you know the expression 'going commando' or 'going regimental?'"

"Yes," Ivy said warily.

"Kilts were part of the Scottish military uniform, and it was against regulations to wear anything underneath them."

"Thus 'going commando' or 'going regimental' became slang for not wearing underwear …" Ivy said, understanding for the first time the how the slang came about.

"But soldiers don't wear kilts today, do they?"

"Kilts are part of the formal dress uniforms, but they were retired from combat in 1940."

"Too much exposed?"

"In a way, but not what you're thinking of! Sadly, chemical warfare became part of the theater, and kilts didn't cover enough skin."

"But today — do soldiers really go without anything underneath their kilts today? What if it's some fancy parade and the queen comes to inspect the troops and a huge gust of wind comes up?"

"Quite honestly, I don't know," Loch answered, "but I do know that there is now a rule that Highland dancers and participants of the Scottish games have to wear something underneath their kilts."

"Thank goodness!" laughed Ivy. There was a moment of silence, and then Ivy asked, "Would you wear anything under your kilt?"

Loch didn't answer Ivy's question. All he said was, "I'd let you look."

Yes, the conversation had been fresh and interesting, but the kiss! It was worth waiting for.

When Loch had first put his lips to Ivy's, she didn't pull away, but she didn't respond either. Loch didn't let that deter him. He had waited a long time for this, and he could no longer hold himself back.

The softness of her mouth drew him in, and with one hand he cupped the back of her head so he could pull her closer to him. When at last she relaxed, leaning forward on her own, he felt a wave wash over him. It was only their lips that were in intimate contact, but it was as if his entire body was being nourished and caressed. Past and future had no meaning, for all that mattered was the immediate passion rising from their shared breath.

It was Loch that initiated the kiss, but it was Loch who pulled back.

"I have to," he said, somewhat abashed. "Otherwise I won't be able to stop."

"Well, then," Ivy said primly, "I will wait for a more appropriate time before I dare you to continue!"

Ten

"At least they know how to greet us at this castle!" Ivy said as Loch maneuvered the car into a parking slot at Castle Douglas. "Everyone should be met with a Highlander in full dress playing bagpipes when they get home!"

"I don't know if I want to get out," Loch said. "Even the closed windows can't keep out that god-awful screech!"

"You don't like bagpipes?" Ivy asked in mock horror. "But you're Scottish! They're part of your heritage!"

"Am I Scottish? There was nothing at Castle Dalziel to prove it." Loch wasn't able to hide some of the discouragement he felt in his voice.

"Maybe you're Italian."

Loch looked at Ivy, dumbfounded. Once again he found himself completely at sea when it came to what would come out of Ivy's mouth. He wanted sympathy! He wanted her to make him feel better by gathering him in her arms and caressing him. He wanted her to leave a trail of soft kisses on his cheeks, his neck, his chest, and even further if she so dared!

But she was giving him none of that! Where did being Italian even begin to enter into his search for his naming?

"Why Italian?" he was finally able to sputter out once he realized Ivy wasn't feeling sorry for him in the least.

"It's believed that the Romans were the ones that originally brought bagpipes to Scotland."

"Is that true?"

"Yep. Roman legions arrived here around AD 71."

"But how does this make me Italian?"

"I didn't say you were Italian. I said maybe you're Italian. There's a big difference."

Loch found himself enjoying his bafflement. "So why didn't you say maybe I'm Swiss or even Tahitian? How is it that my not liking the sound of bagpipes makes it even remotely so that I *might* be Italian?"

"Neither the Swiss or the Tahitians ever invaded the British Isles, so I'd never suggest that! You're the one not making sense!"

"Ivy, you've got to help me out! How is it that you're making sense? How did possibly being Italian even come into this?"

"I told you it wasn't a good idea to look up your history," Ivy said. "I told you to let sleeping dogs lie. I told you that you may not like what you discover.

"So, you do, and what happens? You don't find anything. Isn't that better than finding out something horrible? Flip your perspective. Just be glad that you know you're Scottish. That means that you may very well carry a bit of Roman blood in your veins.

"The Romans were amazing. They invented concrete. They made aqueducts that brought water from 60 miles away to their cities. They developed sewer systems and grid-based cities. They made roads and highways that are still in existence today. Stop wallowing in self-pity and enjoy possibilities."

With that, Ivy got out of the car and began to walk across the gravel lot toward the castle doors and the bagpiper. Loch caught up to her before she was even a car-length away.

"How come you didn't list the exploits of the Scots? They merit some attention!"

"All I can think of right now is haggis."

Loch let out a laugh so loud that even the sound of the bagpipes couldn't drown it out.

Ivy and Loch had spent the night at a bed and breakfast after leaving Castle Dalziel. They had stopped for lunch when they were about an hour away from Castle Douglas. After looking at the menu, Ivy had asked the waitress for a suggestion.

"You have to try our haggis," the waitress had responded enthusiastically. "It's Scotland's national dish, and we make it the traditional way."

"You got me at traditional," Ivy said. "I'll try it."

"Sure you don't want fish and chips?" Loch said. "That's what I'm having."

When Ivy shook her head, Loch asked, "Do you even know what haggis is?"

When Ivy shook her head again, Loch said, "I do, and that's why I'm having fish and chips. My grandmother made me taste it when I was younger. I spit it into my napkin before I could swallow it."

"You're just making me determined to taste it!"

The plate the waitress set before Ivy held a fairly large yellow ball. There was a split in the ball so one could see the grisly grey filling.

"Oh, it's like a stuffed bell pepper," Ivy said. "You just have to ignore the grey color. Should I eat the yellow part?"

"I don't know … can you stomach the stomach?"

Ivy cautiously touched the yellow casing with her fork. "You can't mean that this is a stomach?" she asked.

"The waitress said their haggis was made in the traditional sense. That means the pudding contents are encased in a sheep's stomach."

"Pudding!" Ivy said with relief. "I'll just eat the pudding."

Ivy brought a forkful of the "pudding" to her mouth and then stopped. She put it back down after sniffing it and demanded, "What's in the pudding?"

"Does it matter? I thought you were determined to taste it!"

"Tell me!"

"Ouch! Not even a please!"

"Please tell me!"

"Its ground up sheep's heart, liver, and lungs mixed with onion, oatmeal, fat, salt, and some other spices."

Ivy's face paled and she slowly put down her fork. "I don't think I can do this," she said.

"You don't have to," Loch said, a broad smile across his face, as he carefully placed one of his pieces of fish and half of his chips on their bread plates and slid them in front of Ivy. "Half of mine is yours."

At first Loch thought he had done something wrong. For the moment he had slid half of his portion in front of her, Ivy had tilted her head forward so that he could not see her face. All he could see was that she was sitting very still, motionless except for the slight movement of her chest as she breathed in and out.

"Ivy?" he said her name gently. "Have I done something to upset you? You don't have to eat my fish. You can eat anything you want."

Loch put his hand on one of the plates in front of her, but before he could slide it away, she lifted her head. "No," she said, "I do want it, Loch. I thank you."

"But …"

"It's just that …"

Loch waited.

"… you were so generously kind. You didn't hesitate to share …"

Loch found himself wondering who had treated Ivy so poorly that the simple act of sharing food elicited such a surprising response. He had done nothing out of the ordinary! Didn't she know they were a couple?

It was in that instant that it was Loch's turn to become motionless. Had he really thought: *they were a couple*? He had never thought that before about any woman he had ever been with! Ever!

He found himself somewhat surprised that this realization of his being part of a couple didn't disturb him in the least. He wanted a relationship with Ivy! He wanted her to himself. He didn't want her with any other man. He would go hungry if it meant she wouldn't.

So the big and disturbing question was would Ivy ever think she was paired with him? Obviously, she didn't now – not if she didn't even expect him to share his food. Loch felt his jaw tightening. He would do what he had to make Ivy want only him. He would not fail.

Despite his steely determination, he knew he had to tread gently. For that reason, he did not comment about her unexpected reaction when he divided up his dinner.

All he said was, "Half of mine may be yours, but so is **all** the haggis!"

Ivy's gurgle of laughter broke all tension. Loch couldn't help but join in her mirth.

Loch took Ivy's hand and pulled him to her. "There's got to be something good you can think about the Scots!" he said, wrapping his arms around her. He didn't even care that the bagpipe player was playing with renewed energy now that he and Ivy were out of the car. Loch just wanted to hold Ivy close.

"I only know one thing that will make me forget the haggis."

"And what is that?" Loch asked curiously.

Ivy didn't answer. Instead, she gently pulled Loch's head down while raising her lips to his own.

The burn was instantaneous. Heat from each seared the other as desire sparked and lips adhered. Ivy couldn't help but moan. Her lips were sated and felt complete, but the rest of her flesh was crying out for more. Every inch of her body, from the end of her toes to the tips of her fingers, ached for the same touch of naked skin her lips were allowed. Her legs wanted to feel Loch's bare muscular legs against her own. Her arms wanted to feel his chiseled arms, and her breasts ached to feel the pressure of his taut chest against her own.

Neither Ivy nor Loch knew how much time passed while locked in ardor, but they had to separate out of necessity. The bagpiper had marched across the sandlot and was less than a foot away. Blowing furiously on his instrument, he circled them over and over. The sound was painfully deafening, and in order to protect their sanity and save their hearing, Ivy and Loch were obliged to cover their ears with their hands.

The sound was so loud that at first Ivy did not realize what melody the bagpiper was playing. It wasn't until Loch had grabbed her hand, and they had taken a few steps toward the castle gate that it hit her. The bagpiper was playing the traditional wedding march!

Ivy blushed bright red, but Loch only laughed. For the first time in his life he hadn't minded the screech of bagpipes. Ivy's kiss had made him hear only the beating of his own heart.

Eleven

"The ghost has been very active in the last few days, so if you hear strange noises or see her in the halls, don't be startled. She'll do you no harm. Remember, all she is looking for is her true love."

Ivy put her head down so the tour guide couldn't see her smirk. Loch's face betrayed no disbelief, but he did nudge Ivy with his elbow.

"So, you don't believe in ghosts?" he said to Ivy as the tour guide finished the lecture she gave each tour group in the main foyer before allowing them to roam through the castle halls and explore designated rooms at their leisure. The guide's only admonishment after warning them about the ghost was not to enter into any rooms with closed doors.

"Of course not!" Ivy scoffed. "But ghosts make for great stories, and they add intrigue to any location. People like hearing about them. It makes for a much more interesting walk around the castle if you think you're sharing the space with an eerie specter dressed in white who died of a broken heart.

"And people like to be scared. You want a kid not to get bored touring an old house and listening to history – add a ghost to the mixture who is eternally damned to searching for her lost love, and even a ten-year-old boy who has no interest in history or architecture will start paying attention.

"Even better, there will be someone who swears that they heard something or glimpsed something out of the corner of their eye. Each 'sighting' only makes it easier to believe the ghost is real, and that means even more and more people will spot it hovering at the windows or hear it moaning balefully."

"I don't know about all ten-year old boys," Loch interjected, but speaking strictly for me, a forlorn ghost suffering from heartbreak would have done nothing for me. I would have been much more interested if I were told there was a decapitated specter looking for its head, or even better, a zombie stalking the halls."

"Maybe all the zombies are behind the closed doors," Ivy said laughing. "That's why we're not allowed in."

"In that case," Loch answered, "I dare you to open one!"

"First one I come to!" Ivy answered with a twinkle in her eyes. Gone was her ambling and leisurely examination of a room's content. Instead, she darted down halls looking for a closed door.

"Here!" she cried triumphantly after several turns.

"Ivy, are you sure you …"

Ivy flung open the door and ducked underneath the thick velvet cord that was strung between two moveable gold posts on either side of the portal.

She had no sooner straightened from her crouch when voices could be heard drawing closer. Loch expected Ivy to retreat back into the hall and quickly shut the door so that no one would know of her transgression, but instead, with a broad grin, she stepped further into the room.

It didn't take Loch more than a microsecond to assess the situation. If he was going to keep Ivy from getting in trouble for breaking the rules, he either had to remain in the hall and shut her in or join in her disregard for the regulations and follow her. He chose the latter.

"I think we're in someone's private living quarters!" Ivy whispered.

Spotting a rumpled newspaper and a half-full teacup on an end table, Loch nodded in agreement. Although he kept his voice muffled so as to keep the risk of their presence being discovered to a minimum, he could not keep the mirth from his voice. He was enjoying the antics of this woman and her refusal to abide by rules!

"Most likely human, as I don't think zombies or ghosts keep up on the news or drink tea."

Loch's comment struck Ivy as inordinately funny, and she started to giggle. She clapped a hand over her mouth in an attempt to stifle the sound, but she could not stop her shoulders shaking from merriment.

"Dear God, am I seeing things?"

The shock in Loch's voice was so great that Ivy's hysterical joviality evaporated immediately. She watched wide-eyed as Loch suddenly strode across the room to a large antique bed. The bed was canopied, with four thick intricately carved posts. Plump feather pillows rested against its headboard, and a rose-colored silk duvet covered the rest of its expanse.

Loch paid no mind to the mess he was making up of the bed as he climbed on top of it and sat back, resting on his heels so that he could observe the painting hung on the wall above the pillows.

"It's you."

Ivy wasn't sure she heard correctly. "What did you say?" she asked, as she made her way to the bed.

Loch didn't answer. Without taking his eyes from the painting, he patted the bed next to him. Thinking that perhaps she should remove her shoes, Ivy hesitated.

The concern over her shoes was forgotten when Loch spoke tersely.

"It's you. Unequivocally."

Still not sure she understood because it made no sense, Ivy climbed up onto the bed and copied Loch by sitting back on her heels so she could study the painting. The rectangular canvass was about three feet wide, and despite its ornately carved gilt frame, it fit perfectly in the space on the wall between the bed's two back posts.

It was a sensuous portrait of a woman lying on a cushioned sofa. The woman was naked, her white flesh almost luminescent. Reminiscent of Titian's *Venus of Urbino*, one hand was draped across a pillow while the other was delicately cupped over the woman's most secret parts.

At first Ivy didn't understand what Loch meant. The painting was obviously old. It wasn't just that the paint was cracked in places. It was in the details – the furnishings and the bejeweled ivory combs holding the woman's hair in styled disarray, the bracelet dangling from her wrist. It was also in the woman's body shape. She was voluptuous, an amply curved seductress. Surrounded by a thick fringe of dark lashes, her eyes were mesmerizing. They were a dark shimmery brown that drew one in, and somehow, perhaps because of the delicate stroke of the artist's brush, they crinkled almost imperceptibly at the corners, giving one the sense that the woman was secretly amused at something. Her lips were slightly parted, as if to tantalize by causing one to wonder if she would reveal her inner thoughts or instead choose only to offer words of enticement and cajolery.

"If you're trying to seduce me, it's not going to work."

"It's you," Loch said.

"You know this isn't funny."

"No, it isn't funny. It's incredible."

Ivy looked at Loch whose eyes remained glued to the painting and then back at the painting. Suddenly she clapped her hands over Loch's eyes.

"What color is my hair?" she asked.

"What?"

"You heard me. What color is my hair?"

"Ivy, get serious. Study the painting! I'm right."

"Do you even know the color of my hair?"

"Blond. Like a moon path on water. Makes me want to dip my fingers in it."

Ivy's hands dropped. She didn't know what to say for a moment.

Loch looked at her. "You honestly didn't think I knew the color of your hair?"

Loch sounded so hurt that Ivy felt the need to explain. Gesturing at the painting, she said, "You carried the joke too far. She has red hair."

"And no muscle tone."

"A polite way of saying I have no womanly curves."

"Oh, you're perfectly womanly."

"Thank-you," Ivy said primly, feeling strangely pleased.

"Look beyond the extra pounds, the softness, the hair color, and the white skin. Look at her features. Look at her body proportions. Look at the beauty mark. Look at the things that can't be changed, and it's you. Ivy, I'm telling you, it's uncanny."

"What beauty mark?"

"That one," Loch answered, pointing to the upper right arm of the woman on the canvass. It's only a slight discoloration, like you, but it's a swan. Hers is the same size, location, and shape."

Ivy was silent for a moment. "You don't think it's just a shadow?"

When Loch didn't answer, she asked, "Or a discoloration of the paint?"

"Not even a happenstance of lighting," Loch replied. "Ivy, the man who painted this left nothing out. He got her – her seductiveness and her sexiness, but also her intelligence and strength. She enjoyed posing for him. She didn't mind at all. In truth, I wonder if she dared him to paint the truth."

Ivy shook her head. "I don't see it," she said.

"But you see the birthmark?"

"I see it. A coincidence." There was silence for a moment, and then Ivy said, "I'm surprised you noticed my blemish. Most people don't."

"Beauty mark," Loch corrected her. "It's not a blemish. I noticed it the first time I saw your arms bared. You were wearing the black dress. Though quite honestly, when you walked across that floor, I couldn't take my eyes away from your legs. It wasn't until you sat down and that two-inch band of thigh was hidden that I could concentrate on anything else!"

Ivy laughed, "So maybe I'm a bit of seductress myself!"

"Definitely so, and much more than a bit!"

"Then I'll admit that she looks like me," Ivy said laughingly as she scooted off the bed and made her way toward the door they had come through. "But I'm still chalking it all down to coincidence. We better go before we're caught."

Loch didn't follow Ivy until he had taken several quick photographs of the painting with his phone. When he was done, he walked so rapidly that he was just a few steps behind Ivy when she reached the exit.

Neither one of them was prepared for what happened when Ivy opened the door.

Twelve

"Get out now!"

Ivy once read a sentence in a book where it described one of the characters hissing his words. At the time, Ivy thought it was a ridiculous description. People could sound angry or even bullish, but hiss? Hissing was for snakes!

Now Ivy knew exactly what feeling the author wanted to convey to his reader when he wrote that the words were hissed. It was a terrible feeling that made one's stomach turn. It made one feel as if their hand or arm had just brushed against a rotting carcass or worse, as if one had stepped onto a writhing mass of vipers. It was the feeling Ivy had right now.

Loch couldn't see at first who had spoken because Ivy was blocking his view, but his reaction was immediate. In one seamless movement, he stepped forward and pushed Ivy behind him.

Anyone else might be surprised that it was a seemingly ancient man resting on a cane who spoke so vehemently and with such malevolence. They might think that the man's age and frailty made him less of a threat. Loch knew better. Through his line of work, he knew that appearances could never be trusted. Anger or righteousness, no matter how misplaced, could turn the weakest of individuals into powerful brutes. The desire to live could do the same, too. Loch had seen people emaciated from starvation or bleeding profusely from horrendous wounds furiously hold on to each breath with a strength that belied all medical knowledge or belief.

Ivy gasped when the man spat, but Loch didn't move an inch. Loch waited not more than a second or two, though for Ivy it seemed like an eternity, and then very calmly, Loch raised his arm so that he could wipe the spittle dripping from his cheek off with his sleeve. The entire time he did not once take his eyes off of the man.

"Make one move, and I'll break both your legs."

Although Loch spoke in a normal speaking voice, there was something in his tone that sent a shiver down Ivy's spine. Loch was so calm, and yet the steel in his voice gave validity to the seriousness of his threat.

"Loch, he's an old man," Ivy murmured.

"Which means his legs are brittle."

Ivy was horrified. Would Loch really break the legs of an old man?

Ivy's mind was a mass of confusion, but Loch remained still, his eyes fixed on the wizened being in front of them.

"We're leaving now," Loch said. "One move on your part, and you'll rue the day forever you saw us."

Ivy started to protest, but Loch grasped her firmly and moved her forward, all the while keeping in step with her and using his body to shield her from the man.

Ivy was fuming inside, but she kept quiet. Her passivity ended when they reached the end of the corridor. She stopped short, resisting Loch's pull so that she could look back. Rather than releasing her, Loch turned with her.

"No ghosts," the man said. "No ghosts," he repeated, raising his hand and pointing a gnarled and twisted finger at Ivy.

Ivy was going to ask him what he meant, but she changed her mind when the man spat again. They were too far away for any contact with his saliva, but his action was enough that Ivy didn't need Loch to hasten her exit.

It was rapidly escalating into a full-blown fight.

Castle Douglas was situated on the lee side of a large lake. Built on a huge mound, the castle's backside was nestled against an impregnatable rock ridge. The expanse of the lake lay in front of the castle. A trail circled the entire lake, and Ivy and Loch had walked about a quarter of a mile down it. They had stopped at a small outcropping that one could look from, straight down into the brown-tannin stained water below.

"I can't believe you want to walk away," Loch said, unable to hide the frustration in his voice. "I don't know why you don't want to investigate the painting! You can't tell me you're not curious about the model!"

"I told you," Ivy said, exasperated, "Any similarity to me is just a coincidence. We came here to find out about your family. Not mine. I don't care about my ancestors, and I certainly don't care about that stupid painting!"

"And you don't find it interesting that the old man called you a ghost? Was that also just a coincidence?"

"You treated him despicably," Ivy chided. "Shockingly so. Loch, he was an old man!"

"And," Ivy continued, pursing her lips, "He didn't call me a ghost! He said, 'No ghosts.' And despite his obvious senility, it just so happens that I agree with him on this one matter. There are no ghosts! There's no such thing!"

Ivy spun around. She meant to walk back to the car park, but someone was blocking her path.

"So some say."

Ivy stared at the man in front of her. He appeared so suddenly that it was as if he was some apparition sprung from the forest, but Ivy knew that couldn't be. Looking closer, she saw that although this man looked as ancient as the man in the castle, this man had a pleasant face. He, too, needed support, but instead of a cane, he had a walking stick cut from a branch. The wood where his hand rested had been worn smooth and shiny by years of use. He was dressed in swarthy outdoor garb, with dark pants tucked into Wellington boots and a tam, or Scottish cap, on his head.

"So some say what?" asked Ivy.

"That there is no such thing as ghosts."

"And you say there are?"

"So some say. Is that the same as I?"

"No, it isn't," Ivy said, laughing with delight. Normally, Ivy would not have invited a conversation with a stranger, but at this moment, she wanted the diversion. It was a way of reducing the tension rapidly escalating between her and Loch.

Smiling broadly, Ivy looked at the man and said, "I'm here to listen about what some say if you desire to say!"

"We will sit," said the man, pointing to the stone ledge of the outcropping Loch and Ivy had been previously standing on. Nodding agreement, Ivy sat, with Loch on one side and the old man on the other. She didn't even have time to cross her legs before the man began his oration.

"The lass was naught but a peasant child, sired and birthed in a crofter's cottage. Nothing separated her from the mud floor but the pile of straw her mother lay on. According to legend, the wee bairn was made most of big eyes and a mess of carrot hair. An ugly thing all spotted with freckles, but oh, the life in her. She had a laugh that made even the dourest of men break into a smile. Kind, too, she was. Always showing up if one was sick and an extra hand needed. Heard too much and saw too much for being such a little'un, really, but no one seemed to mind.

Then one day, without anyone knowing exactly when or how, she was grown. Turned from ugly duckling to a swan. Freckles had faded, and her hair, her hair was a silken mass of copper and gold."

The man was silent for a moment. Then he said, "The Roman's left their wall …"

When he didn't speak for a moment, Ivy filled in for him. "Hadrian's Wall," Ivy murmured with a smile.

"Yes," said the old man, nodding. "Construction commanded by General Hadrian. Started in AD 122 and marked the end of Roman expansion. Stone, with forts every five miles. Across the entire island, from the Irish to the North Sea."

"So do some say there are ghosts of lost Roman soldiers doomed to patrol for eternity?" Loch asked. His enjoyment with the raconteur and his tale was obvious from his tone of voice. He, too, had been uncomfortable with the disagreement Ivy and he had been having, but Loch felt he had done nothing wrong. Yes, the old man had looked frail, but his spitting was a vile and vicious act. In Loch's mind, it was a situation to be faced, not fled from.

"I'm not here to say," the old man answered. "But the Romans left us more than the Wall."

"Ivy's filled me in on some of their other great feats. I had no idea Roman merits were going to come up again so soon. Good thing I've been tutored," Loch said, a burst of laughter escaping as he grabbed hold of Ivy's hand, raised it to his lips and kissed it.

Still feeling miffed at what Loch said to the old man they met in the castle and his insistence that she should care about the similarity he saw between her and the woman in the painting, Ivy didn't feel like holding Loch's hand at that moment. She tried to pull away, but she couldn't – at least for a moment. Loch didn't release her until he had once more raised her hand to his lips and kissed it.

"Ah, love," the old man said, noting the give and take play between Loch and Ivy. He sat for a moment in a quiet reverie until Ivy queried him further, encouraging him to speak again about the red-haired lady.

"And what else did the Romans leave besides Hadrian's Wall?"

"We're sitting on part of it right now."

"You mean these stones …" Ivy said with astonishment.

"Yes," the old man said. "Collected and stacked and waiting for you to sit on for almost one-thousand years."

There was silence for a moment while Ivy and Loch thought about what it must have been so long ago when the wall was constructed. The man's next comment brought them back to the present.

"Those soldiers left us this, but they brought us something, too. They brought us red-hair. We're a nation of red-heads, and that's what the Romans brought us. They brought us red-hair."

"Didn't red-hair originate in Central Asia?" Loch asked.

"Don't know where it sprung," the old man said, "but it was the Romans who brought it here to the highlands."

"Yes, they did," Ivy agreed. "And we just saw a painting in the castle with a red-haired woman. I think she might be as beautiful as the woman you were just telling us about."

"She's the one. The one in the painting she is. A swan she became."

"Can you tell us more about her?" Loch's voice was persuasive.

Ivy got an unsettled feeling in her stomach. Was Loch going to goad the old man simply because he had the ridiculous notion that in some way she was tied to the woman in the painting?

Ivy began to get up. She was going to say that it was time for them to go, but the old man began to speak. Not wanting to be rude, Ivy sat back down.

"You're as impatient as she was," he said. "But then you've got the sign."

Ivy would not have asked, but Loch didn't hesitate. "What sign?"

"You know fair well," the man said nodding at Ivy. "The mark of the swan."

Ivy almost burst out laughing. This was getting completely out of hand. This was like a huge joke that someone was carrying too far. This old man probably did this same type of thing to every tourist he spotted. She didn't know exactly what it was he wanted or how he was going to go about it, but she was sure that before they left the castle grounds, there would be a request for money. Probably some scam where they have could lay claim to having noble ancestry. For enough cash, they could be assured of having a duke, duchess, or even a beheaded queen as antecedents!

"The Lord saw her here for the first time. He had come up the path on his horse, riding home late at night. He was alone, but the moon was full, and he had no fear of brigands. His steed was quick, his sword was mighty, and he was eager for his own home after defending his king.

"He pulled up on his horse, stopping close to the edge so he could look down into the water. A strange ripple had caught his eye, and he wanted to know what matter of beast was making it."

"And it was a cousin of Nessie, the Loch Ness monster?" Ivy asked, unable to keep the mirthful tone from her voice.

The man shot Ivy such a look of reproach that Ivy instantly felt ashamed. No matter how she felt, she was a guest in this country. No matter what she thought, she should show respect to its inhabitants. The Loch Ness monster had been proved a fake, but still people insisted on believing in it. If this man thought it to be true, Ivy shouldn't jest. She should just keep her feelings quiet.

"I'm sorry," she said. "It's just that you said it was night, and to see the water rippling down below while on horseback …"

"And I said the moon was full," the man said in a chiding voice. "You're not paying attention. *She was swimming in the moon path.*"

"Oh," Ivy said. Afraid of being chastised again, she waited for the man to once again take up the tale.

"He stopped his steed and waited. He didn't know what was going to emerge, but when she did — with water dripping off of her lustrous skin, her hair burnished with moonlight, our Lord was taken. He had to have her.

"She had no idea she was being watched, but when she stepped onto the land, he was waiting for her. He told her forthright that he wanted her. She could be his, and riches and unheard of luxuries would be hers."

"Naked, sleek water still dripping down her alabaster skin, she told him that she would never be with him. Lords were with Ladies, and she was nothing but a peasant girl not to be abused.

"The Lord had never been spoken to in such a way. Instead of driving him away, her fearlessness only made his desire grow. She was naked, but she showed no shame. She didn't try to cover. Instead, she kept her hands by her sides and boldly looked directly at him."

Despite believing it just to be a legend, Ivy found herself worried that the next part of the story would tell of the woman being raped. At that time, women were nothing but chattel. What could a landless peasant girl do against the advances of a man of nobility? Ivy found herself holding her breath as the old man continued with his tale.

"Just as boldly, she dressed in front of him."

"What?" Ivy couldn't help but interject.

"Some say," the old man said with a mischievous smile, that seduction is when the clothes are taken off. But *with every article of clothing this woman put on, always with her lips upturned, her eyes on the Lord's face, she drove the Lord closer to madness with desire. With every layer, she was showing him what he could not have. With every lacing, she was teasing him with what he could not and she would not ever allow him to touch or even see again."*

The old man stopped speaking, and this time it was Loch who broke the silence.

"What happened to her?"

"'I'll wed thee then,' the Lord said, sweeping her up with one hand and placing her on the saddle in front of him.

"She didn't protest?" Ivy asked, scarcely breathing.

"She believed him."

"He wouldn't have," Loch said, shaking his head in disbelief. "At that time, no, he wouldn't have."

"The Lord took her straight to his castle. That very night he sent word for dressmakers and a parson. He took great care in having her sleep in a different wing. He posted a female servant and a guardsman at her door.

"They were wed the next day, in the garden. The Lord swept his bride off of her feet, and he carried her into his chamber. It was two days before they came out, but the servants heard great merriment from behind the bed curtains when the master rang the bell and they hurried in to take his orders for food and wine."

"Oh my," Ivy said. "Two days! How scandalous!"

"I'm sure the Lord would have had it longer, but a messenger arrived with the King's business. The Lord had to return to Court immediately, but he assured his love he would return as quickly as he could.

"Just a few days after he had gone, his now Lady was walking round this very loch. Dressed in her new finery she was, with a maidservant and guard following close behind. She protested the company, but the maid and the guard had been ordered by the Lord himself. She allowed them only because they told her they would be punished if they disobeyed the Lord's orders.

"There was a troupe of actors camped in one of the old forts along the Wall. She would have passed them by, but a young woman called out, begging her to look at her sick babe.

"The babe was sickly looking and mute, but when the Lady undressed it and examined it, it let out a whimper. That was when the Lady said, 'Why this babe isn't sick! It's in pain! She did something then, to its elbow, and the wee bairn's whole body seemed to relax, and then the wee thing cooed and gurgled, just like that."

"A partial dislocation of the elbow joint." Loch said, nodding sagely. "It happens when a ligament slips out of place near the elbow. The medical term is *annular ligament displacement*. It can happen quite easily in babies and toddlers, as people forget that babies shouldn't be tossed around or swung by their arms as their ligaments are still loose. She was a wise woman if she knew how to slip the ligament back in place."

"Oh, please tell me she wasn't called a witch!" Ivy burst out.

"No," the old man said, shaking his head, "but she might have preferred it."

"Why?" Loch asked.

"I don't know if I want to hear it," Ivy said, shifting uncomfortably on the stones. "This isn't going to turn out well, I have a terrible feeling."

Unconsciously, Ivy reached for Loch's hand. The instant her hand was linked with Loch's, he felt an immediate surge of heat and emotion course through his veins directly to his heart. She had reached for him! She had sought him out for comfort. It was such a small thing. He had held so many ladies' hands and had done so much more to so many women, but this simple touch made his blood surge and his heart quicken. He could not explain it, but he knew he would not be the one to let go.

"The young mother was so astonished and grateful," the old man continued, *"that she offered the Lady a gold coin.*

"The Lady was surprised at this, for a gold coin at that time was more than most peasants would ever see in their lifetime. And actors often received their pay in barter — food and drink.

"Where did you get this?' the Lady asked. And it was her answer that made the Lady go that night to the very spot where the Lord had first seen her, fill a bag with heavy stones, and jump to her death."

"Aye, she drowned herself," the old man said when Ivy gasped in dismay.

"What did she say?" Loch demanded.

"She said the coin was one of six, as they had just come into fortune. They had never had such riches. It had all come from her husband. He had, just five days prior, been paid to act the part of a parson. All he had to do was perform a wedding ceremony. The surfeit of coins was to keep his silence."

"How horrible!" Ivy said with dismay. "That poor woman! She was just being used! What a ghastly and unscrupulous trick!"

"Aye, but the trick was not just on her alone."

"What do you mean?" Loch asked.

"The Lord had no intention of deceiving his lady. He did not know the parson was naught but an actor."

"But why …" Ivy asked, her voice trailing off.

"The Lord was devastated. Even more so when they dragged the weeds and couldn't find her body. Wasn't until months later that it rose, all rotted and wrapped in weeds, half-eaten by the foul creatures of the deeps. His Lord swore over her remains that all those who had partaken in the cruel jest would be cursed. His love would be avenged."

There was silence for a moment, while Loch and Ivy took in all that the old man had told them. They were so intent on their thoughts that it took a moment for them to realize that the old man had started speaking again.

"He was a man driven, with heart left only for vengeance. It didn't take him long to ferret out the truth. It was his own brother. His only one. 11 years younger, and because of the rule of primogeniture, nothing to inherit."

"Primogeniture?" Ivy asked.

Loch answered. "The right, by law, of the legitimate firstborn son to inherit his parent's entire or main estate. A younger brother or an illegitimate son or daughter was out of luck. At that time, the only way a legitimate younger brother could inherit the estate was if the elder brother died without producing an heir."

"But how did he avenge his Lady's death?" Ivy asked, puzzled. "If he killed his younger brother, wouldn't he go to jail – or the gaol as they called it then?"

"*The Lord drove his brother off,*" the old man said. "*Forbade him or any of his ancestors to ever enter the estate again for all eternity. Other nobles followed suit, and it is believed he may have drowned at sea. As for our Lord, he made sure to produce sons. He wanted it ironclad that no one but his progeny would come to own the land. Seven of them, he had, and three daughters. Two wives it took to produce them all, as the first wife died birthing his fourth son. And both wives were legal, you can be sure of that.*"

"Those poor women," Ivy said, shaking her head. "To be thought of only as breeding machines. I hope he showed them some kindness."

"They had riches," the old man said, shrugging. "They had titles. Their children were well-treated. As for the bedding, each and every time it was a reminder of their purpose."

"But how do you know he didn't treat them tenderly?" Ivy asked.

"He may well have been gentle on the flesh," the old man said shrugging, "but they knew where the Lord's heart was. How could they not when each time they lay with him it was if they were there with a ghost – that huge portrait of his love hanging there on the wall between the bed posts.

"He painted that portrait himself, you know. In the evenings and months he couldn't sleep soon after she died. There's not one of his sires he didn't begat under her watchful eye."

"How utterly callous," Ivy exclaimed, "and demoralizing."

"It's been said," the old man said, "that even the darkness of the night didn't relieve his wives of his one true love's examination. The Lord always lit a candle and set it beside the bed before doing his business."

"This just keeps getting even more insulting," Ivy said.

"And eerie," Loch agreed. "Think of the flickering light reflecting off the white paint of her skin."

"Mocking them," Ivy said, sadly. Pulling her hand from Loch's grasp, she made a spreading gesture with her hands and said, "At least they had this beauty to console themselves with. They could walk around this lake – or loch as you call it," Ivy said, smiling at the old man. "I know that would make me forget my troubles. At least for a little while."

"Probably not," the old man said. "Or if they did, only in the daylight.

Before Ivy or Loch could ask why, the old man continued. *"They say her wraith haunts this loch still, always walking this path when the moon is full. Waiting, always for the Lord to find her again."*

"Wraith?" Ivy asked.

"Scottish for ghost," Loch answered.

"Right," said Ivy, shaking her head, but smiling to take the sting away from her words. "Wraiths always bring in the tourists. If I were running a tour service, I'd be sure and make sure we came to this castle during the full moon. Then everyone could look for the ghost."

"But only some people would want to see her."

"Right," Ivy said nodding, "not everyone likes to get scared."

"I don't know about being scared. It just depends on one's situation," the old man said.

"What do you mean?" Loch asked.

"According to legend, she is only interested in lovers. She appears only to caution those whose love will not last. If her warning is not heeded, the entire family will be put at risk. Anyone of them might take their own life so as to escape the wraith."

Ivy grinned. "She's a safety net! If anyone really doesn't want to marry someone or wants to back out, all they have to do is say they saw the ghost!"

Ivy was silent for a moment before continuing her thought. "However tragic this lady of legend's life was, I'll bet a lot of women are grateful for it. I wonder how many young girls got out of unwanted or arranged marriages by saying they spotted the ghost!"

"In years past, I'm sure that more than a few came so they could claim they saw the wraith, no doubt," the old man said. "But times have changed. Now they come with different purpose."

"What purpose?"

"The legend goes that if two hearts belonged together, then even if they were split asunder, if they were ever to be reunited, they would have to come here first. To Loch Douglas where the lady could fix them — just as she did with the baby — and make them whole again."

Thirteen

It was the second time that morning she almost died. The first time Ivy put it down to chance. She ran a yellow light, but she was alongside a taxi. There was no way Ivy could know that when the driver was more than two-thirds through the intersection that he would decide to make a left-turn, especially as he neglected to signal with either his rear blinkers or his arm. The car hit Ivy's right handle bar, and it was only Ivy's quick reflexes that allowed her to control the swerve and turn with the taxi.

Ivy banged on the side of the taxi once she had control of the bike, but rather than acknowledging her, the driver accelerated. Ivy pulled over to access the damage. Except for the handlebars being knocked out of alignment, the bike was fine. Ivy didn't concern herself with the physical damage until she had straightened the handlebars – an easy fix. Her right knee and upper leg were bruised were the taxi had made contact when it turned, but Ivy had suffered worse. She could wait until the evening to ice her leg, but she gulped down two ibuprofens from the supply she kept in her messenger bag for the pain now, as well as to keep the swelling to a minimum.

The second bout with near-death was much more serious. Ivy had just dropped off a package at the front desk of the Waldorf Astoria Hotel on Park Avenue. It was more common for Ivy to take packages up to rooms or suites, but this one had come with instructions to leave it at the front desk. Ivy assumed it was because the recipient might be out. The Waldorf Astoria was so upscale that Ivy knew the package would be safely kept until the guest picked it up.

Ivy had planned her lunch break to coincide with the Waldorf Astoria delivery because of the hotel's proximity to the Museum of Modern Art. If one walked, the distance was ten minutes, but on her bike, Ivy could do it in a mere few.

Ivy often spent her free time roaming the MoMA. She loved the 5th floor, especially with its collection of paintings spanning the years 1880 to 1940. Although Ivy detested many of Picasso's later works, she cherished most of his paintings from his Blue Period. She also had a favorite – *Family of Acrobats* – which he painted in 1905 during his Rose Period. There was something about the desolate landscape and the way the family seemed so disconnected despite being grouped together that touched a nerve in Ivy. She felt that it was one of the most poignant depictions of loneliness she had ever seen.

Ivy was already on 53rd Street when she nearly collided with a motorcycle. What frightened Ivy the most was that she was sure the driver had seen her. He was wearing a helmet with dark glass so that his face was hidden, but just before swerving toward her, he had turned his head so that she could see her reflection in the dark glass. His maneuvering of the motorcycle had to be deliberate! There was no way he could not have seen her!

Due to sheer instinct for survival and without thought of consequence, Ivy let go of the handlebars, pushed off of the pedals, and as the bike went forward, dove off sideways onto the sidewalk. Despite her long-sleeved shirt and leggings, she left skin on the pavement. Her helmet was the only thing that kept her skull from cracking.

The driver of the motorcycle ran over her bike, but he didn't stop. Ivy could hear his engine rev as he twisted the grip of his accelerator and raced away.

Several pedestrians stopped, two of whom offered to call an ambulance. Ivy shook her head in the negative while slowly rising. Straightening her messenger bag, she pulled out her phone while gingerly walking over to the remains of her bike. A man had pulled the twisted wreckage out of the street and onto the sidewalk.

"Thanks," she said to the man. "So very much, thanks, but I've got it from here."

Ivy first texted her boss that she would be out for the day, possibly longer because of a wreck, but that she was fine. As she was paid by the delivery, taking a day off of work presented no problem at all. All the messengers supported and provided back-up for each other. Ivy being out of the queue would just mean that her workmates would have extra opportunities to make money.

Finished, Ivy looked up from her phone. Her plan was to drag the remains of her bike to where she could set it beside a garbage can or dumpster. To her surprise, the man who had pulled the bike onto the sidewalk was still there.

"Oh," Ivy exclaimed. "I told you, I'm fine, but once again, thank-you. Thank-you very much."

"It wasn't an accident."

"Excuse me?"

"He ran over you on purpose. I saw it."

Ivy was silent for a moment. "Well that's interesting," she said slowly. She bent down to pick up the carnage of what remained of her bike.

"You're bleeding."

Ivy grimaced. "I know."

"Are you okay?"

All Ivy wanted to do was get home and take a bath. The last thing she wanted to do was have to deal with this stranger. Trying to keep the irritation out of her voice, she said, "I'm fine, thank-you. I told you."

The man took the bike from her and said, "Allow me."

Ivy looked around and then pointed to a dumpster down an alley. "In there," she said. She followed the man as she did her bidding.

"It's just that you're so calm," he said as he threw the bike into the bin. "I'm worried you have a concussion."

"Wouldn't be the first time," Ivy had said in a nonchalant tone. Before turning to go, she extended her hand and shook the man's hand to show her gratitude. "Thanks."

"I'm a doctor."

Ivy pulled her hand away, took a step back, and eyed the man warily.

The man put up his hands, holding them shoulder high and palm out to show that he was defenseless. "It's just that you hit the pavement hard. It was quite a tumble. I really think you should see a doctor."

"I'm seeing one."

The man looked at Ivy quizzingly.

"You said you're a doctor," Ivy said breaking into a grin. "I see you. Just you. No stars. No dizziness. I'm fine."

"Right," the man said nodding. "Obviously you've been through this before. Seeing stars and feeling dizzy are often signs of a concussion."

"Good-bye again," Ivy said, once more beginning to walk away.

"At least take my card. That way if you need anything, you can call."

Ivy knew she would never call, but she didn't want to appear rude. After all, the man had come to her assistance. She took the card and shoved it into her messenger bag. As she made her way down the alley, she knew that when she came to the street, she would need to turn without hesitating. If she didn't, the doctor – or at least the man who said he was a doctor – might think she was confused, a sure sign of concussion.

Without thought, she turned to the left. It wasn't until she had gone a block that she realized what she was doing. She was making her way to the Chrysler building where Loch worked.

It was two blocks later that the hair began to rise on the back of her neck. She had the uncomfortable feeling that something was wrong. It was the same feeling she got on her bike sometimes when she was being followed too closely by a car or truck. The prickly feeling always made her hyper-alert, and Ivy felt the need for the same vigilance even though she was on foot instead of on her bike.

She had been limping slightly since she started walking, but she had kept up a steady pace. Now, as an excuse so that she could go more slowly, she began to walk with a more pronounced limp. The slower pace allowed her to examine the reflections in the store windows. It also made her stops to "rest" seem needed, and it was at these moments that Ivy would examine her surroundings by causally glancing around her.

Although Ivy had turned in the direction of Loch's office without thinking, she hadn't been exactly sure if she would enter the building and ask him for his help. The two of them had gotten in an argument, and it had left Ivy feeling defensive.

The argument hadn't manifested itself until they were on the plane returning from Scotland, but the disgruntlement that led to their disagreement had begun immediately after their encounter with the old man at Loch Douglas who had recounted the story of the ghost.

When the old man had finished his tale, Loch had begun to question him for further details. At first Ivy stood quietly, but when Loch pressed for more information about "the mark of the swan," she had had enough.

Without caring how short she sounded, she said, "This interrogation has gone on long enough." When Loch started to protest, Ivy cut him off abruptly.

"I'll be in the car," she said.

It was several minutes before Loch caught up to her. She had no idea what he and the old man talked about during that time, but she didn't care. She had told Loch that she had no interest in delving into or even discussing her family history. She had only agreed to accompany him on this trip so that he could research his *own* history. He should be thinking about why his grandmother insisted that he be named *Loch Douglas*. Did it mean that Loch's grandmother had loved someone else? Was the name of her grandchild a sign to some lost lover that he was not forgotten? That despite the years that had passed, that she still felt broken and incomplete without him? Whatever the case, it was Loch's concern. She wanted nothing to do with this!

When Loch finally caught up with Ivy, she immediately vented her anger. She told him exactly what she had been thinking, her sentences coming in a rapid staccato. Loch started to say something when she finally stopped, but Ivy's look of fury silenced him.

Loch did not speak again until they were in the car, about to turn left out of the castle parking lot. "Okay," he said, looking at her. "Okay."

In retrospect Ivy should have known better, but at the time, Ivy took Loch at his word. She thought it was over. She thought his saying "okay" meant that Loch would only seek answers about his own heritage and his grandmother. He would no longer pursue any line of questioning or investigation that was connected to herself.

But, of course, it wasn't over for Loch! He had only postponed the discussion he was intent on having with Ivy until she was someplace where he was certain she couldn't walk away. He waited until they were over 40,000 feet above the Atlantic Ocean and captive in a thin shell of an airplane.

Perhaps, Ivy thought, when she went over all that had occurred, Loch hoped that the last two days they spent in Scotland would soften her attitude. Whatever Ivy felt at this very moment while she walked away from the wreckage of her bicycle, she knew that those days were nothing short of magical. In truth, it was in part due to those days that she felt so conflicted now.

Loch had been nothing but solicitous and kind. He had remained silent after his turn out of the car park until they had gone about a mile.

"I thought," he said, "that we would go to the town of St. Andrews next."

"Why?" Ivy tried to keep the wariness out of her voice, but she couldn't quite do it.

"Because," Loch answered, fully cognizant of Ivy's apprehension, "of its links, and it's my way of starting over."

Loch laughed at Ivy's puzzled expression. Loch's laughter did not make Ivy feel small. Rather, it had such warmth to it that it felt like a soothing balm. She felt all her tensions and frustrations over what had transpired in the last few hours begin to dissipate.

"Links, as in St. Andrews Links. Regarded as the 'home of golf' because one of the courses there is believed to be the oldest in the world. People have been playing on it since the 15th century."

Ivy didn't answer, but she reached out across the seat and placed her hand on Loch's thigh. She could feel his muscles flex as he pushed down on the clutch as he changed gears.

"Starting over," Loch said as he kept one hand on the steering wheel and picked up Ivy's hand with the other so he could bring it to his mouth and kiss it.

"Starting over," Ivy agreed. Just as Loch had kissed her hand, she kissed Loch's.

Ivy had never played golf, but Loch had insisted they play the Old Course. Ivy didn't mind her poor play because she was so entranced with the history behind the sweeping greens.

"Tell me more!" she said to Loch as they walked down a fairway. "And then tell me how you know so much about this place."

"I'll answer your question first," Loch said, enjoying thoroughly Ivy's delight. "None other than my grandmother. To call her a fan of golf is to put it mildly. Go past fanatical all the way to maniacal. She plays several times a week, and she takes her game seriously. There's little about the game that she doesn't know."

"The same grandmother that …"

"The one that named me, yes."

"Hmmmm …"

"That's all you have to say? Hmmm?"

"You're the one supposed to be telling me things!"

"Did you know that because of this course, the standard for every golf course in the world is 18 holes?"

When Ivy shook her head that she didn't, Loch told her that the change came about in 1764. At that time, the course had 22 holes. Members decided that the first four and last four holes on the course were too short. They combined them, making the course 18 holes. From that time onward, 18 holes was the standard for any course.

"And what about all these sand pits?" queried Ivy.

"You mean bunkers. There is a total of 112 of them on this course. They are all named, and each one has a unique story and history behind it. You can't believe the number of Open Championships that have been lost because of a ball hit into one of these 'sand pits' as you call them. Trust me, it's much more difficult to put a ball into play when it's on sand rather than grass."

"Oh, I'm finding out!" Ivy said as she cheerfully wacked at a ball.

Later, when a beautiful stone bridge came into view, Ivy didn't even bother to play. She set down her club and walked back and forth along the arch. "This belongs in a fairy tale!" she said. "I'm enchanted!"

Loch couldn't take his eyes off of Ivy. She was so happy and seemed so carefree that he felt something quicken inside of him. He wanted her to feel this way every day. He wanted her to feel this way about him!

It took him a moment to realize Ivy was saying something to him.

"Facts!" she was calling out. "I want facts!"

When Loch didn't answer right away, Ivy stopped and stood facing him, arms akimbo. Eyes twinkling, she said, "Dare I give one kiss per fact?"

"You'll dare!" Loch said before he began his recitation. "30 feet long, eight feet wide, six feet tall. Built over 700 years go to help shepherds get livestock across. Spans the Swilcan Burn, and thus the name the Swilcan Burn Bridge. A burn by the way is a Scottish term for a watercourse.

"It's customary for every champion to show respect and some type of homage to this humble and unimposing structure. Tom Watson has been photographed kissing this bridge, and Jack Nicklaus said his final goodbyes standing on its hallowed stones."

Loch paused only to take a breath before saying, "Eleven."

"Eleven?"

"I'm owed eleven kisses."

"Ten."

"Eleven."

"Not by my count," Ivy said, shaking her head.

Loch wasn't going to compromise. He wasn't going to give up a one! He began to recite the facts again, but this time holding up a finger and keeping count as he progressed.

"But I already knew that a burn was the Scottish term for a watercourse!" Ivy protested when Loch got to that part of his litany.

"Doesn't matter. It's a fact. You asked for facts."

"I'll concede!" Ivy said, "but only because you're so enjoyable to kiss!"

Ivy started on the downward slope of the bridge so as to fulfil her promise, but Loch had already started up to meet her.

They may have met half-way, but each could not help but give all when first they touched. It was if their bodies were drawn to fit, and it was only right that they hold tight and cleave to the other.

Ten kisses owed, or eleven, the number was meaningless, as passion overrode all thoughts of counting. Lips were warm and delicious, and the touch of skin was silken. Hearts beat so powerfully that each could feel the other's throb. Nerve endings ignited, sending sparks that even through the thickness of their clothes warmed to flames. Neither one of them knew how long they had embraced, for with each breath of shared air, each gentle nibble on tender lip, their senses became immune to everything but the one they were holding. They were naught but a mere speck in a vast sea of tended green, but within each other's embrace, they were safe at shore.

"Coorie up!"

The words were spoken so loudly and brusquely that they could not be ignored. When Ivy and Loch turned to face the man who had said them, the look on his face was so stern that they had the feeling he had spoken them more than once. When he began to lecture them on respecting the game of golf and the hallowed ground they were standing on, they were sure of it.

Apologizing profusely, they grabbed their clubs and crossed the bridge for the last time. As they exited the field under the disapproving eyes of the man, Ivy whispered to Loch, *"Coorie up.* What does that mean? Was he calling us names?"

"No," Loch said, trying not to laugh as he did not want to give the man more fodder for his disapproval. "It means *Hurry up.*"

Ivy obediently quickened her pace.

"Ivy!" Loch protested, pulling her to a stop. "Enjoy the scenery!"

Loch pointed to the grand Royal and Ancient Clubhouse that sat adjacent to the magnificent stone Hamilton Hall. Then, turning her, he said, "It's the North Sea. It's too spectacular to rush. If you're going to remember it you've got to absorb it all with leisure."

"You're right," Ivy said as she slowly turned full circle. "Loch," she said softly, "I'm truly glad you brought me here. It's … it's … enchanting."

"Enchanting," Loch agreed with a smile. "Yes, it is."

"Enchanting," Ivy repeated to Loch that night after they were exhausted from their spent passions. She curled up under Loch's arm and nestled herself against him while he pulled the thick damask sheet up to her shoulder so as to keep her warm.

"Are you going to sleep?" he asked, bending his head a bit so that he could plant a kiss on the top of her head.

"Just thinking."

Somehow Loch knew she wasn't finished with her thought, and he waited patiently.

"You were right to make me stop and take in the view. No matter what direction one looked, it was spectacular."

"Speaking of directions, there's a fact I forgot to tell you."

"And that is?"

"One of the unique features about the Old Course is that it can be played in either direction."

"What do you mean?"

"You start on Hole One, but from there you can play in either direction. You can go clockwise or counterclockwise."

"That's unusual?"

"Very."

There was another pause.

"I'm owed."

Ivy raised herself up on one elbow. "What are you talking about?"

Loch put his arm around her waist and pulled her on top of him. "I told you another fact. I'm owed another kiss."

"Just one kiss," Ivy said, feigning disappointment. "I so wanted to do much more, but if that is all you want."

It wasn't all that Loch wanted. He made sure to let Ivy know it, and later, when Ivy called out his name and could not control her shuddering, Loch felt content, knowing he had given her as much as she had given him.

Ivy had never given herself so freely to anyone before. She hid it, but it made her feel vulnerable. Before, she had always kept some feelings in reserve, for that was safer. Nora had always told her that true love required a leap of faith, but Ivy had never felt that final step was worth the risk. Her last two days in Scotland with Loch were the closest she had ever come. Perhaps that is why she was so angry at Loch for what had transpired on the plane on the trip home. Ivy felt Loch had blindsided her, and she still harbored resentment.

"I want you to look at something."

Ivy had taken the window seat. She had heard Loch typing madly on his computer, but she had ignored him. Instead, she kept her eyes fixated on the view outside the window.

"I'll never get tired of flying," she told Loch as she finally turned to look at him. "I know this is only my second time, the first my arrival to Scotland, and now my departure, but I never want to lose this feeling of magic. This plane must weigh thousands of pounds, and we're flying! Flying, Loch, flying!"

"More like hundreds of thousands of pounds. All told, this carrier probably weighs about 735,000."

"And you just know that figure off the top of your head?"

Loch shrugged.

"So how do you know that? And come to think of it, how did you know to put duct tape on Vinny's leg when he was run over by the wheelchair? We never did finish that conversation!"

"It helps in my line of work."

Ivy tried not to scoff. "Loch, you're a trader. Okay, maybe you were dealing in airplane stock so you had to learn plane facts, but duct tape? If there's a commodities or futures market in duct tape, I've never heard of it."

"I don't deal with commodities or futures markets."

"What then?"

"People."

"What do you mean people? Are you trafficking sex workers?"

"Ivy!" Loch was indignant and hurt all at once.

"You're the one that said you don't deal with commodities or futures, and you do work at Dalziel Traders …"

"The name reassures my clients. It's circumspect."

"Circumspect? Doesn't that mean cautious and guarded? I thought traders were supposed to be daring and take risks."

"I do, and my clients want me to, but they also want their privacy. The name is respectable, and it's discreet."

"Circumspect, discreet," Ivy said shaking her head. "It shouldn't be this hard for you to tell me what you do. I'm a bike messenger. I get on a bike and deliver messages and pick up packages. Now it's your turn to tell me what you do just as frankly and just as simply."

"I get people back."

Loch expected Ivy to object that his explanation wasn't enough. Instead, she only spoke one word.

"Cults?"

"At times."

"Kidnapped children from angry ex-spouses?"

"At times."

Asking only so that Loch would have to say something other than "at times," Ivy asked, "Victims of Somali pirates?"

"At times."

There was a moment of silence while Ivy thought about Loch's response. When she finally asked her next question, she spoke the words slowly.

"Brazilian kidnapping victims where the kidnappers send pieces of their victims' ears back to the family?"

"At times."

Once again there was silence, and Loch could see a wave of emotions washing over Ivy's face.

"Well," she said primly. "I've read about the plastic surgeon there who pioneered the procedure to reconstruct the victims' ears and is now quite wealthy. I just hope your fees aren't so exorbitant that not everyone can afford to get new ears after you get them back. It seems to me that it would help one to recover from the psychological trauma of being kidnapped if they had two ears."

Loch didn't know what to say for a moment. Out of all the things that Ivy could have said, this is not what he expected. Most people would have gasped. They would have mentioned danger. They would have asked how he entered into this profession. The boldest would have asked if he had ever had to kill. Ivy only expressed concern for the rehabilitation of those he got back.

"To be honest," he said slowly, "my only concern has been retrieval."

"You make it sound so business-like!"

"I have to think that way. The minute one makes it personal one lessens the chance of choosing the best option."

"And duct tape has come in handy in your line of work?"

"Yes."

"This is all making me suspicious."

"What do you mean? You don't believe me?"

"Of course, I believe you," Ivy said impatiently.

"Then why are you suspicious?"

"Obviously you're successful in your business. That means you have a very unique skill set. That same skill set would make it very easy for you to find out anything you want about your family and your grandmother's history."

Loch knew immediately what Ivy was getting at. "It drove my grandmother crazy that I didn't ask. My lack of curiosity was like a thorn in her side."

"I remember you telling me you were in constant battle, but I also recall you agreeing with me when I said that I thought you enjoyed her indignation."

"Your memory is correct."

"But if you really didn't care about knowing the secrets from your grandmother's past, why did we go to Castle Dalziel and Castle Douglas?"

"I wanted to make love to you."

"But we'd just slept together!"

"Three times."

"What?"

"We made love three times. I remember vividly and fondly each and every time. It made me want more."

"But why …"

"I had to think of something to make you want to go off with me instead of returning with the team. I only used visiting Castle Dalziel and Castle Douglas as enticement. My friend Robert would have jumped at the chance, but you – you told me to let sleeping dogs lie. I wasn't expecting that at all."

"But I went with you anyway because you said it would be an adventure."

"I would have said anything to get you to go with me. And having said already I was interested in looking for clues to my family history, I couldn't change my story."

"It seems an extraordinary effort just to sleep with me," Ivy said with a slight grin.

"Well it would have been pretty bald of me to just come out and say stay in Scotland so I can bed you!"

"And most certainly that would not have worked!" Ivy said laughing.

Ivy felt so good at that moment that she didn't think anything could ruin her mood. Loch may have had to concoct a plan to get her to travel through Scotland with him, but he had come up with a good plan. He had enticed her with the thought of an adventure. It had been an adventure! And truth be told, the love-making had been extraordinary. Ivy had never felt so close to another human being in her life.

"How fleeting that moment of bliss," thought Ivy as she looked down again at her legs. Both knees were bleeding, but the left one was the one that concerned her the most. The blood had seeped through what remained of her leggings and was dripping into her shoe. She needed to wash and bandage it as soon as possible. Loch's office was less than a block away, but still, she wasn't sure yet that that was where she was going to go. If only Loch hadn't done what he had done!

Fourteen

Ivy was pleased with the ample room between rows in the first-class cabin because it was very easy to turn in her seat so she could kiss Loch. She had intended on just giving him a quick kiss on his cheek — a way of showing she wasn't angry at all for him enticing her to travel with him over the Scottish countryside. No matter the false pretenses, it had been a wonderful escapade!

It was Loch who made the kiss something more. Once Ivy's lips touched his, he felt his passion rise. He knew there was a limit to how far he could go when it came to crossing over the line of public respectability, but he was willing to take it to right to the edge. Lips met lips; pressure deepened. Bolts of warmth spread like lightening to the tips of every digit. The new becoming familiar, the familiar only making it more new.

Ivy only came to her senses when Loch, lost to the world except the passions of that very moment, brought a hand up to her breast.

"Enough," she said, pushing his hand away. "Enough."

Loch sat back immediately. Abashed, he ran his fingers over the top of his head and through his hair. "I'm sorry," he said after a moment. "I forgot where we were." He didn't tell Ivy that it was the first time that had ever happened to him.

Of course, Ivy didn't know what Loch was thinking, but she could tell he was a bit embarrassed. Wanting to put him at his ease, she said, "You wanted to show me something."

"Right," Loch answered, straightening his computer and hitting a button so the screen that had darkened lit up. "I just got a little side-tracked, that's all."

"My fault," Ivy said cheerfully. "But now that I know what you do for a living, I'm glad of it." "So," she said again, nodding at the computer. "What did you want to show me?"

Her smile disappeared the instant she looked at the screen. "What is this?" she demanded.

"Sometimes in my line of work I need to use some pretty sophisticated facial recognition algorithms. It's the only way I can be certain of identity, especially if the body has decomposed or been mutilated."

"Enough!" Ivy's tone was curt and Loch mistakenly thought it was because she was upset about his talking so casually about a possible corpse. Because of this, he changed his focus.

"There are several different types of algorithms. I use a combination of geometric and photometric. The geometric looks at distinguishing features, while the photometric distills an image in values and compares the …"

Loch was silenced when Ivy slammed down the lid of his computer. She had seen enough when she saw her face and body diagrammed and overlaid upon another figure.

"I'm not your work."

"But Ivy, you're an exact match! It doesn't matter if I use the geometric or photometric algorithms or even the latest 3-D software.

You're the lady in the painting! Ivy, you've got to be related! You have to be!" Loch couldn't keep the excitement from his voice.

"I told you to let sleeping dogs lie." Ivy was so angry her voice quavered.

Loch looked at her, astonished. "Ivy," he said earnestly, "I know this has something to do with your family. I don't know what happened there, and why you close down when any mention of your family comes up, but it's a serendipitous find! How can you walk away from it?"

"Serendipitous?"

"Discovered or ..."

"Occurring by happy chance. I know what serendipitous means. If you didn't notice, my tone was caustic. Do you need me to define caustic? It means acidic and corrosive."

"Now you're sounding sarcastic, but you're not."

Ivy didn't bother to ask what she was. She just glared. Loch answered the unspoken question on his own.

"You're afraid."

"What?"

"You're afraid."

Ivy was so angry she turned toward the window even though it was completely dark and there was nothing to see but the blinking red light on the plane's wing. She sat motionless, facing the black. She tensed when she Loch leaned forward and gently rested his chin on her shoulder.

"I've always enjoyed reading about Franklin Delano Roosevelt," Loch said, speaking softly into her ear. "We were in the depths of the Great Depression when he was elected, but he made people regain faith in themselves. In his Inaugural Address, he said something that I believe every school child in America should have to memorize. He said, *'The only thing we have to fear is fear itself.'*

"Ivy, I don't know what went on with you and your family. You can go on closing up and shutting everyone out, but that won't make whatever you're afraid of go away. If anything, it makes it worse. Whatever you're afraid of, it's better to face it. I'll do it with you."

Ivy didn't respond, but Loch refused to be dissuaded. "Ivy," he said, the tone in his voice persuasive but gentle, "You can't hide. You were in a castle in Scotland of all places for God's sake, and you met a piece of your past. I don't know where that piece fits, but I do know this. If you confront it – face it on your terms, you are the stronger foe. Don't, and you might be blindsided. You'll never know who might come looking for you one day. And much worse things might happen than being spat upon."

When Loch stopped speaking this time, he expected Ivy to open up. Loch's experience with other women had been that with the right mix of attention and cajolery, secrets dropped as easily as oranges from a netted bag with a tear along the bottom. If anything, they revealed far more than he ever wanted to know.

"Ivy?"

"No," she said, pushing him away. "I told you I would not discuss my family, and I won't."

The remainder of the flight had been an uncomfortable silence, but Ivy had refused to engage in conversation. Instead, she had put on headphones and feigned sleep. When they landed, Loch insisted on driving Ivy home, but she did not invite him in. Loch had phoned and sent text messages, but Ivy had ignored him.

Ivy knew that she was being unfair to Loch. She knew that he was only trying to help her. Part of her fear came from the fact that she had never felt so close to anyone before. It made her feel vulnerable and weak. She wanted to believe that she wasn't yet ready for that leap of faith that love takes. The truth was though, that without Loch she felt that something vital was missing from her very being. That was what scared her the most.

Yes, she had cut him off since the return flight from Scotland. Yet when she was hurt, she had instinctively turned to where his office was. Didn't that mean something? It had to!

"I'm going to Loch," Ivy thought to herself with resolve. "I'm going to Loch." She straightened and took a few slow steps, trying not to grimace at the pain. Then she had a horrible thought: what if Loch wasn't there? What if he was in some faraway jungle in South America or shell-shocked city in the Middle East? With his line of work, he would have to leave in a moment's notice. He couldn't wait around for Ivy to finally respond to all his messages.

It made no sense for Ivy to quicken her pace if Loch wasn't there, but Ivy found herself speeding up regardless. "Maybe he's just leaving," she found herself thinking. "I can catch him before he leaves."

Ivy's anxiety about missing Loch made her momentarily forget her concerns about being followed, but they returned full force with her accelerated pace. She was being followed! Ivy was sure of it!

Several times when Ivy had looked around and seemingly glanced casually into store-glass reflections, she had spotted a woman on the other side of the street. There was nothing about the woman's attire that stood out. She could have been any New Yorker in ballet flats, t-shirt, and blue jeans carrying a nondescript knapsack over one shoulder. It was that she was always there, more or less the same distance behind no matter Ivy's length of stride or pace. It was unlikely that anyone else would have noticed. It was just that Ivy was used to taking in details about vehicles and people around her and then mentally calculating where they would be depending on her own speed. Ivy practiced this type of calculation without thinking. It had been practiced and honed on every bike run. It was what allowed her to slip between cars, shoot across intersections, and sometimes even take a quick dash up a sidewalk.

It was easy for people to call her lucky, what with all the seemingly near misses, but Ivy knew better. When Wes had taken her under his wing when she first became a messenger, he had told her, "Ivy, be Larry Bird."

When Ivy asked who Larry Bird was, Wes at first thought she was kidding. Once he found out that Ivy really didn't know, he subjected Ivy to a lesson she would never forget.

"Forward for the Boston Celtics in the 1980s. Not a flashy player. Not very fast. Not a remarkable jumper."

"But I want to be like him?" Ivy asked, confused.

"Yes!"

"I don't understand."

"Bird spent hours practicing with his team. He didn't stop there. He practiced hours on his own. Hours, Ivy. Hours and hours. His timing and feel for the game became legend. He just *knew* where the ball should be and where it was going to be. And it wasn't due to talent he was born with or illegal steroids pumped into his body. He achieved his greatness the old-fashioned way. He attacked – yes, attacked – every second of every game with every ounce of effort. He was consistent. No feeling poorly and playing subpar. And he never grandstanded. He was a team player. If someone could get a better shot, the ball was passed.

"You're going to be a great bike messenger, Ivy. So, learn to be Larry Bird. Know where you should be. Know where every moving object is going to be."

Of course, Wes had been right, and when Ivy had given this same lecture to her wheelchair rugby players, she had seen Wes nodding in approval.

The woman with the backpack on the other side of the street should have long passed Ivy. Her careful maintaining of the same distance back was what made her stand out. "Larry Bird, I did you proud," Ivy thought to herself. "I spotted her, and I know just where she is going to be."

As Ivy drew very close to the entrance of the Chrysler Building, she stopped. She made it look as if she was resting, but really, she was waiting for the pedestrian crossing sign to change to green. She waited, her timing perfect, until the mass of crossing pedestrians converged on her. Right when she was in their midst, she bent, leaning forward so her height was no longer visible. Moving with the crowd, she remained hidden until she reached the entrance door. Once at the door, she pushed her way inside the building's portal well before the back half of the crowd had passed by.

Ivy pushed the button for the elevator, but while she was waiting for it to arrive, she stood to the side where her position hid her from outside viewing but allowed her to look out onto the street. It was only when she was sure that she had not been followed and had not been seen inside the building did she enter the elevator and push the button for the floor occupied by Dalziel Traders.

Ivy didn't think about how startling or shocking her disheveled and bloody appearance might be. When she quietly opened the door, all was she thinking about was Loch. Would he be there?

Ivy couldn't have stood for more than a half a second before she was noticed.

"Loch!" The name was spoken in a firm and commanding tone by the woman Ivy had brought the pizza for the day she had brought Loch lunch.

The name and the tone were enough. The woman didn't have to say anything else. Loch turned, and before Ivy could take a step he was at her side.

"My God," he said, picking her up. Ivy sagged with relief, pressing her head against his chest. She started to say something as he carried her across the room to a couch, but he shushed her. "Later," he said gently but firmly. "You can tell me later. Now let's just clean you up."

The surge of adrenaline that had been keeping Ivy going suddenly evaporated, and Ivy found herself trembling. Loch felt her fear, and he felt a cold rage sweep through him. Who had done this to her?

He put her down and gently felt her limbs. "No broken arms or legs," he said with a cheer he did not feel. "So now all we have to do is wipe off that blood and see if you need stitches."

"You don't keep duct tape in your desk?" Ivy smiled, albeit wanly, as she asked the question.

"Duct tape?" asked the woman who had called Loch when Ivy opened the door. Unbidden, while Loch had gone to Ivy, she had gone to the restroom to get the first-aid kit as well as some other supplies. She now stood next to Loch. In addition to the first-aid kit, she had a pail of hot, soapy water and a bundle of clean cloths.

"Instead of stitches," Ivy said. "I learned that from Loch."

The woman gave Loch a look of disapproval. "Don't even think about it," she said. "Move!"

To Ivy's surprise, Loch obeyed. He sat on the couch next to Ivy and put a comforting arm around her.

"You'll need stitches on both knees. The arm can get by with butterfly bandages. I'm going to have to pick out some gravel first, though, and that's going to hurt. If it's okay with you I'll give you a shot of local anesthetic. I'll warn you in advance that it is going to hurt, but the shot will lessen the pain in the long run."

"Marcella's a nurse," Loch explained.

"Was," Marcella said, continuing to swab at Ivy's lacerations. "Now I'm just the office manager."

"She's more than that," Loch said, squeezing Ivy closer to him. "She's a whiz on the computer. Does a lot of our preliminary fact finding, and when we call for help in the field, she tells us what our best options are."

"Duct tape," Marcella snorted as she filled a syringe and jabbed it into Ivy's knee. Ivy stiffened, but she didn't show any other sign of distress despite the pain the needle must have caused. Marcella noticed, but she didn't say anything. Instead, she looked quickly at Loch. He nodded to her, letting her know that he, too, had observed Ivy's grit.

Ivy didn't say a word as she eyed Marcella threading a needle, but Loch saw a tendon tighten in Ivy's neck. To take her mind off of being sutured, he said, "Don't let her fool you, Ivy. There was a time when Marcella didn't sound so disdainful about duct tape. In fact, she ordered me to use it!"

Loch was relieved that Ivy finally turned away from her injuries so as to look at Loch questioningly. He didn't need any more encouragement to continue.

"I was in Colombia, two years ago. I got too near a tarantula. Next thing I knew I had this burning pain."

"I would imagine a tarantula bite would hurt," Ivy said.

"I wasn't bitten."

"Then what?"

"I didn't know what it was, but Marcella told me to put duct tape all over my …"

"Bottom!" laughed Marcella. "He had dropped his pants and was going to the bathroom!"

"I was in the middle of the jungle! That's what you do! You drop your pants and squat!"

"But why duct tape?" asked Ivy, oblivious to the fact that Marcella had started on her second leg.

"It took me a couple of minutes to figure it out," Marcella admitted. "But I put it all together once I got the details. Tarantellas are nocturnal, and I'm guessing he squatted too near a brooding female. They get very aggressive."

"So, the stupid thing shot me!" Loch laughed.

"What?"

"Urticating hairs," Marcella said. "In lay man's terms, barbed bristles. They're a tarantula's first line of defense. They throw them."

"They throw them?"

"Yes. It's like being hit by a mist of microscopic barbed hairs. Extremely painful, especially if they go into one's eyes or nostrils. People have lost their sight. Fortunately, Loch was only hit on his posterior."

"When she told me what to do, I thought she was crazy," Loch said laughing. "I felt ridiculous enough putting strips of tape all over my butt, but when she insisted I make sure they were tightly adhered before ripping them off with as much force as I could muster, I knew I was at the point where all dignity had been lost."

"At least your bottom isn't hairy," Ivy mused. "It could have been a lot worse."

Startled, Marcella's eyes grew momentarily wider. "Hmmm …" she said unable to keep the amusement from her voice.

Ivy didn't realize what her words had revealed to Marcella about her relationship with Loch until she saw Loch blush. His entire face and even as much as she could see of his neck grew a deep red.

"Oh," Ivy cried in dismay, "I didn't mean to …" She broke off, as her own face became warm, and she too began to blush.

"I love it," Marcella said, sitting back on her heels after tying off another suture. "FARC didn't faze you, but this little lady mentions your bottom, and you can't keep your cool!"

"Enough," Loch said. "Marcella, enough!"

"I've never seen him this way before," Marcella said, eyeing Ivy with increased curiosity.

"FARC?" Ivy asked, hoping to change the subject.

"Just a day's work," Loch said, shrugging.

Marcella snorted again. "Just in a day's work, he says." As she worked on Ivy's arm, Marcella explained. "FARC is the Revolutionary Armed Forces of Colombia. In Spanish it's *Fuerzas Armadas Revolucionarias de Columbia*. They've been active since 1964.

They fund themselves by kidnap and ransom. Loch was there for two children who had been taken on their way to school. Their father was a judge who had refused to be intimidated by those devils."

"Marcella, I said enough!"

"Oh no, not yet!" laughed Marcella. "I'm not done. There's more to say!"

"You've said enough," Loch grumbled.

"Loch took this one on all by himself. No one knows what he did."

"You're making me out to be better than I am," Loch grumbled. "It's better that I'm unknown. Makes the risk of retaliation less."

"He wouldn't even take payment," Marcella said as she gathered up all her supplies and stripped off her rubber gloves.

"Ivy, what happened to you?"

It took a moment for Loch's question to register. Ivy had been so caught up in what Marcella's tale of Loch that she had momentarily forgotten her own woes.

"Someone tried to run me over — twice."

"Ivy, you're a bike messenger. Everyone's trying to run you over!"

"No," Ivy said slowly, shaking her head. "I was targeted. Perhaps because I was on a bike, but then why follow me?"

"Ivy, I know you're upset, but think for a moment how you're sounding. Accidents happen all the time. This is a huge city with lots of congestion. You're still probably suffering from a bit of jet lag. I can't believe that you went back to work already. Jet lag can put anyone off their game."

There was something in the tone of Loch's voice that Ivy did not expect. She had come to him for support and help, but there was something wrong. His voice was tender, but he wasn't taking her seriously! He sounded … was it … could it be … a bit patronizing? Did he really think that she was being melodramatic just because of jet lag and having had a few patches of skin scraped off? Or even worse, did he think that she was competing with him – after Marcella's tales of his heroics that she had to make her own accident into something more exciting and dramatic?

Wearily, Ivy closed her eyes for a moment. She felt a great sadness inside, realizing she had been wrong to come. Loch did not believe her.

"You're right; it sounds crazy," Ivy said opening her eyes. She stood up gingerly, ignoring the hand Loch had extended for her to grip so he could help her stand. "Marcella, I can't thank you enough. You saved me hours waiting in urgent care. Loch, it's good to see you're not suffering any ill effects from jet lag."

"Ivy! You're still mad at me!"

After Loch spoke, Marcella started to say something, but she decided better of it. "I'll leave you two," she said grabbing hold of all her medical accoutrements.

Marcella didn't take more than a few steps before she changed her mind. She stopped, looked appraisingly at Loch, and then took one step forward. When she was sure that Loch was looking at her, she flashed a wide grin and said, "You might want to rethink your words. Right now you're not doing too well, and Loch, this is one time where you really don't want to blow it."

Fifteen

Ivy averted her eyes from Loch's gaze as she began to walk to the door. Her first step made her grimace, but she quickly bit down on her lip so as to still her face. The men on the team she coached and suffered far worse, and she never allowed them to whine. Their fortitude was what she would reach for.

"Ivy, you're not going anywhere!"

Ivy didn't answer, concentrating on forcing herself not to wince.

"You're being ridiculous," Ivy heard Loch mutter before swooping her up in his arms.

It hurt too much for Ivy to struggle, but that didn't stop her verbal protests. "Put me down!"

Loch didn't bother to answer back. Continuing to hold her, he walked to the door, his stride easy. It was as if he was holding nothing more than a half-empty grocery sack. When they reached the door, Marcella was already there, holding it open.

"Relax," Loch said, as they crossed over the threshold. "I'm driving you home."

Ivy thought Loch would set her down when they reached the elevators, but once again Marcella was there. She had hurried through the portal behind Loch and then went ahead of him so as to push the call button before they got there. Loch spoke to Marcella. His tone of voice as well as his body was so relaxed that no one would know unless they witnessed it that he was carrying an adult human being.

"Call Wes first. Tell him what happened. He can call Nora and find out if I should bring Ivy to their house or hers."

"My house is fine," Ivy said, finally speaking.

"Nora will decide."

Ivy wasn't sure whether to protest or not. If Loch had told Ivy directly she had no choice in where she was to go, she would have objected. Nora being the arbitrator changed things a bit. Why was Loch leaving the decision making to Nora? Ivy didn't understand.

It was as if Loch could read her thoughts. "Nora will be staying with you. I don't know if it will be easier for her to care for you at her house or yours."

"I don't need a babysitter!" Ivy protested. "And besides, Nora might be busy."

"It's Nora or me."

The words were said with such finality that Ivy knew there was no other option. Wearily, she shut her eyes and laid her head back on Loch's chest.

When Ivy accepted Loch's decision so readily, Loch had a thought so sudden and terrible that it made him feel as if a knife had just been slipped under his ribs and twisted into his heart. Was the thought of staying with him so terrible that it had quelled all Ivy's protests of not needing help? Did Ivy really feel that the only alternative was to be with Nora?

The thought that Ivy might find his very presence odious was so painful to Loch that he blurted out the words, "I believe you."

Ivy waited until the elevator doors shut behind them and they were alone before she asked, "Believe what?"

"That you were targeted. Someone tried to run you over twice. You were followed."

"No, you don't."

"Yes, I do!"

"You think I'm off my game. You think it's jet lag."

Loch did think exactly that, but he realized what he thought didn't matter. The hurt he had felt when Ivy so readily accepted Nora as caretaker over him was something he had never felt before. The pain was acute and penetrating, but it was also shocking. He didn't want to feel it again. Loch waited until they were in his car before speaking.

"It doesn't matter what I believe. It matters what you believe."

Ivy was silent for moment, mulling over what Loch had just told her. She said slowly, "And what if I told you I believed I was the Queen of England?"

"You are royalty to me."

"Very clever answer," Ivy said dryly.

"Look, Ivy," Loch said earnestly, "The bottom line is that you don't feel you're safe. I'm willing to do whatever it takes to make you feel safe. You believe you're being targeted. So, allow me to protect you.

"You just can't claim to be Emperor of Antarctica. That I can't accept."

Ivy couldn't help but be curious. "But what if I want to be Emperor of Antarctica?"

"Nope! That position has already been claimed."

"By whom?" For the first time, Ivy's voice sounded normal – exactly what Loch was striving for.

"John Nash."

"Who?"

"Nash was one of the greatest mathematicians of his time. He was tormented by schizophrenia, but despite that won a Nobel Prize in 1994. He was offered a faculty position at the University of Chicago, but he turned them down.

"Why would he turn Chicago down? It's a great university, and it's a great city."

"Nash told the University no because he said he was about to be named Emperor of Antarctica."

"You're not making this up?"

"No. In truth, he is one of my heroes. He transformed the field of economics. His work on game theory is nothing short of brilliant. It's become a crucial aid in high-stakes contests such as arms talks, trade negotiations, and elections."

"So, you apply it in your line of work?"

"Yes, I do and have many times."

Ivy was silent, pondering the information Loch had provided.

"I'm not schizophrenic," she said finally.

"I know that," Loch said laughing. "You're missing my point."

"Hey," Ivy said with the feistiness Loch was familiar with and had been seeking, "I may not ever win a Noble Prize, but I got your point!"

"Which is?"

"Even if one is suffering from delusions, one's thoughts may have great merit."

"Smart girl," Loch said smiling. "Smart girl."

"I don't want you to go home. You're not ready."

Ivy started to laugh. "You're just saying that Nora because you don't want to cook!"

Nora looked around at the bouquets of roses filling every vase in the house. Breathing in deeply, she said, "Maybe I just find the scent of roses sublime."

"No," Ivy said, standing up from the kitchen table and beginning to collect the dishes, "It's the food."

"I probably gained a pound a day since you've been here," Nora agreed, "but how could I not? All the roses Loch sent were romantic, but the meals! Ivy, you have to admit it was very thoughtful. Nothing I would have prepared for you would have come close to what Loch has provided for all of us since you've been here."

Nora leaned back in her chair and closed her eyes. "Braised salmon with melon, rice with peanut sauce, curried cashews and snow peas, sushi trays, fish tacos," she said dreamily.

"Enough!" Ivy said. "It's back to cold cereal and pizza!"

"I still have to go nostalgic over breakfast and desert," protested Nora. "Whole wheat bagels slathered in whipped cream cheese, crusty croissants that melt in one's mouth, berry smoothies, fresh squeezed orange juice, bacon sandwiches topped with fresh avocado …"

"Those were for Wes," Ivy giggled. "I've never seen him eat so much!"

"White chocolate cheesecake with raspberry topping," Nora continued, as if Ivy had never interrupted. "Blueberry tarts, pound cake covered in dollops of cream and piles of strawberries, hazelnut torte …"

"Enough!" Ivy said, laughing. "If I stayed any longer, it would be impossible to go back to normal."

"Maybe with Loch this is normal."

"Then it's not for me."

Nora sat up and opened her eyes. "What's wrong with Loch?" she asked cautiously. "Don't you think it can work out?"

"What can work out?"

Nora appraised her friend with narrowed eyes. "You know," she said slowly. "A future. If it's not Loch, then who or what are you looking for? It seems to me you can't do much better."

"That's your stomach talking."

"No, it isn't."

Ivy turned from the sink that she had filled with hot soapy water. Facing her friend, she said, "I have a question for you. If Loch's so perfect how come he isn't already married? If he's the catch you think he is, then it seems to me that some other woman would have already found him."

"Maybe," Ivy said, "Loch has lots of women. After all, so many women chase him that he dallies with one until he's bored and ready for the next one."

"Did you say dally?" Nora asked with a giggle. "I don't think men dally."

Ivy's response was to smile and turn back to the sink and plunge her hands into the water. She pretended she didn't hear what Nora said under her breathe.

"If it weren't for Wes, I'd gladly be one of Loch's dalliances."

Sixteen

Vinny rolled up to Ivy who had come early, as it was her first day back at practice since her accident. "Coach," he said, "we need to talk."

"I know," Ivy said. "And you're here early! You're never early. Are you sick?"

Ivy's tone was full of jest, but when she saw the look on Vinny's face she lost all sense of levity. "What is it?" Her voice was soft and full of concern.

"It's just a feeling."

Ivy waited patiently. She had no idea what was wrong, but she knew that Vinny had a better feel for what was going on with the team and other players than anyone else. Vinny seemed to inspire confidence. When it came to Post Traumatic Stress Disorder, he seemed to do more for others with a few simple words or a pat on the leg than hours spent in a psychiatrist's office. Once, when Vinny was joking around and feeling expansive (in part due to several bottles of beer), he told Ivy he was thankful for other people's demons.

When Ivy had looked at him quizzically, Vinny explained. "There's a voice in the mind of every veteran that wonders why he or she is the one who survived. When we think about if we deserved it or not, we all come up short. Sometimes the voice is so loud that it can't be borne. I don't wish that voice on any veteran or any person, but I know that every time I can quiet it for one of my fellow soldiers, my voice is easier to bear."

Any words Ivy might have chosen to say could not and would not have been adequate. She stared for a moment at Vinny who, despite the beer bottle in his one good hand, suddenly looked abashed at what he had revealed. When Ivy leaned forward and kissed him on the cheek, Vinny remained still for a moment with his eyes closed. When he opened them, he said brusquely, "Don't go soft on me coach." Then he winked and rolled his wheelchair toward the ice chest, calling for another beer.

That was the first and last time Vinny had revealed something personal to Ivy. Ivy had kept it confidential, as she knew Vinny wanted. It was one of the few things she had never discussed with Wes or Nora.

Ivy was worried now that perhaps the voice of Vinny's demons had become stronger, but as Vinny spoke, she realized Vinny was concerned about a completely different matter.

"It's this feeling," he said again. "Hard to explain. Like the air is wired somehow. I got it several times in Iraq. Not a good feeling, Coach. Something always happened when I felt it."

Ivy still didn't speak. She knew Vinny would tell her all that he wanted her to know. Asking questions or pressing for more information would not loosen his tongue.

"Makes me hyper-vigilant," he said. "So, I can protect myself. Though there's not much left of me to protect," Vinny said a bit ruefully.

"Your heart."

Vinny looked at Ivy, puzzled.

"Your heart," Ivy said again. "Your mighty heart. It's worth protecting. What can I do?"

"Well, that's the thing," Vinny said, "I don't think it's me that needs protecting. It's you. I'm sure of it."

Ivy took a deep breath and then said slowly but matter-of-factly, "No one else believes I'm in danger."

"But you think you are." Vinny made a statement. He didn't ask, but he looked at Ivy curiously.

"Your accident," Vinny said suddenly. "You think it was intentional?"

Ivy nodded. "Someone went for me twice in one day, and then I was followed."

Even as Ivy said the words out loud, she knew how crazy they sounded. Loch hadn't believed her, and though he had made sure that he, Nora, or Wes was with her at all times since then, she could tell that all three of them thought she was reacting to her close call, not any perpetrated danger.

"You back at work?"

The change of subject was abrupt, and Ivy decided that for Vinny, too, it was too much of a stretch to believe that she was followed.

"I'll go in tomorrow," she said. "I'll do a run or two and see how I feel. If I'm okay, I'll stay all day."

Vinny nodded, and then hearing his name called, gave a cockeyed grin to Ivy and wheeled himself to where a mass of other players were laughing at something Torrance had put together.

Ivy worked the men hard, but she could tell they were as happy as she was that she was back. None of them had asked about the mottled bruises that were still fading, but Ivy knew they were all curious.

She didn't provide details or tell them about any of her concerns. Slyly smiling, she simply said, "Just so you know, I made the delivery before I hit the pavement."

"And that's all that counts!" Dance yelled out. Dance was a 22-year-old double amputee whose real name was Pete. Dance had lost both his legs to a staph infection. "Best man at a wedding," he had explained when he first joined the team. "On line-rental tux and shoes. Tux was fine, but the shoes were too tight. Danced the night away, and when I took the shoes off, bloody blister on the end of each big toe. Went to sleep, and when I woke up four days later I didn't have any legs.

"My friends thought I had just passed out from too much drinking. When they couldn't wake me, they called an ambulance. Ends up I was fighting a bacterial infection – MRSA. Methicillin-resistant staphylococcus aureus. Ate my flesh. All from two goddamn blisters."

Dance had hoped for prostheses, but as the infection had made it necessary for part of his left hip to be removed, artificial legs were not an option. After one game where Dance had flown out of his wheel-chair and his torso and spun on the floor like a child's top before coming to a stop, Vinny had called out, "Look there! Pete's trying to dance!" That was the last time anyone on the team ever called Pete "Pete." From then on, he was known as Dance.

"That's right," Ivy said yelling back at Dance, "No slacking on the job and no ..."

Ivy didn't need to finish her sentence, as the entire team joined in rowdily with Dance to finish it for her.

"... slacking on the court!"

"So, what's the plan for tonight?"

The men, sweaty but content, were making their way off the court. Ivy, just as beat but feeling better than she had since her accident, was at the far end of the gym packing her duffle.

"I'm going home tonight," Ivy said, turning toward Vinny who was waiting for her answer. "Nora would have me stay longer, but she and Wes need their privacy."

"Benjamin Franklin said it," Vinny agreed. "After three days any guest smells like rotten fish." "Though I'm not saying you smell like rotten fish," Vinny said quickly.

"Why?" Ivy asked.

"Coach!" Vinny said. "I'm not letting this feeling go. I'm taking you home, and then I'm sticking around until it doesn't feel wrong anymore."

Ivy was so touched that for a moment she couldn't say anything. She had been completely wrong about Vinny. He had taken her concerns seriously! He did think she was in danger! Loch had made sure she was surrounded by people she felt safe with, but he was only doing it for her mental well-being. He didn't think it was really necessary. When it came to relationships, was that enough? That someone would care for her even when they felt the problems were all in one's mind? Was it asking too much for one to also sense the same fears? Ivy's thoughts were interrupted by Vince.

"I'll take you home and spend the night."

Ivy was silent for a moment, thinking it over. She had made sure after Wes's accident that her apartment was wheelchair accessible so that wasn't the issue. It was just that she was ready for some alone time. She loved Nora and Wes, and she would never compare them to rotten fish, but still, she had been looking forward to a quiet evening in her own apartment where she could nestle under a blanket on her couch and eat over-salted popcorn and drink cinnamon tea while streaming a romantic movie.

"You have to think about this?"

The voice sounded somewhat like Loch's, but the tone was so clipped and frigid that when Ivy turned to see who had crept up behind her, she half-expected to see an unfamiliar stranger.

"Loch!" she said, her voice a bit befuddled because of her uncertainty about his voice, "I wasn't expecting you! Nora said you weren't coming back until tomorrow."

"Obviously."

"Obviously what?"

"You didn't think I was coming back until tomorrow."

Ivy took a step back. "You're angry with me!" she said, surprised.

Loch's eyes narrowed. "I didn't know my coming back early would interfere with your plans."

"What plans?" Ivy asked. "What in the world are you talking about?"

"Do you want him to leave?" Vinny inched his wheelchair up closer to Loch and put his hands on the wheels, ready to propel himself forward.

"What?" Ivy said, turning her head to look at Vinny. "Why would I want Loch to leave?"

Loch answered. "So you can sleep with him."

This time when Ivy turned her head again so that she could look at Loch, she felt as if was in some bizarre comedy that had the fuzziness of a Shakespearean comedy being performed underwater. Her reaction time may have been a bit lagging, but when she spoke her words were an unequivocal demand.

"You owe me and Vinny an apology. Now."

Loch looked first at Ivy and then at Vinny. Vinny had the same type of grin on his face that Tom Sawyer would have made when he tricked the neighborhood children into whitewashing the fence he had been ordered to paint while paying him for the "privilege."

"I'm sorry."

There was a moment of silence, and then Vinny spoke. "It's all cool. Coach, I'll wait for you by the door."

Loch waited until Vinny was out of earshot before he said incredulously, "So you are going to sleep with him?"

Ivy said slowly, "I'm not sure I like this side of you."

"I'm jealous. I admit that it's a new feeling for me when it comes to women. It makes me angry. Really angry. I thought …"

"That we had something special?"

"Yes."

"We do. We did."

"Did? So, you're going to sleep with him?"

Ivy picked up her bag and slung it over her shoulder. She walked up to Loch who was standing rigid and gave him a soft peck on the cheek.

"There's a big difference," she said, unable to keep the mirth from her voice, "between someone spending the night and sleeping with someone."

She took a step away toward the door before turning her head and flashing a smile. "The only reason I'm accepting your apology is because you admitted that you're jealous."

She took a few more steps before she turned again. "So, are you coming? Or not?"

Seventeen

Ivy woke to an empty bed. She felt a twinge of disappointment that emanated in her stomach and then coursed to the very tips of all of her extremities. Sighing, she pulled the pillow that still smelled of Loch to her chest and clasped it to her chest while she lay back and thought about what Loch had made her feel last night.

Loch had brought her home after she had explained the situation to Vinny. Vinny had nodded acquiescence, but he had told her, "The feelings there, Coach; I'm not going to let this go until it's gone."

"And I thank you," Ivy had answered simply before leaning down and hugging him.

Loch didn't speak to Vinny, but he had nodded respectfully.

"It's all cool," Vinny said again before wheeling himself out the door to his van.

When Loch and Ivy reached Loch's car, Loch had courteously held the door open for Ivy. He waited until she was seated so that he could shut it for her before walking to the driver's side so he could seat himself. Ivy thanked him while Loch was putting his seat belt, but just as he had with Vinny, he didn't respond verbally. He only nodded.

Loch spoke so little on the way home and while Ivy was getting ready for bed that Ivy could not help think about what she had asked Nora. *If Loch's so perfect how come he isn't already married?*

Loch had been awful quick to jump to the wrong conclusion when it came to her and Vinny. Was Loch's problem jealousy? Did it ultimately drive other women away? Yet Loch had apologized to Vinny, albeit she was the one who had told him to. Despite Loch's lack of conversation, he had behaved as a gentleman, opening and closing the car door for her.

Ivy had still been uneasy, not sure of what to think when Loch, freshly showered, had joined her in bed. She was lying on her side with the blankets pulled up to her neck. Loch had immediately reached for her as soon as he crawled in the other side. Ivy had remained still and mute, but Loch wasn't deterred.

To say that Loch was overly aggressive was incorrect, but there was something about his determination that made Ivy wonder what would have happened if she had objected to his lovemaking. There were no words. It was almost as if Loch was acting on some primordial need. Ivy couldn't help but feel excited, as Loch's urge was so fierce. Their passion was raw, and when release came upon them uncontrollable, they collapsed back onto the sheets with their hearts racing and their skin covered in a sheen of sweat.

Ivy lay quietly, unsure of what to say. Usually she nestled up under the crook of Loch's arm and laid her head on his broad chest after lovemaking, but for the first time she remained on her back. As she felt the thumping of her heart slowly return to normal, she felt completely spent. Loch had demanded and taken, but during that time, Loch had made a world where she and Loch were the only two inhabitants. Nothing else or no one else existed in the universe.

As delightful as that pocket of time had been, Ivy was mature enough to know that it wasn't enough. Physical ecstasy was not enough to maintain a relationship. There needed to be comprehension, compassion, kindness, and generosity. There needed to be intellectual mating too, where curiosity could be sparked and humor shared.

Suddenly feeling bereft, Ivy sighed. She was about to turn away from Loch and face the wall when Loch stilled her, laying his heavy arm across her stomach.

"I lost her."

The words were mumbled and spoken so quietly that Ivy couldn't make out what Loch had said. Although she could not explain how or why because Loch had been incomprehensible, she knew that Loch was in need. She put her own hand on Loch's arm and squeezed gently.

"I didn't hear," she said.

"I lost her."

Ivy understood instantly how terrible the words were. For Loch to have lost someone, it meant that someone had died. No wonder he had behaved so strangely.

"Was it your fault?"

For the first time Loch sounded normal – astonished, but normal. "Aren't you supposed to say you're sorry? Aren't you supposed to comfort me?"

"You don't need me to feel better. Accept that it's over but learn from what happened."

"It won't go down as my error," Loch said.

"That makes no difference."

"I know."

There was a miserableness in Loch's voice that Ivy had never heard before, and it made Ivy want to comfort him. She turned so that she could nestle in the crook of Loch's arm like she usually did after their lovemaking.

"I'm listening," she said, her breath gentle on his chest.

Loch absently stroked Ivy's hair as he spoke.

"In country."

"You mean the US?"

"Yes. Domestic kidnapping. It's not a case I would have usually taken, but I wanted to stay close to you."

"And you normally wouldn't have taken a case like this because …"

"Families get messy. With a Somali pirate or a terrorist kidnapping, it's clear cut. There's a bad guy and a victim."

"And this family was messy?" Although Loch's nod of agreement was almost imperceptible, Ivy could feel it. "Go on," she said.

"So, the father hires me. Says his ex-wife has kidnapped his 12-year-old daughter. All checks out. Courts had given the girl and her 14-year-old brother to the father because the mother was a heroin addict.

"But the mother wasn't really an addict?"

"Oh no, she was. Real loser. Actually tried to pimp the girl for cash."

"That's horrible!"

"I find the girl, but she doesn't want to go back."

"What?"

"Tells me she'd rather stay with her mom."

"So, her mom had cleaned up?"

"Nope. Still an addict."

"I don't understand. The girl's own mother tried to turn her underage child into a prostitute and is a heroin user and the girl doesn't want to go back?"

"That's right."

Ivy was silent for a moment, visualizing the girl despite never having seen her. After pondering the girl's plight, she said slowly, "And the brother? Where was he?"

"With his father."

"But you never factored him into the equation?"

"Didn't think I had to."

"You're saying that like you made a mistake."

"I did."

Ivy heard pain and regret in Loch's voice, but she also heard anger. Suddenly understanding, she said, "The girl didn't want to go back because of the brother."

This time when Loch spoke his voice was only filled with rage. "He was raping her."

"And the father knew?" Ivy asked, tears in her eyes.

"He knew. Didn't care. Told the girl it was all her fault. Just didn't want his ex-wife to get the girl."

"You brought the girl back," Ivy said softly.

"And she killed herself. Just like she told me she would."

There was nothing Ivy could say. It was too terrible. As there were no words, Ivy sought to comfort Loch in the only way people can be when the tragedy is so immense or the loss so great that one is left feeling as if there is a space missing or cut out of one's soul. Ivy gave Loch her body, all the while taking his. After, exhausted but replete, they fell asleep still joined together as one.

Ivy took one final deep breath of the pillow Loch had used before putting it down and sitting up in the bed. However much she would have liked to have woken up with Loch beside her, they had last night. It was hers to remember forever, and no one could ever take it from her. Standing, she stretched and walked over to her dresser. "Second best thing," she thought to herself, as she grabbed her clothes for biking and began to put them on. "Air on my face, trucks to dodge, lights to run – work!"

"No."

The single word was spoken decisively. It booked no argument.

Ivy stood, her mouth open in surprise. Loch was standing in the kitchen, a cup of coffee in his hand. Vinny was at the table.

Ivy was surprised at Vinny's presence, but she was also surprised at Loch's reaction to her entering the kitchen. This was the first time he had seen her since their passionate love-making of the night before. It's not that she wanted him on his hands and knees swooning about how she made him feel, but he could have been a bit more tender! He could have least had said, "Good morning!"

Usually Ivy would have bristled at being told *no* in such a decisive fashion, but still remembering the feel of Loch's hands roving over her body, she decided to forego her usual response. Instead, with a huge smile breaking across her face, she turned to Vinny and asked, "May I bring you a cup of coffee?"

"No." Loch spoke the directive again.

"I'm asking Vinny," Ivy said. "You've already got a cup. You're holding it."

Vinny shook his head. "Keep it in the bedroom, you two. This isn't the time or place."

"Excuse me?" Ivy spluttered, her face reddening.

"The tension," Vinny said. "I can feel it. You two are just sorting out how to fit together."

The sudden image that came to Ivy's mind was so intimate that Ivy's face turned an even brighter red. Before she could tell Vinny his comments were out of line, Vinny turned to Loch and spoke again.

"You could use a little help."

There was a shocked silence until Vinny started laughing. "I mean with words! I figure you two have the bedroom thing going just fine."

"We do!" The response from both Ivy and Loch had come simultaneously, pitched with the same level of indignation. When they realized that they had parroted each other, they looked from Vinny to each other. Ivy was sure that the satisfied glint in Loch's eyes matched her own. When a smile skirted across her face, Loch nodded approvingly.

"Just a bit sparing with the words," Vinny said, as if Ivy and Loch had never responded. "You should know that you can't just tell Coach *no*. She'll do the opposite just to spite you."

"She's not going to work!" Loch said curtly.

Vinny didn't answer, but with one brow cocked he looked at Ivy.

"How I so enjoy being talked about in the third person," Ivy said dryly.

"This is exactly what I mean!" Vinny said, speaking directly to Loch. "You've got to work on your words." Vinny waited a second and then added, "And your tone, man. Honestly, you're a bit abrasive."

Ivy felt a sense of satisfaction that Vinny was reprimanding Loch, but then he pointed one of his remaining fingers at her. "He's not in this alone, Coach," he said. "You're not telling him everything."

Ivy's face paled, and Loch noticed immediately. "What isn't she telling me?" he thought. And then a more disturbing thought flashed through his mind. "Why hasn't she told me?"

"I'm confident you can sort it out later," Vinny said. "Or not. Doesn't matter."

"It does matter!" Ivy's interjection eased some of the tension Loch was feeling. Maybe Ivy was going to share something with him.

Did he finally earn enough of her trust that she could freely reveal herself to him?

"It does matter," Loch said. "It matters a lot."

"What I meant," Vinny said, "is that it doesn't matter when it comes to Coach going to work."

"Ivy," Vinny said, drawing attention to the seriousness of what he said by using her name for the first time instead of calling her Coach, "Loch was right when he told you no. You're not going to work. Too easy to knock you off. Luck never lasts, and that's all you were before – lucky."

Eighteen

"So, these four tourists decide to have a picnic dinner. They set out chairs and a tiny folding table on the edge of a glacier."

"We can do that if you want."

Ivy rolled her eyes and said, "I think not. Listen to what happened. A huge gust of wind comes, and the edge breaks off! The tourists started drifting away!"

"You're kidding me!"

"No. It's right here in the magazine. Fortunately, one of the tourists was able to leap to shore before they floated too far out. He went and called for help. The rescuers said it was the strangest sight when they spotted the other three tourists still sitting in their chairs. There they were, huddled around the table, barely fitting on the tiny ice floe."

"Okay, so we'll set our table far back from the edge."

Ivy didn't respond the way Loch wanted her to. She didn't laugh or even break a smile. Instead, she just bit her lip. Loch wasn't used to Ivy showing any nervousness, and he didn't like it.

"Play and playwright: *Journeys end in lovers meeting.*"

Startled, Ivy looked at Loch. "Is this some type of test?"

"No," Loch said, a teasing smile breaking across his face. "You seem nervous. Thought I'd give you something else to think about."

"You don't think I know?"

Loch paused for a moment, thinking carefully about his answer. "You might," he finally answered.

Ivy started laughing. "Ah, such tact! But then your job is diplomacy." She waited a second before saying, "It's got to be Shakespeare. Everyone quotes from Shakespeare. You mention love, so I'm thinking *Romeo and Juliet.* Am I right?"

"It's Shakespeare. *Twelfth Night.*"

"Half-right," Ivy said. She took a deep breath and then said, "Half-wrong, too. Loch, should we really be doing this?"

Loch took Ivy's hand and gave it a firm squeeze. "Yes," he said. "Yes."

"But running away to Iceland?"

Loch had brought Ivy home from practice, but Vinny, unable to shake the feeling that something was wrong, had followed them. When he saw Loch follow Ivy into the house, he didn't leave. Instead, Vinny pulled his van up closer to Ivy's door but away from any streetlamps. His plan was to spend the night. The first time someone drove down the street on a motorcycle, Vinny didn't really pay attention. When the driver of the motorcycle made a U-turn at the end of street and then started back down, Vinny took notice. He felt a surge of adrenaline when the driver slowed the motorcycle down considerably in front of Ivy's door and once past, accelerated quickly and sped away.

Vinny remained vigilant all night, but the motorcycle was not to be seen until early morning. Vinny knew it was the same one because of the make. He couldn't be sure that it was the same driver, but he suspected it was because he was wearing the same black helmet with the dark face glass that hid his face. As it had begun to dawn and there was more light, Vinny hoped to be able to read the number on the license plate.

Vinny did get a good look at the plate, but he still couldn't read the numbers or letters — they were covered in dirt. "Not a coincidence," Vinny thought, starting up his van. Using the controls designed for his stronger hand, he set the van into motion and started down the street. When he got to the corner, he turned just in time to see the motorcycle making a right turn at the end of the next block.

"He's circling," Vinny thought. Ignoring traffic rules, Vinny drove the van in reverse, backing up until he could park where he wanted. He slid down in the seat, remaining hidden. When the driver of the motorcycle came around the corner, Vinny was able to see what he did.

First, the driver squeezed the motorcycle between two parked cars. Next, he took something out of the bike's seat compartment before walking to the edge of the building on the corner. When the man raised his face mask, Vinny saw what the man had retrieved from his bike. It was a thermos, probably filled with coffee. From where the man was standing, it was obvious that he was doing his own stake-out. He would be able to see Ivy quite clearly when she left her building.

Vinny started up his van when another truck came down the street. He was sure that the man standing vigilant at the corner never noticed, especially as he was not behind him but ahead of him down the street. Just in case, Vinny parked his van after going three-quarters around the block. Once parked, he used his wheelchair to go to Ivy's.

Loch had answered the door. Vinny didn't waste time with small talk. Wheeling himself in, he said, "There's a man waiting to run her over."

"We were just deciding the best course of action when you came down dressed for work," Loch had explained after Vinny had left. "That's why I told you *no*."

Loch had cocked a half-smile before adding, "And Vinny's right. I should have used more words. I should have explained that I didn't want you going to work because I was afraid of what might happen to you. I wasn't saying *no* just so I could order you around."

Ivy understood now, but when the two men first told her what they had been discussing and then revealed to her their plans, she was too stunned to do more than offer a feeble protest. Now, sitting on a plane making its way to the tiny island of Iceland, she needed reassurance that there was indeed some sanity to what now seemed nothing more than madness.

"Yes," Loch said again. "Yes, we should be going to Iceland. I can keep you safe here while Vinny and my staff find out what's going on."

"But it's so small, and it's so open. Isn't it like the most sparsely populated country in Europe? I don't think there are more than 330,000 people there. We'll never be able to hide, and we'll certainly be easy to follow."

"Which is to our advantage."

Ivy was silent for a moment pondering what Loch said. "Oh," she said suddenly, "I'm bait."

"I like the word alluring better."

When Ivy didn't say anything, Loch expanded on what he liked better. "Think lure instead of bait, and you are enchanting and fabulous, so …"

"I get it; I get it," Ivy said. "Alluring, huh?"

"Yes. Definitely alluring."

"I'd like it better if you were the one who was alluring."

"I'm not?" Loch's look of mock dismay still didn't put a smile on Ivy's face, but, at least for the moment, she did seem less distraught.

"It's a good place, Ivy. You're looking at it with the wrong perspective. You say we can't hide, and we'll be easy to follow. I say the person who is chasing you will be easy to spot, and he won't be able to hide! Whatever it seems, we're not just on the defensive here. We're on the offensive, too."

"And he can't eat at McDonald's or go to a strip club."

Loch shook his head. "You've done it again," he said. "I don't think I'll ever know what you are going to say next. What in the world are you talking about?"

Ivy finally laughed. "There's more in this magazine about Iceland than just the dangers of erupting volcanoes and glaciers calving. They have a whole section on fun facts."

"I'm still at a loss."

"So, if your ploy works and someone really does come follow us here, they won't be able to eat at McDonald's because there are no McDonald's in Iceland. There was one, but it closed in 2009. It couldn't make a profit."

"And the strip clubs? Sad to say I can't see those not making a profit."

"Oh, they made a profit, but Iceland banned them. In 2010 the Icelandic Parliament made it an offense for any business to profit from the nudity of its employees.

"Brave move. And a good one."

"I couldn't agree with you more. They quote Iceland's prime minister as saying that the Nordic countries are leading the way on women's equality, recognizing women as equal citizens rather than commodities for sale."

"At any moment of time you can tell me that you're really glad we're going to Iceland."

Ivy said, "Nope. The verdict is still out. It all depends on what happens and what doesn't happen while we're there."

"You know if someone came after me right now, I don't think you're going to be of much help."

"My mind's on other things."

Ivy sunk further down into the hot water she was soaking in. Even her upper lip was under water.

"You can't hide," Loch said, stretching out his legs and fondling Ivy's with his feet.

Ivy grabbed one of Loch's feet with her hands and pushed it away. She sat up a bit, but not so much that her breasts were uncovered. "I still can't believe that we are actually sitting in a running creek with water the temperature of a hot bath! A creek!"

"Don't forget the being naked part," Loch said, "and in broad daylight." He grinned lasciviously.

"All the more reason to stay submerged."

"You're going to have to get out some time!"

Ivy moved just a bit further down the creek so as to be out of Loch's reach – at least temporarily. "I'm glad we came."

"So, the verdict is in? I thought you were going to wait till we left. We have one more night."

Ivy lay back in the water completely supine and then raised her toes so that that all ten of them were sticking out of the water. She wriggled them happily before sitting up so as to hold herself against the gentle current a bit more easily.

"It's truly a land of fire and ice. I never in my entire life expected to see such pristine wilderness. Glaciers, hot pools, waterfalls. And once we're off the Ring Road, it's as if we're the only people in the entire world."

Ivy continued to reminisce. "And the only sign of danger came from the Arctic Terns! You never warned me about them!"

Loch could have pointed out something to Ivy that might have made her feel less complacent, but instead he only smiled ruefully and felt the top of his head. "The scab's still there. I only wish I had known to warn you! I would have stayed in the car!"

Ivy and Loch had come across a scene that had made Ivy cry out in wonder. "It's like a snow globe! But it's huge, and we're in it!"

The "snow specks" were Arctic terns. Just as the white specks swirled in the liquid of a snow globe when shaken, these terns filled the air in masse. There were thousands of them, their small delicate bodies forming a huge cloud of streaming white.

"They migrate father than any other bird," Ivy said, her voice dreamy as she watched them. They get two summers a year."

"That's right," Loch agreed. "They nest here, but they migrate down to the Antarctic coast for the southern summer. I read somewhere that the average roundtrip distance for terns nesting in Iceland is about 44,000 miles. They take some convoluted route so as to take advantage of the prevailing winds. Arctic terns live about 30 years, so that means that in their lifetimes they've traveled farther than to the moon and back!"

"Let's get out!" Ivy said, "But we have to stay on the road. They're ground-nesters, and we don't want to step on a nest."

Ivy and Loch may have had no intention of inadvertently crushing an egg or harming a chick, but the terns had no idea that Ivy and Loch weren't intent on making a meal out of their young. When the two human intruders got out of their car, the birds attacked. The majority of the birds dive-bombed Loch, as he was the taller of the two. Ivy was able to retreat to the car unscathed, but one of the birds attacking Loch succeeded in drawing blood.

Ivy stayed submerged, but she moved closer to Loch. "Do you want me to kiss it and make it feel better?"

"Only a kiss?"

"You think you deserve more?"

"I saved you from thousands of terns! Yes, I think I deserve more!"

"You didn't! Your height did!"

"How do you separate me from my height?" Loch asked laughing. "I don't think that's possible."

"You're right," Ivy said. "I concede. You saved me from thousands of terns."

She leaned over to kiss Loch on the back of the head. Then she whispered softly into his ear, "I've never made love on the Arctic tundra."

The sun never set, as it was the height of the Arctic summer, so neither one of them knew when the day ended and the night began. All they knew was that the water was there to warm them each and every time the tundra was their bed.

Nineteen

"Will we be able to find our way back?"

"Yes."

Ivy pulled on Loch's arm, necessitating his stopping. "We've walked for over an hour. We haven't seen a soul, and I'm not sure I can find my way back to the car. I think we should turn around."

Loch looked at Ivy, surprised. Perhaps she knew more than he thought she did. "I know the way back to the car. You're the one that wanted to see these bird cliffs. How come you're so nervous? We've been in much more desolate areas before. Reykjavik isn't more than two hours away. We have plenty of time to get to the airport before our flight."

"I know I'm the one who wanted to come here," Ivy said. "It's just that when that fisherman told me these bird cliffs where the best kept secret in Iceland, I never thought we were the only ones let in on the secret."

"I also thought there would be a trail," she said. "There's nothing but lava fields and piles of rock. There's not a living thing anywhere – plant or animal. Loch, this is creepy. I can't even tell where we've just walked!"

"But we know we're going in the right direction," Loch said soothingly. "We haven't lost sight of the ocean once."

"I know we've been walking to it," Ivy said, "but I thought it was only about twenty minutes away. For all our trekking, it doesn't seem to be any closer."

"In this type of landscape distances can be deceptive, but we're closer. I'd say only twenty more minutes at most."

"And you can find the way back to the car?" Ivy asked again for reassurance.

"Yes, I can."

"How?"

Loch started laughing. "I wasn't going to say! I just wanted you to be impressed that I could find my way back. I should have known that with you the truth will out! I have a GPS tracking system. It's never failed me, but if it does, we can go back to the old ways."

"A compass?"

"Built into my watch."

"Ah. Old school."

"Is that good or bad?"

Ivy smiled. "Good. I'm reassured. Now I see why you were so quick to agree. I really thought you'd say we should spend our last hours doing something else."

Ivy saw something in Loch's face she didn't understand, but she didn't dwell on it. "Let's go!" she said with renewed enthusiasm. "The cliffs are waiting!"

Just as Loch had estimated, the ocean was not much more than twenty minutes away. The land ended abruptly, with just a small strip of green before the sheer 1,500-foot drop-off. Loch strode right up to the rim and peered over. "You've got to see this, Ivy!" he said straightening up with excitement. "I've never seen so many birds in one place! And they're fearless!"

Ivy came close, but instead of standing like Loch she laid down flat on her stomach before peering over. The height and the sheer drop almost made her feel dizzy, and she didn't want to risk losing her balance and falling. Once she was lying down, it was easy to look over the cliff edge and see the masses of birds perched on ledges so narrow they were almost nonexistent.

"Guillemots!" Ivy cried in excitement. "And Razorbills! This is amazing. There must be millions!"

"They're fearless," Loch said. "I've never seen anything like it. They don't seem to even notice us."

"No predator can get to them," Ivy said. "There's not a fox or a mortal that can scale that cliff. It's a vertical drop down, and that water looks deep!"

"Very," Loch said. "And cold."

"That's enough," Ivy said. "Loch, get away from the rim. It could crumble at any moment, and where would I be?"

"Safe here, lying on top."

"I wouldn't be able to get to you, and by the time I found the car – if I did – you'd be …"

"Dead from hypothermia," Loch said cheerfully, "if not eaten by an orca first."

"An orca?"

"Killer whale. There's a huge population of them out here."

"I suppose they feast on any bird that slips off a ledge." Ivy shivered at the thought though she well understood the role of the carnivore in the food chain. "Loch, you've got to get away from the edge. I don't care if you're uneasy. I am."

"It'd be best if you stood next to me."

There was something so chilling in Loch's voice that at first Ivy wasn't sure what he had said. She felt a twinge of fear in her stomach. The memory of how angry Loch was when he thought she was going to sleep with Vinny flashed through her mind. And Vinny had warned her that something was very wrong! He had said that she was in danger! Had, Vinny, too, been tricked by Loch – the master of negotiation, the man who could modulate his voice to best sway any situation so as to negotiate the deal that he wanted? Loch's tone now, when he said, "It'd be best if you stood next to me," was worse than bone-chilling. It was menacing, the words more terrifying because they were spoken at a tightly controlled normal level rather than at a raised decibel.

This was a perfect site to murder someone. No one knew they were there, for they had no set itinerary. They had left no trail. All it would take was a simple push. One simple push, and then it would all be over. One would be lost to the grey, icy depths of the North Atlantic Ocean.

Ivy tried to grip the grass she was lying on with both hands. A hysterical voice in the back of her mind scoffed at her attempt. "That's not going to hold you down!" it said.

"A rock," a voice from a more sensible part of Ivy's brain was saying. "Sit up casually, but find a rock!"

The entire situation had so quickly turned surreal, that Ivy wasn't sure she wasn't dreaming. Did Loch really tell her to stand next to him, high on the cliff where he could so easily push her in and feed her to the orcas? Was she really thinking she needed a rock to protect herself from the man who had convinced her to travel with him to Iceland so that he could protect her?

Ivy turned her head away from Loch and forced herself to breath normally. She put her right hand out, as if to support herself, while she put her other hand under her belly and felt for a stone. When her fingers felt one she thought she could manage, she used her thumb to loosen it by digging under it and the rest of her fingers to grasp it and pull up. With the heavy weight firmly in hand, she rose to a squatting position.

Her face was still turned away from Loch. She took a deep breath and was preparing to slowly turn to Loch as she stood. Her arm was tensed and ready. She would have only a split second to decide if she should heave the stone with all her might or if she should try to use it as a hammer, holding onto it while striking Loch repeatedly. If she was going over the cliff, she wasn't going to make it easy. She would have to be forcefully thrown, and if that was going to be her end, then she wasn't going alone. She'd pull Loch down with her.

Ivy felt something begin to grab at her, and all thoughts disappeared from her mind. She was nothing but action, her head whipping around while she scrambled back from the ledge and raised her arm. What she saw was so unexpected that for a moment she thought she was seeing a ghostly apparition.

Loch was not alone. There was another man. The two were a tangle of arms and legs, and because they were utterly silent, it took Ivy a few seconds to realize the intensity of their conflict.

As the men continued to grapple, straining against the other, Ivy realized with sudden clarity that this was not a simple case of strong-armed robbery. The two men were trying to kill each other. One of them was going to die.

Ivy wanted it to be a nightmare. She wanted someone to wake her up and reassure her with a warm cup of cocoa. The certainty of it being real became concrete when Loch was suddenly pushed to the brink of the cliff edge. His right foot slid off the edge, and he fell to his knees. One strong push to the chest, and he would topple backwards into the grisly depths of the unforgiving seas.

Ivy let out a scream and plunged forward. With an outstretched hand she grabbed the leg of the unknown assailant and began to beat on the back of his calf with her rock. Over and over she pounded. She didn't let go, even when the man jerked his leg back and kicked her so hard under her chin with the heel of his boot that she felt her mouth fill with blood. Eyes shut and tears streaming, she swung blindly, smashing through cloth, skin, and bone.

Ivy raised her arm, set to chop again, when suddenly she lost her grip on the man's leg. At first, she didn't understand why or how, and it wasn't until it was all over that she realized what had happened.

Loch had stood up. As Loch rose, he lifted his assailant up with him. When Loch stood at full height, he didn't stop. In seamless motion and with one mighty toss, he heaved the man over his head.

Ivy caught a glimpse of the attacker's face as he fell from view. His expression wasn't fearful. He didn't even seem surprised. What he looked was malevolent and furious.

"He didn't scream; he didn't scream," Ivy said fearfully, backing away from the cliff. "He didn't scream!"

Loch peered over the edge. "He can't," he said simply.

Wide-eyed, Ivy stared at Loch. "He can't," she repeated, feeling slow and stupid. Then she sounded her own conclusion. "Because he's dead."

"He's dead," Loch agreed. "Or soon will be."

Loch's conversational tone only added to the surrealness of the situation. A man had just fallen silently to his death, and Loch confirmed it as matter-of-factly as one would the time of day.

The rock Ivy had been holding dropped from her hand. "Why didn't he scream?" she asked, backing away from Loch. "I would have screamed."

"You're not a professional assassin. He was well-trained."

"No one's going to believe us Loch!" Ivy said, a twinge of hysteria entering her voice. "There's so little crime here that policemen don't even wear guns. They're not going to know what to do with us. They're going to think we murdered him in cold blood!"

"Ivy, there's nothing to report."

Ivy shook her head. "What do you mean nothing to report? We killed a man. In self-defense, but we killed him. He's dead."

Loch took Ivy's arm and pulled her forward to the cliff edge. "Look," he said. "Look down."

Reluctantly, Ivy peered over the edge. It was exactly as before. The birds were perched on their ledges, the young ones balls of fluff waiting impatiently for their parents to return with their evening meal. The grey ocean looked just as empty and merciless as it had before. The midnight sun still sat low on the horizon.

"Ivy, there's nothing to report," Loch repeated.

Ivy took one last searching look before nodding dumbly and backing away from the cliff. Still without speaking she began to walk inland. She walked quickly, her pace almost a run. After about twenty minutes, despite stumbling a few times on the rough ground, Loch spoke.

"Turn a bit to the right, Ivy. About ten degrees. That way we'll skirt that rock outcropping, and we'll get to the car a bit sooner."

Ivy didn't answer, but she followed Loch's instructions.

"Or was it a command?" she thought suddenly to herself. *Instruction, command, instruction, command* ... the words seemed to alternate in her head with each step like a deranged form of tinnitus. She couldn't stop them, but she felt if she didn't, her head would explode.

Unable to stand it any longer, Ivy stopped so abruptly that Loch almost walked into her. "Instruction or command?" Ivy asked in a demanding voice.

Loch was used to dealing with people in shock. Despite being completely baffled by Ivy's question, he recognized from her voice that he had to answer carefully. Most people who had witnessed someone dying would be trembling and skittish, but with Ivy he never knew what to expect. She had only shown vulnerability once — when she was upset that the attacker had not screamed. Since then, she had exhibited nothing but stony resilience.

"It's almost as if this isn't the first time ..." he thought suddenly. He looked at Ivy, thinking of her refusal to talk about her family and how her body tensed to the point of rigidity if the slightest mention of kin ever came up.

"It was advice," he said, finally answering Ivy's question.

Ivy didn't comment, but she pointed in the direction she thought the car was in and looked at Loch inquiringly. When he nodded, she turned and once again resumed her quick and determined stride. She didn't speak again until they reached the car, but every ten minutes or so, she would stop and point. If Loch felt a slightly different direction was needed, he phrased his words carefully, wanting to avoid anything that Ivy would take as a command. "A slight yaw to the right might help," he would say gently.

Once at the car, Ivy said, "We're really not going to report this?"

"I don't think we should," Loch said, still wary about sounding too commanding. "But perhaps we should drive up and down the road a bit and see if we can spot another vehicle."

"If he's a professional assassin like you said, he will have hidden his car. It could be parked in any dip or behind any rock formation and it might be years before anyone sees it."

"Or someone dropped him off," Loch said.

That thought hadn't crossed Ivy's mind, but she understood the implications immediately. She quickly got in the car and buckled her seatbelt.

"If you watch your side, I'll watch mine," Loch said. "Then when we backtrack, it will be fresh eyes and a different angle."

Ivy nodded, as it made perfect sense.

"If I was Icelandic, my grandmother's money might not have been enough to get me named Loch."

Although Ivy did not respond verbally to Loch, she did look up at him. Loch was encouraged, as Ivy had remained silent and averted her eyes whenever he had tried to engage her after they had returned from the bird cliffs. She had remained mute the entire time they had searched for their unknown assailant's vehicle, and when they returned to their hotel room, she had locked herself in the bathroom. Hearing the water in the shower, Loch hoped that the hot water would have a soothing effect.

When she had come out, hair still wet, draped in a tightly belted over-sized bathroom, Loch did nothing to break her silence. It wasn't until he was freshly shaved and showered and had made them both a cup of hot tea using the kettle in the room that he made the comment about his grandmother.

He took a sip of tea, and then said, "I don't know if you remember the story of how I was named, but my grandmother paid my mother for naming rights."

Ivy nodded.

Encouraged, Loch went on. "In Iceland, within six months of a baby being born, the parents have to submit their newborn's name to the National Registry. If the name isn't on the registry, they have to fill out an application and pay a fee. The fee doesn't guarantee them the use of the name, but it does mean that the Personal Names Committee will evaluate it.

"If this committee doesn't approve of the name, it's a no go. This is because under Icelandic law, *a forename may not be such as to cause the bearer embarrassment.*'"

"I suppose that makes sense," Ivy said slowly, "You wouldn't want some child named Nipple or Breast."

Loch said, "In the article I was reading, they said that one of the more recent names they rejected was the name Satanía for a girl. The committee's concern was that the child would be called Satan."

"So why wouldn't they approve Loch?"

"Loch would probably pass the playground teasing test, but it might not fulfill other requirements. For example, just recently a girl named Harriet was refused a new passport because her name couldn't be integrated into Icelandic grammar. There are name requirements that deal with Icelandic grammatical endings, linguistic structure of Iceland, and Icelandic orthography."

"You're kidding me!"

"No, I'm not. I'm guessing the name Ivy wouldn't make it either, so we have at least one thing in common."

Ivy stiffened slightly at Loch's last comment. Most people would not have noticed it, but Loch did. He felt as if he had been skewered by her rejection. Was Ivy that averse to having such a small thing in common with him? Was she repulsed by him now that he had done what he had to do to protect her? There was no other way he could have dealt with what had happened on the bird cliffs. And as for going to the police, no matter what Ivy felt, he knew it would not help.

Iceland didn't require visas so it would be very difficult to find out who their attacker was, especially if he had used an alias. Loch had noticed him the second day they were there, but he had chosen not to tell Ivy. Instead, he had contacted Marcella, and she had gotten his staff started on looking for a trail. Perhaps Loch should have told Ivy so that she could have been forewarned. He had opted to remain silent because he wanted Ivy to appear normal. He didn't want her acting skittish. She might not have been so willing to explore the more isolated landscapes of the island if she had known that their peregrinations made her the more tempting bait.

"I think he was the same man who tried to run me over on the motorcycle."

Although Ivy used the phrase *I think*, she sounded certain. Loch was surprised at the relief he felt that Ivy didn't sound angry.

"He was."

Ivy looked at Loch and raised an eyebrow. "Perhaps," she said slowly, "you should take Vinny's advice and be less sparing with the words."

Loch felt a twinge of irritation and jealously. Once more it was Vinny he was being compared to, and at least to Ivy, Loch was the one coming up short.

Keeping his face free of his inner frustration, Loch said, "Whoever he was, he was very good at his job. Marcella's still trying to figure out who he is, but when I sent a photo, Vinny said it was the same man he saw."

"What photo?"

"The second day we were here. We were at Gullfoss on the Golden Circle."

"I remember Gullfoss," Ivy said. "How can I forget? It's only one of Iceland's most famous waterfalls! I wanted to wait to see it until dinner time so all the tourist buses would be finished with their routes, but you wanted to see it in the middle of the day."

"You made sure to express your dissatisfaction to me," Loch said with a smile, "but even you admitted it was a sight worth wading through the tourists for."

"You told me to go on ahead while you went to the restroom," Ivy said, giving Loch a hard stare.

"I never took my eyes off of you," Loch said, reassuring her. "But I needed us to separate so I could look over the crowd. Once I spotted him, I took several photos and sent them on to Marcella."

"You were expecting him?"

"You were the one that called yourself bait. I was never far behind, and I knew that he couldn't do anything because of all the tourists."

Ivy retied the sash around her bathrobe. She thought about Loch refusing to turn around when she felt the Bird Cliffs were too far. She wondered now if he already knew what the outcome was going to be before they arrived there.

"Is it over?" she asked.

Loch knew Ivy was asking if she was safe.

"I don't think so."

Ivy made a sudden fist and smashed it into a pillow. "I can't stand this," she cried in frustration. "If this all doesn't end soon I'm going to go berserk."

"Berserk?"

"Yes, berserk!"

Several days earlier, Ivy and Loch had wandered into a small historical museum. When they entered the small building, Ivy thought that the entrance fee would allow them access to some historical structures strewn around the grounds. It wasn't until they had paid the exorbitant admission fee that they found out what it was they had paid for – access to the basement and a set of head phones with a recorded summary of the epic saga of Egill Skallagrímsson. There were eight small, dark exhibits cobbled together that were supposed to depict important parts of the saga. The exhibits were laid out chronologically, but the workmanship was crude and amateurish.

"Almost as if a Cub Scout group put them together," Ivy whispered to Loch. "Just so they'd earn some kind of badge."

Loch and Ivy were the only two visitors, but as they had the musty room to themselves, they could freely make merry of having spent an outrageous amount of money for something that no matter how well intended was clearly nothing more than a local tourist trap.

Despite their revelry, Ivy found herself getting caught up in the saga. Over and over, Egill is described as exhibiting berserk behavior. Perhaps the most notable time was when he was only seven years old. Egill was playing a game with some local boys, and he became enraged when he felt one of them had cheated. Egill went home, but it wasn't to pout. It was only so he could grab an axe.

Then, axe in hand, Egill returned to where the boys were playing. Once there, Egill "split the skull to the teeth" of the boy who had cheated on him. The voice on the tape did not express any horror at Egill's young age or revulsion at what he had done. It simply said that Egill had gone berserk.

Murder and mayhem followed Egill throughout his life. He killed without hesitation those he felt grievously insulted him, and he slaughtered easily those he once considered friends. Over and over, the voice on the tape explained, "Egill went berserk."

"And these are the stories they tell their children?" Ivy said aghast to Loch.

"We have folk tales, too," Loch pointed out.

"But Paul Bunyan didn't go around axing people at the age of seven! He made the Great Lakes when he needed watering holes for Babe, his great blue ox. And this same ox is the one that pulled on the twisty roads and straightened them," Ivy protested. "John Henry helped build a railroad, and Wild Bill Pecos rode tornados. They didn't kill people!"

"Maybe Egill gets mellower with age," Loch said.

Shaking her head, Ivy took a couple of steps to stand in front of the last exhibit. It consisted of a small hole, bucket-sized treasure chest, and a plastic skeleton.

"I'll bet you the skeleton isn't Egill's!" Ivy said to Loch, squeezing his arm in jest.

The voice on the tape explained that Egill lived until his 80s. Just before he died, Egill had a servant help him bury all his silver treasure near Mosfellsbaer. Egill showed his gratitude to his servant by murdering him soon afterward.

"They never once said Egill was bad!" Ivy exclaimed after they returned the headphones and they were walking out. "Or a terrible man! They just said he went berserk!"

"I've been thinking about that word berserk."

Ivy looked at Loch warily. She hit the pillow again, but then she threw it on the bed. "So, what have you been thinking?" she asked.

"I googled it," Loch said, "after we left the museum and you were in the bakery. We typically use it as an adjective. You already know that it means frenziedly violent or destructive, but did you know that it can also be a noun?"

Ivy shook her head in the negative.

"The word's origins are Icelandic, a combination of their word for bear and shirt. If you're berserk or a berserker – they mean the same – you're a member of a class of ancient Norse warriors. Guess what these warriors did before battle?"

Ivy shrugged her shoulders.

"They worked themselves into a frenzy. Their heightened rage meant that they fought with insane fury and courage."

"So maybe," Loch said slowly looking at Ivy, "it's a good thing that you're feeling as if you're going berserk. It means you're ready to protect yourself."

"But that's the thing," Ivy said, her voice filled with frustration, "I don't know from what! That's what I can't stand."

There was a moment of silence, and then Ivy said someone bitterly, "It's hard for me not to blame you."

Loch looked at her, his face showing no emotion. Ivy stared back at him, suddenly fearful, though she wasn't sure of what.

"That's patently unfair," Loch said quietly, but firmly. "The man was after you, Ivy, not me. I had no choice."

"But it all started after Scotland!" Ivy cried in defense of her accusation. "And you're the one who insists I'm connected to that stupid painting!"

"I'm still working on that."

"All you did was open up a hornet's nest!"

"What is it about your family that you don't want me to know, Ivy?" Loch asked quietly. "I didn't press it when you didn't want to talk about it before, but think for a moment before you clam up and refuse to talk. There have been three attempts on your life in a very short time period. They may be connected to our trip to Scotland, or they may not. All I know is that if I have all the information, I have — we all have — a better chance of protecting you and keeping you safe. You've been lucky so far, but I don't trust luck."

"Maybe I don't trust you."

For the first time Loch sounded weary. "I would never hurt you, Ivy. If you don't know that, then there is nothing more to say."

Loch got up without another word and began to get dressed. It wasn't until he was tying his shoelaces that Ivy realized he intended on leaving.

"Where are you going?" she demanded.

"Does it matter?"

Ivy said something that she never expected to say to anyone.

"I don't want to be alone."

There was a slicing silence while Loch looked at Ivy appraisingly. Ivy felt her stomach churn in painful contortions while she looked at Loch in mute appeal. Had she driven him away?

Finally, Loch spoke. "Enemy or friend?"

"What do you mean?" Ivy asked, puzzled.

His gaze still intent, Loch said, "About 400 BC there was a Chinese general and military strategist named Sun-tzu. Sun-tzu said *Keep your friends close, and your enemies closer.* I'm asking you if I'm enemy or friend."

Ivy was the one who couldn't meet Loch's gaze. Dropping her eyes, she said softly, "I don't want you to leave."

She was painfully aware that Loch knew she hadn't answered his question. There was so much unsaid, that she had kept covered, that it had become too big. She didn't know quite where to start, and she felt that as soon as she opened her mouth, it would all come pouring out in an incomprehensible and confused garble. It would be like a Pandora's Box — flies and wasps and all kinds of vile and horrible creatures — that would drive one to madness before one realized that hope remained. Still, Ivy so hoped, so wanted, so needed him to stay.

Loch stayed immobile for what seemed an eternity, Ivy afraid to breathe, but then he stood and walked over to the bed. Taking a pillow from it, he said curtly, "I'll sleep on the floor."

Twenty

It seemed as if the night would never end. The steady stream of light from the unsetting sun only made the hours seem all the more interminable. Ivy contemplated getting up to adjust the curtains so they covered more of the window, but she was afraid her stirrings would disturb Loch. As Ivy had tossed and turned, she cursed Loch's steady breathing. How dare he fall asleep so easily!

"And yet I'm afraid to wake him," Ivy said somewhat ruefully to herself as she turned once again in the bed. "Where's the sense in that?"

Suddenly she could stand it no longer. She sat up abruptly, and burst out a single word. "Okay."

There was an instant change in Loch's breathing, but he didn't answer.

"Okay," Ivy said again, this time leaning over the bed and reaching out with her arm so she could nudge Loch. "There are things to say."

"I'm listening."

"You're staying on the floor?" Ivy said incredulously. She could not hide the shock in her voice. Ivy had expected Loch to sit up, and if not join her in bed, at least get off the floor! He could at least show a semblance of courtesy by sitting in a chair!

Loch didn't answer, but when Ivy patted the bed, he got up slowly and then walked to the opposite side of the bed. He sat down beside her, resting his back on the headboard, but he didn't get under the covers. Instead, he stretched his long legs over the top of the duvet.

Ivy lay down. She avoided Loch's gaze by looking up at the ceiling. "I don't have a family," she said slowly.

Loch didn't respond. Ivy wondered if he believed her. She waited for him to say something, but he remained mute. It was up to Ivy to share what she wanted.

"I had a family, once," she said. Ivy closed her eyes, staying still except for her fingers — she had interlaced them with the satin edging of the blanket and kept bunching up the material between them.

"There was Alberta and Hugh, who used to be my parents, and Preston. Preston was ..."

Loch could see that Ivy's hands had clenched around the blanket edging. He didn't say anything, but he reached over and covered her closest hand with his own. His touch seemed to be the reassurance that Ivy needed.

"Preston was younger, but only by ten months. I often wondered if it would have been different if there had been a greater age difference."

Loch finally spoke. "How so?"

"He hated me. Perhaps he thought I had usurped his position by being older. But it made no sense because there was none of that primogeniture inheritance stuff that you told me about in Scotland. He was clearly the favorite, and if anyone had the advantage it was him.

"I should have been a year ahead of him at school because of the birthday deadline, but Preston was so upset that I would be ahead of him that he was sent to a private school where he was allowed to start early. Pay enough, and one always gets what one wants.

"I would come home from school, and there would be things missing from my room. I'd find them later, under my covers or when I'd open a drawer. Torn up or ruined in some way. The worst were my dolls. He'd chop off a leg or take out an eye."

"Your parents didn't say anything?"

"Alberta and Hugh blamed me. I was sent to a counselor."

"Sociopaths are good liars."

"I was the one diagnosed as antisocial personality disorder."

"Pay enough, and one can get any diagnosis they want for one's child."

Ivy looked at Loch for the first time. "There's nothing wrong with you," he said gently. "You know that, right?"

"I stepped out of the shower once, and he was in the bathroom. I screamed and pushed him out the door. I was told I was over reacting. I started locking the bathroom door and my bedroom door, but he would rattle the knob, just so that I knew he was outside waiting.

"He asked for a lock picking kit for his twelfth birthday. He made sure everyone saw him reading books about Houdini before he asked."

"So, everyone thought he just wanted to emulate the greatest escape artist of all time. Very clever, but it also shows the depths of his evilness."

Ivy sat up suddenly, pulling the duvet up so it would cover her breasts. "Yes," she said. "That's what he was. He wasn't sick. He was evil. Pure evilness."

"Whatever he did to you, it wasn't your fault"

"It's what I did to him."

"Throw him over a cliff?"

For the first time Ivy smiled, albeit weakly. "No," she said, shaking her head. "My methods were more devious."

It was hard for Loch to show patience. He wanted to shake Ivy by the shoulders and demand that she tell him all that she had refused to bare. It was only because he knew how skittish she was that he forced himself to wait silently, hoping she would explain. When she finally spoke, he sat quietly.

"I braced a chair against my door before going to bed at night. I'd do the same when I showered. I had to because the locks on the doors were so simple that they were no deterrent. I knew Hugh and Alberta wouldn't help. I heard them showing off about how clever Preston was when it came to deciphering lock mechanisms and how hard he practiced so as to make their unlocking appear so effortlessly seamless. Hugh would scour second hand stores, antique stores, and even police equipment stores so as to purchase locks and handcuffs for Preston to practice on. He would take Preston into fancy hotels, and he would rent a room just so Preston could practice picking the door locks.

"I loved the book *The Swiss Family Robinson*, and the movie was even better. In the movie, the youngest boy Francis, after the family gets ship-wrecked and ends up on that tropical island, sets up a pirate trap by stringing some bells along a tree branch. The trap is much maligned and scoffed at, as it is so innocuous and simple compared to the pit with the enraged tiger and the rock and log piles designed to crush the oncoming pirates with one fell swoop. Unlike all the bombs made from hollowed out coconuts and filled with gunpowder, the trap took only seconds to set up, and yet it was the single string of bells which provided the clarion call that thwarted the surprise back door attack of the pirates and ultimately saved the family."

Loch smiled at Ivy. "That book is one of the few I kept from my childhood. A great read. My goal was to grow up and live in a tree house just like they did."

"So, I set up some bells," Ivy continued, her voice soft and devoid of inflection, "because I knew it was only a matter of time before the chair slipped, or Preston would figure out a way to get the door open."

"Those bells saved me three times. I was asleep each time, but I had so many tied together that the noise of their jangling was enough to wake me up."

"And the noise was enough to make Preston leave?"

"I'm not sure. I wasn't going to wait to find out. What I did was just start screaming. I'd scream loud enough to wake everyone up."

"And even then Preston didn't get in trouble?"

"I got in trouble for having nightmares. Preston was lauded for coming to my aid so quickly. I was made to thank him."

It was Loch's turn to be incredulous. "Ivy," he said gently but firmly, "what you're telling me is a nightmare! No child should ever have to be under such duress or suffer the way you did. Your parents should be in jail!"

"They're not my parents. I told you I don't have a family," Ivy said, her voice short.

"You wouldn't want to have them as family," Loch said, agreeing. "They sound despicable and odious."

"When they returned me, I told myself I was lucky not to have a family. I still feel that way."

Loch was momentarily confused. "They returned you? Like a bottle with a deposit?"

"I was adopted. I didn't know until I was relinquished. Ends up lots of children are returned. The worst cases hit the news of course — like when that nurse from Tennessee put her seven-year-old adopted son on a plane, alone, and sent him back to his native Russia. The truth is that something like ten percent of all adoptions are dissolved — the parent-child relationship completely severed."

"I would think that happens most with children who were adopted when they older or are disabled," Loch said thoughtfully.

"You're right," Ivy said. "The international adoption pool has shrunk due to tighter restrictions, so there's been a rise in adopting more challenging children. Some overseas agencies have fees of over 40,000 dollars. They are more than willing to lie about a baby's age or what conditions it has been living in. Some of the kids are nothing more than feral. They won't make eye contact, they spit and bite, and they can't stand to be touched."

"I was adopted as a baby," Ivy said. "Just a week old and here in the U.S. Alberta thought she couldn't have children. She and Hugh had tried for years, and after they had gone through every infertility treatment possible, they decided to adopt."

"Was Preston adopted, too?"

"No. He was Alberta's and Hugh's. Alberta thought that if she adopted a baby she would get pregnant. She had heard that having a baby would somehow relax her, and it would be easier for her to get pregnant."

"I'm pretty sure that's a myth," Loch said.

"Pretty much," Ivy agreed. "But it's a pervasive myth. The truth is that the women who conceive after adopting fall within the percentages of spontaneous pregnancy, even if they didn't go through or stopped infertility treatments."

"It's pretty bold to assume adopting a baby is relaxing," Loch mused.

"And that reasoning is even worse for a woman who is raped and gets pregnant. Think of those idiots like Todd Akin and Pete Nielsen. Akin said, 'If it's a legitimate rape, the female body has ways to shut that whole thing down.' Nielson said he was 'of the understanding that in many cases of rape it does not involve any pregnancy because of the trauma of the incident. That may be true with incest a little bit.'"

"Akin was a Missouri Representative?"

"Yes, and Nielsen was a representative too, but he was from Idaho."

"I'm in complete agreement; they are both idiots. Worse, actually. I've always liked the magazine *Scientific American*. It's known for its rigorous fact checking, and according to them, women get pregnant from rape as frequently as they get pregnant from consensual sex."

"Whatever the facts, Alberta believed adopting me would help her to get pregnant. And she did, very soon after I arrived."

"Thus explaining the ten month age difference between you and Preston."

There was a silence. Loch wanted Ivy to continue. He wanted her to tell him what she had done to Preston, but he knew that if he asked there was the very real possibility that Ivy would once again retreat into sullen silence. After some minutes had passed, he chose his words carefully.

"That myth hurts the adopted child most. Adopted kids aren't a means to an end."

"What do you mean?" Ivy asked.

"Infertility is a disease. No child wants to think of themselves as a cure for a disease. No child wants to think that their highest worth is to help their parents achieve their real goal – that of having a child of their own.

"Every child deserves to be an end to him or herself. Every child, adopted or biological, is a miracle that makes and enriches a family."

"True," Ivy said, thoughtfully. "But in my case, I was glad I was adopted. Maybe not when I first found out, but I think that was mostly because of the shock. It didn't take me long to get used to the idea, and then it made sense. Alberta and Hugh, and especially Preston, never liked me, and no matter how hard I tried, they were never going to. Very soon that fact that I was adopted became a relief. I was glad there wasn't one shared drop of blood between us. I wanted no ties to any of them."

"You're a strong woman."

"They made me strong."

"No," Loch said. "They didn't make you strong. You made yourself strong. It's like what Frederick Douglass said. *The soul that is within me no man can degrade.*"

"I like that," Ivy said slowly. "I like that a lot."

Ivy was still for a moment, and then she suddenly sat up. "This talking out is amazing," she said, her lips beginning to form a smile, and her eyes taking on a mischievous glint. "Nora's always spouting out whatever comes to mind. She comes off as a scatterbrained airhead at times, but she's one of the strongest and most perceptive women I know. When Wes was hurt, she never kept anything in. She wept and cried, but she was steel. She was the one who wouldn't let any of us admit defeat."

Ivy sat back and positioned herself so for the first time she could look directly at Loch. "I'm babbling," she said, "but I feel this sense of lightness. I'm speaking of things I've kept bottled inside so long that their weight had become part of me."

The words were said softly, but there was no belying the force of the sentiment behind them. "If I can carry all the load for you, it is done."

"Or toss it over a cliff."

Ivy had responded so quickly and flippantly that Loch was startled. Did she think that he was only posturing and his words were not truly meant? Or that he was incapable of helping her? Or was she still in shock about all that had so recently occurred and she had witnessed?

Loch stared pensively at Ivy for a moment, considering his words carefully before speaking. He knew that emotion could cloud one's judgement, and he had already felt his blood begin to roil as Ivy had recounted only a partial part of her sordid history. If Ivy continued to trust him enough to expand on her personal history, Loch was braced for hearing far worse. If she spoke of sexual assault, he just hoped he could keep his anger in check and instead concentrate on insuring Ivy that the fault of it did not lie with her. She did not invite it. All blame rested with Preston and the adults who were supposed to care for her.

Very slowly and with measured but even tone, he said, "If Preston needs to be dinner for an orca, consider it done."

This time it was Ivy who couldn't answer right away. With brow furrowed, she finally spoke. "And do you make this kind of offer to every girl you bed?"

"You're the first."

"Ah," Ivy said, "it wouldn't behoove a mercenary to offer his services for free to just anyone."

"Is that how you see me? A mercenary?" He couldn't hide the hurt in his tone.

"Thin-skinned, are you?"

Loch opened his mouth to say something, but then he just shook his head in disbelief. Ivy thought Nora was strong, but Ivy put all to shame when it came to resilience. Someone had attempted to kill her, she had witnessed a gruesome death, she was ordered to break from all societal mores she had been raised with and not report it, and now she had the temerity to be teasing him?

"I've met my match," Loch said reaching forward and taking Ivy into his arms. His head on hers, his arms stroking her back, he realized that he was feeling something for this woman that he had never felt before with any other being. He wanted her safe, he wanted her desiring him the same way he craved her, but more than that, he wanted her by his side. Forever.

It was that thought of time and eternity that jolted Loch back to reality. This was not the time to speak of love. This was time the time to defend. If defending involved attacking, then so be it.

"Don't you want to know what I did?"

Loch was so caught up in his own thoughts that it took him a moment to realize what Ivy was asking. Smiling gently, he pulled back and tenderly tucked an errant tendril of hair behind Ivy's ear. "I'm sorry if I seemed inattentive," he said. "I was thinking of keeping you safe. If you're ready to tell, I'm ready to listen."

Ivy nodded, and then moved away a bit so that once again she could meet his gaze as she spoke.

"I told you how Preston was always after me."

"Yes."

"I realized it was only a matter of time before he hurt me. No matter how careful I was, there would come a day when I would slip up. And Preston was getting another growth spurt. He was getting stronger and bigger. If he caught me unawares, I wouldn't be strong enough to get away from him.

"I told you already I was being sent to a counselor. I suppose there are some good counselors out there, but this woman was an idiot. She was so sure that I was lying that I knew there was nothing I could do to change her mind. She had it in her head that the family needed protection from me! From me! When I'd try and tell her how I couldn't be the one who had stolen the money from Alberta's purse, she would sit back in her chair. 'Tell me,' she'd say with a smug smile on her face, 'how is it then that the money came to be in your backpack? Did it fly there?'

"Looking back on it, I think that Alberta and Hugh must have told her that the problems all lay in the fact that I was adopted, and I hated Preston because somehow I sensed that I wasn't his equal. I was jealous of his very existence. And as she wasn't very smart, she just jumped to the conclusion that I was the one acting out. In her view, it was Preston who had to be kept safe!

"She claimed that my nightmares were due to my fears of being abandoned because I was so unworthy of my younger brother! I couldn't figure out at first why she kept asking me if I minded there being so many pictures of Alberta pregnant with Preston while there were none of me. The truth is that there were hardly any pictures of me at any stage of my life. All the pictures were of Preston.

"When I pointed that out, all the counselor did was sit back in her chair the way she always did and say in her smug little voice, 'So, you've always felt that you were being treated unfairly. You're going to have to learn that the world does not revolve around you.'"

"You didn't have a chance."

"I could defend myself, but …" A look of pain crossed Ivy's face. She started to speak several times, but each time her voice would begin to tremble, and she would stop abruptly. Loch moved forward to take her once again into his arms, but Ivy only held her hand up, palm flat and out, as a silent sign to keep him a bay. She sat that way for a moment, and then she nodded, as if agreeing with an internal voice that she was strong enough to break her silence.

"I was walking home from school. It was late because I had to stay after school to serve detention. Preston had taken my homework that morning from my backpack without me knowing, and I was being punished for not having completed it. Preston had done this before, and consequently I had a reputation for not being responsible.

"I heard some rustling next to a large hedge at the corner of our yard, and the next thing I knew was that I was falling forward. Preston had whacked the back of my knees with a broom handle. I heard my wrist snap as I fell on it, and the pain burned through me like molten lava. Preston had hold of both of my feet, and he was dragging me into the hedge. I was still so dazed and shocked from the searing pain in my wrist that at first I didn't know what his intentions were. He had hurt me before, but all the bruises I had been marked with previously were nothing compared to this. It wasn't until he began ripping at my pants that I understood.

"You have to remember that Preston was given everything. He never had to work or put any effort out. He demanded, and he was given. Toys, electronics, clothes, trophies, all were showered upon him. He could break them in seconds and leave the discarded pieces strewn about, and all that happened was that a new and better one would appear.

"Preston wasn't used to resistance, and that is what saved me. I kicked as hard as I could, and I think the fact that I wasn't just lying there startled him more than the impact of my flailing feet. Before, if I had tried to stand up for myself, I was the one accused of being the aggressor. This time, I tore at the dirt and threw it into his face as I twisted and turned. When he cried and put his hands up to his face I grabbed the broom and began to pummel him. I whacked him over and over, and I didn't stop until he was a whimpering mass."

"Thank God," Loch said fiercely. "I hope you crippled him."

"It gets worse."

Loch didn't give Ivy a chance to put up a hand and ask him to keep his distance. In one fluid motion he pulled Ivy into his arms. "Whatever you're going to tell me, know that it is in the past. It's all over."

"Is it?" Ivy asked quietly. Pushing away, she turned and looked directly at Loch. "How can you out of all people say that the past is over? You berate me for not delving into the painting, while you're the one who lets your grandmother taunt you with secrets that I know full well from the little time I've known you that you are very capable of finding out.

"We're more alike that you want to admit. The past isn't ever over. It is a part of us that cannot be denied. What we can do though is bury it. I had buried mine. You had buried yours, too.

"You hid from it like a child. You didn't cower under a blanket, of course, but you hid from it, nevertheless. You hid from it by pretending you didn't care. You say your passivity and refusal to question was to infuriate your grandmother, but I don't buy that. Mature adults don't take pleasure in making others angry. You made her angry because you do care, and more than that, you wanted to taunt her the same way she was taunting you. She taunted you with what she wouldn't say, and with your indifference, you taunted her right back.

"My adoptive mother was cruel. There is no denying that. But at least I know why she hated me. She hated me because she never wanted me. My presence was only due to her infertility. I was second choice to begin with, and once Preston was born, I was naught but a painful, despised, and ever-growing canker sore."

There was a long, protracted silence, and then Loch spoke quietly. "I admit it."

Drawing Ivy back into his embrace, he repeated himself. "I admit it. I am angry at my grandmother, and I'm angry at my mother, too. Hell, I'm angry at my father and grandfather come to think of it. There was no reason to be told that my name had been paid for if no one was going to tell me why."

"Perhaps they all hoped you would uncover the truth. Perhaps they hoped you would help them deal with their past. After all, you know what Carl Jung said."

"The Swiss psychiatrist and psychoanalyst?"

"Yes, that's him — the founder of analytical psychology. He said, *'The greatest harm to a child is the unlived life of a parent.'*"

"You're a wise and well-read woman," Loch said.

"As was Carl Jung — wise and well-read, though not a woman!"

There was a moment of agreeable silence. Then, bracing himself for a cold refusal, Loch said quietly, "You were going to tell me how Preston's story got worse."

Twenty-one

"I was punished, of course, for attacking Preston. Locked in the basement and told I couldn't come out. There was a bathroom in there with a toilet and a sink, but there wasn't any food. I don't know how many hours passed before the door opened. Alberta stood at the top of the stairs looking down while Preston came down carrying a tray. 'See what you did to him,' Alberta said, 'See how he is hobbling and bruised, and yet he insisted that you be fed, and he be the one who brings it to you. You don't deserve your brother.'"

"I remained mute as Preston made his way down the stairs. I saw him grimace in pain a few times, but I also saw something in his eyes. It took me a moment to realize what it was. When I saw his smug smile, there was no question. It was triumph."

"Because you were a prisoner in your own home? A fly caught in his web?"

Ivy shook her head impatiently. "No, not that. It was the food. Preston would have never been concerned about any hunger pangs I might be feeling. He had no interest in mitigating any punishment Alberta inflicted on me, so for him to suggest that I needed food meant only one thing."

Loch knew instantly what it was. "Poisoned. Not to kill, I'm sure, but a date rape drug. Unfortunately, predator drugs are all too easy to get hold of."

Ivy nodded. "And they metabolize quickly so if they are tested for, there is often no trace left to find."

"So, what did you do?"

"I thanked Preston, the way I had been ordered. I made sure to keep my eyes downcast, my face averted, and my hands tremble when I took the tray. I had to appear weak and afraid."

"I'm going to kill him." Loch said the words quietly, but they were said so forcefully that there was no doubt that he would do it.

"He came for me that night," Ivy said, continuing as if Loch had never spoken. "I was waiting for him. I had scraped all the food into the toilet and flushed it away. When he first opened the door and used a flashlight to come down the stairs, I thought I was wrong about the food being drugged. But then when he got to the bottom of the stairs and flicked on the light, I realized that he had only kept quiet so as not to wake Hugh and Alberta. Now that the door was shut and his privacy insured, he could molest me at his leisure. I might be sore and hurt, and even bleeding in the morning, but I would have no proof."

Loch's arms were so taut that every tendon and vein seemed to be bursting from the skin. He had to force himself to control his breathing. It was a good thing Preston wasn't here right now because if he was, Loch would tear his limbs from his body. If there was anything left to his torso at that point, Loch would stomp on him, crushing his rib cage to a pulp. There would be nothing left but a bloody pulp. Better for Ivy not to see such carnage.

"I waited for him to come close to the old sofa I was lying on. Then I threw off the afghan I was using as a cover and stood up. I had a piece of wood in my hand with nails sticking out from the end – it was the leg of an old coffee table. I had broken off the leg by stomping on it when I was looking for a weapon. I held it like a bat, and I just looked at him.”

“Good girl,” Loch murmured. “Good girl.”

“He didn’t say anything, but I could see the surprise on his face. I’m sure he stood there for only a few seconds, but it felt like forever. He backed up slowly, never taking his eyes off of me. When he got to the stairs, he said, “Look out the window, tomorrow after school.”

“It was a horrible night,” Ivy said softly. “I kept telling myself that the wondering was worse than the knowing. I kept telling myself that no matter what Preston tried, I would be able to defend myself. I just never knew …” and here Ivy’s voice faltered for the first time. “I just never knew it was someone else I should have been worrying about.”

Ivy took several deep breathes. When she again began her narration, her voice was filled with anguish. “Our neighbors had a daughter with Down’s syndrome. Her name was Tricia, and she was eight years old. She was so sweet. Always smiling. Clumsy, but she loved bubbles. I would often blow them at her with one of those hand wands. She would stand in the middle of the floating spheres and twirl, her hands up high. I think they made her feel like she was a princess. She was so easy to please, and her laugh was so innocent and joyful. Her delight was infectious. She just … she just made the world a happier and better place.

“He enticed her with the bubbles. She was laughing, batting at them so carefree as he stayed a few steps in front of her, leading her along. He led her right into the bushes surrounding the basement window. They were shielded from the street, but I could see them. He … he … he …”

Ivy paused and shuddered, and for a moment Loch thought she would not be able to continue. “It’s not your fault,” Loch said softly, but his voice firm. “The blame does not rest on you.”

"I was frozen at first," Ivy said. "I couldn't believe what I was seeing. Her pants were down. Preston's pants were down, but it wasn't until I saw the sudden panic and fear on her face when she suddenly realized that something was very wrong that I could act. I shattered the window with that table leg I had broken off. The window was too small for me to crawl though, but I was able to reach my arm through. I grabbed at pieces of glass and heaved them at Preston, all the while screaming as loud as I could.

"There was so much blood, and I couldn't tell whether it was Preston's or mine. I was so fueled by adrenaline that pain couldn't enter."

"It was both of ours," Ivy said after she took a deep breath and looked Loch in the eyes. "But it was also Tricia's."

Had Ivy inadvertently sliced one of Tricia's arteries while blinding stabbing with a piece of glass? Had she killed her? Had Ivy had to watch as the little girl she tried to save bleed to death on the ground in front of her? Loch's face remained stoically passive, but his insides were a churning tangle of anger, horror, and sorrow. "You were only trying to protect her," he said quietly.

"Preston called Alberta from his cell phone. I don't know how much time passed before she came flying up into the driveway, but none of us were thinking clearly as all three of us were in some form of shock. She wasn't there, and then she was there. It felt to me though of course I know it is impossible that there was no time in between.

"I don't know what she said or how she covered it up, but Alberta was a master of deceit. She had to know what was going on because although Preston had gotten his pants up, Tricia's were still down. She had Tricia fully clothed before the paramedics arrived."

"I'm guessing …"

Loch interrupted in surprise. "Guessing? Were you in such a state of shock that you don't remember?"

"I'm guessing," Ivy continued, as if Loch had not spoken, "that Alberta told everyone that I had hidden in the basement so as not to be caught skipping school. When I realized that I had somehow locked myself in, I broke the window and called out to Tricia who just happened to be passing by. When she came to investigate, she accidently cut herself on a piece of glass. At that point, I started to panic so I started screaming at Tricia to get away. Preston, alerted by my screaming and Tricia's wailing, came onto the scene. While striking blindly with the glass in my attempt to drive Preston away as well as Tricia, I sliced up Preston, inflicted more damage on Tricia, and cut myself. Preston had only been trying to help."

"I'm guessing that is what she said because all I know is that the paramedics knocked me out with some kind of a sedative, and I woke up in a psychiatric ward. My psychiatrist made sure to tell me that Preston was a hero."

"And Tricia?" Loch asked quietly. "What happened to her?"

"I never saw her again. Hugh and Alberta filed the papers for relinquishing me while I was still in the psychiatric ward. At the suggestion of the psychiatrist Hugh and Alberta had me seeing, I was transferred to a group home for juvenile delinquents after my release. I never saw Hugh, Alberta, or Preston again."

"I built a wall," Ivy continued. "I built it brick by brick in my mind. Hugh, Alberta, Preston – they're all on the other side. They have nothing to do with me now. I have barred them. They don't exist."

"You're not curious?"

"How can one be curious about something that doesn't exist?"

Loch said slowly, "I'm not one to judge. I've never gone through what you have. That said, I think it is better – not just better, but safer – to keep up to date information. Knowledge provides the foundation of protection."

"I filed for a release of documents when I turned eighteen," Ivy said. "I was described as a potential murderer, as Preston needed over 300 stitches and several surgeries to restore movement to his right arm. I don't need protection from Preston. If anything, he needs protection from me."

"From me. He needs protection from me. Preston and anyone else who wants to harm you."

Unbidden, a single tear slipped from Ivy's eye. Uncomfortable with showing any form of weakness, she turned her head so as to hide it and all the others she felt welling up inside her. She did not want Loch to know how overwhelmed she was at his determination and willingness to protect her. Despite the wall that she had so solidly constructed, there were times when she felt flawed. She knew there was nothing wrong with her, but still, there it was on legal documents that she was a potential murderer.

Ivy turned her head, but she should have known that nothing, not even a single tear, would escape Loch's notice. Gently, he kissed it away. "In a perfect world," he murmured, "there would be no cause for a vigilante or even anyone in my profession. Despite people's good intentions, despots like Hitler, Idi Amin, and Pol Pot still emerge. They are balanced somewhat by people like Gandhi, Martin Luther King, and Jane Addams, but the truth is that it comes down to common individuals doing what is right in their daily lives. Ivy, you did right."

As some more tears began to well up in Ivy's eyes, she raised her face to Loch's while pulling his down to meet her own. "I have to kiss you," she said, "because these are tears of joy."

Loch was an experienced lover. He knew full well how to pleasure a woman and how to take his own pleasure. Yet in all his life, in all the beds he had shared, he had never felt what he had just felt with Ivy. He had never really been interested in the history of whom he was bedding. He was intent only on the pleasures of physical release. He wanted things simple. Now, as he lay exhausted, with Ivy breathing on his chest, their limbs all tangled together, he had never felt more joined to anyone in all of his existence. With every kiss, with every trace of a finger against skin, he had experienced the fire of lust, yes, but he had also sensed something more. For the first time, with every thrust, he felt as if he were being seared together as one.

It wasn't complicated. It was right.

Twenty-two

"I'm not Sherlock Holmes."

Loch's face remained stoically still, but Ivy could not hide her concern about Vinny's mental health. She and Loch had gone directly to Loch's office after their return from Iceland and arrival in New York. Marcella had been waiting for them at the airport, and once they were in the car, she had informed them that she was taking them straight to the office because Vinny was there. He wanted to tell them something important.

Ivy had hoped that Vinny would tell her why the man in the black helmet on the motorcycle had tried to run her over, or at least tell her that he had found out his identity. Instead of revealing anything of importance, it seemed that Vinny was simply babbling nonsense.

"You are better than fiction, though I'm not sure by much," Marcella said. Smiling, she patted Vinny gently on the shoulder and then left her hand draped there as she leaned against his wheelchair and waited for Vinny to explain further. Both Ivy and Loch were very conscious of Marcella's position. Ivy because she knew that Vinny's wheelchair was part of his personal space, and ordinarily Vinny would have objected if he felt it had been invaded. Marcella was not just touching his wheelchair – she was leaning on it! Loch noticed because he had never seen Marcella give anyone a pat, let alone rest her hand affectionately on someone's shoulder!

"We work well together," Marcella said, looking directly at Loch. "We'll see what happens after this case." Turning to look at Ivy she explained, "Nothing personal until this is finished. Loch may be breaking company policy, but I am not."

Even if Ivy couldn't understand what Vinny was talking about, she wasn't too tired from the plane trip to understand what Marcella was referring too. Her cheeks reddened, but she didn't look down. If anything, she stood straighter. Ivy had learned long ago how to deal with insults. She thought of them as water on a duck – it slid off. The duck remained dry. It never got wet.

Loch put his arm around Ivy and said in an authoritative voice, "Marcella said that to remind Vinny to keep his distance. She meant no harm to you."

"Oh!" Marcella gasped, looking at Ivy in dismay. "I never meant to slight you! Loch is absolutely right. It's just that Vinny gave me some line about *what's good for the goose is good for the gander*, and I ..."

"Am not a goose," Vinny cut in laughing. He grabbed Marcella's hand with his one real arm and brought it to his lips.

Ivy had never seen Vinny so relaxed and at ease, and she was happy for him. Yet at the same time, she couldn't help but feel ire. Someone had tried to kill her! Loch had killed for her! She wanted Vinny to have a good life, but she wanted that very same for herself, too. This was not the time to be entertained by two blossoming lovebirds!

"And you're not Sherlock Holmes," Ivy snapped. The brittleness in her tone surprised and silenced everyone.

Loch started to say something, but Vinny understood how men and women who had been in battle or under siege could feel. "It's on me," he said firmly. "Sit down, and I'll give my report."

Vinny waited quietly while Marcella brought bottles of water for everyone and then took a seat next to Loch and Ivy.

"Sherlock Holmes – yes, I know he is a fictional character – said, 'When *you have eliminated the impossible, whatever remains, however improbable, must be the truth.*' I said I wasn't Sherlock Holmes because I didn't try to eliminate anything. I approached the problem very differently."

"Coach, it was a team effort," Vinny said looking at Ivy. "At practice I just asked the team why anyone would want to kill you."

"He did," Marcella said, nodding her head. "I was there. He just called everyone over before practice and told them you weren't there because someone was trying to kill you. Then he said that after practice, no one could leave until they offered up a possible explanation."

Loch was shaking his head, not sure whether to be aghast, amused, or amazed. A sliver of a smile passed over Ivy's face. How she would have enjoyed seeing the men's reactions to Vinny's news and instructions!

"Body parts."

"What?" Ivy's smile was replaced by a confused grimace.

"Body parts," Vinny repeated. "Not one person said revenge – you're too sweet, Ivy. It's good to be sweet.

"Not one person said money. You're definitely not rich, Ivy. Maybe that's not so good, but no one is certainly trying to off you for your wealth.

"But everyone said body parts. Hearts and livers were mentioned, but the consensus of over half was for a kidney."

"That's ridiculous," Ivy snapped. She started to say that Sherlock Holmes would have been better at getting results, but she stopped short. Sherlock Holmes couldn't eliminate anything because he was fictional! Shaking her head, she said ruefully, "Vinny, I apologize for sounding so harsh, but that's the most ridiculous thing I've ever heard. Do you really expect me to take you seriously?"

She expected Loch to back her up, but instead he said thoughtfully, "There's currently over 94,000 people on the kidney transplant waiting list in the United States alone. The average wait for a deceased donor could be five years, but in some states, it is closer to ten.

"Hearts – that's a different matter. Someone is added to the national waiting list every ten minutes. 22 people die a day waiting for a heart on the average. The statistics on livers are pretty grim, too. The sicker one gets, the higher one gets up on the list, but then of course, the sicker one is, the less chance of recovery."

"I thought I was going to be the one telling you this!" Vinny said. "I didn't expect you to be able to rattle of numbers."

Loch shrugged noncommittedly, but Marcella spoke up. "Loch's had several cases where people have been kidnapped for procurement of their organs. Children have been left outside emergency rooms in countries on the opposite side of the globe with an open wound and minus a kidney. It's heinous what some people do.

"Some people sell their body parts, of course, but that rarely gets them out of poverty. The cost to their own health is usually so great that they are never able to recover completely. And the doctors that perform these surgeries – they are despicable. They only care about the person paying for the transplant. They care nothing about the donor. They have to know that the donors aren't voluntary!"

"I agree with you completely," Ivy said, "but I don't see how this has anything to do with me. "It's recorded on my driver's license that I'm an organ donor, but lots of people have it listed on their licenses. What's so special about me?"

"You're a perfect match," Vinny said. "That's what makes you special."

"How could one know?" Ivy scoffed. "I've never heard of anything so ridiculous in my life."

"Blood marrow registry."

"Yes!" Vinny said, nodding his head emphatically in agreement with Loch.

"How do you know I'm on the blood marrow registry?" Ivy demanded.

"Probability," Loch said calmly. "You have a job where the mortality rate rockets off the charts. Your best friend being in a wheelchair is proof of the risk. When Wes was hurt, you didn't even think of getting off your bike. You did start coaching though — a team where all the players are alive due to major medical interventions. You are the type of person who routinely donates blood because you know how important it is. You'd also not hesitate when asked if additional blood typing could be done so as to add you to the bone marrow registry."

"The data is supposed to be confidential," Loch continued, "but trust me, in today's world, a middle-schooler could hack into most medical record systems. Transplants have a much higher success rate when blood type, immune system activity, and other factors are matched. You're someone's close match, there's no question there. We all are."

Turning to Vinny, Loch continued. "Okay, you crowd sourced for a reason, but now it's time to think like Sherlock. What have you done to start eliminating the possibility that Ivy's being sought for organ harvesting?"

"Organ harvesting?" Ivy said, shuddering. "It sounds so gruesome. I really can't believe …" her voice faltered and then trailed off into silence.

"That's the official term," Marcella said. "The fact is that just one organ donor can save eight lives, and the same donor can also save or improve the lives of 50 more people by donating tissues and eyes. Whatever it is called, it is truly the gift of life."

"Or not," Ivy said dryly.

Twenty-three

Loch divided up the tasks. Vinny and Marcella were told they were responsible for following up on the possibility of there being a body part connection. "I'll take on the possible Scottish connection," Loch said. "The two may be connected. Of course, they may have nothing to do with each other and there is no intersection at all," he said, giving a nod to Ivy before continuing in a firm voice that booked no dissent, "but I don't want to leave anything to chance.

"There's one more thing that needs checking, but on this, we have to leave no trail. The investigation has to be kept so secret and confidential that the people being investigated have no idea. Nothing is to be written down or typed into a computer."

Marcella cocked an inquiring eye at Loch, but she asked no questions. Instead, she asked succinctly, "Name or names?"

"Hugh, Alberta, and Preston …" Loch looked at Ivy, waiting for her to provide the last name. There was a long awkward pause, but finally Ivy spoke.

"Richards."

"Birthdates, last known whereabouts?" Marcella asked, her voice impersonal and clipped.

When there was yet another pause, Loch said gently, "Trust me, Ivy."

"Trust us," Vinny said. When Ivy remained mute, Vinny continued in a lighter tone. "I've read that silence can be deafening, and I never believed it. I thought it was oxymoronic twaddle! Now I know it's true! Ivy, you have to talk because your silence is deafening."

Ivy couldn't help but smile. She could tell why Vinny had been such a leader of men. He knew just when to infuse humor, and he knew how to make one know they were not alone.

"Oxymoronic twaddle," Ivy said, laughing. "How often have you used that expression?"

"First time!" Vinny said, a grin stretching across his face. "I made it up, but perhaps we can make it so popular that it wins a spot in the Oxford English Dictionary's annual list of new words! It's at least as good as *unlawyerly* and *toeside* – two very recent additions."

"Enough said!" Ivy said. Taking a deep breath, she gave Marcella as much information as she could. Marcella wrote nothing down, but she repeated everything to Ivy, making sure that what she heard was what Ivy meant to say.

When Ivy had nothing left to say, Marcella turned to Loch so that she could broach a completely different topic. "Ivy's safety?" she asked. "I'd be a poor office manager if I didn't know what was going on there."

Loch answered without hesitation. "She'll be with me."

Vinny gave a low whistle. "You're a slow learner, Loch. You've got to work on the words and the tone, I'm telling you! You have to ask her, not command her!"

Ivy shook her head in mock dismay. Turning to Marcella she said, "He's talking about me in the third person, again. Does Loch always do this?"

"No," Marcella said slowly. "No, he doesn't. Loch keeps his distance when he is working. He doesn't mix business with personal. He thinks only in terms of retrieval. Getting personal makes things complicated."

"So, I've put myself at risk by sleeping with him?" Ivy said musingly.

"I'm right here!" Loch snapped. "I can hear everything you're saying."

"I never equated abstinence with safety," Ivy said, continuing to speak to Marcella and refusing to meet Loch's gaze. "But, I'll be sure to keep that in mind!"

"Winner gets her kidney!"

"I just want her leg!"

"They can't transplant legs yet, you idiot," Dance said. "The most you could hope for was her hand."

"Or face!" someone cut in. "They've done some full-face transplants. Do you think if Terry got her face he'd still have to shave?"

Ivy loved it. She stood on the bottom bleacher looking down at her team. "I've missed you, too!" she said, her eyes twinkling. "And I can tell by your raucous comments that though Wes make a great substitute, he's been too soft on you. Whatever happened to fearing one's coach? Be warned that you're going to work up a sweat like never before. You're going to be crying for mercy before the night is over!"

Ivy was true to her word, but no one complained. Even as men were knocked to the floor and scrabbled to stay clear of steel wheels, they shouted not from frustration but only that they were just getting started. It was Ivy, who had been running back and forth down the court shouting orders who had to call time. "I've been bested!" she said, wiping her sweat drenched brow. "I can't keep up."

After the men collected their belongings and various bags, she waited for the men to make their way to the door. Ivy had made it her habit to never leave until she was sure that those who couldn't drive had been picked up by a family member or a transport service. When she saw Wes and three other men lingering close to where she had placed her possessions, she went over to them and asked if something was wrong.

"We're taking turns," one explained. "It's our night to keep you surrounded until Nora gives us the okay.

"Nora?" Ivy was too surprised to be angry. She looked at Wes, but he didn't say anything. A saucy grin flashed across his face. In an instant, Ivy knew what was going on. Loch knew she would object to being babysat. He also knew that Ivy would never hurt Nora's feelings or do anything that would publicly embarrass her. Now that Ivy knew the men were waiting for Nora, there was no way she could leave without her.

"Very clever," she mouthed silently to Wes. Wes just shrugged, but Ivy could tell he was trying hard not to laugh.

It wasn't until Ivy was sitting in the back of Wes's van, with Nora driving, that Wes spoke. "Nora, you should have seen her face! Ivy would have smacked us all on our heads and pulled us out of our chairs if your name hadn't been mentioned! Your name had power!"

Nora tossed her head disdainfully. "Wes, I'll tell you what has power. It's not a name. It's female friendship. There's nothing stronger."

Ivy started to laugh. "I wish you could see your husband's face," she said to Nora. "You've hurt his feelings."

"You have."

The pain in Wes's voice was so palpable that both Ivy and Nora weren't sure how to respond. A few interminable seconds passed, and then Ivy reached for Wes's hand and pulled it close to her heart. Nora also reacted physically rather than orally, but her action had much greater consequences.

Nora pulled the van to the side of the road and slammed on the brakes. Putting the van in park, she unbuckled her seatbelt with the other hand. Her intent was to take Wes's face in her hands, tell him she was his alone, and then kiss him. She never got the chance, for just as she turned and faced the interior of the van, she was catapulted forward. If Ivy hadn't been belted in, she, too, would have been knocked from her seat, although she would have gone forward into the windshield instead of, like Nora, the opposite direction.

Ivy was conscious of Nora's confused and fearful face, Wes swearing furiously, and the sound of metal on metal. Any sort of understanding all became a blur when the door slid open and a man in a black ski mask reached for Nora. Screeching in terror, Nora flailed helplessly as the man put his arms around her and began to hoist her out. Wes didn't let the fact that his wheelchair was locked into its electronic docking system hold him back. Using every muscle in his abdomen he literally catapulted himself out of his wheelchair. With a thud, he landed on Nora, trapping her under him. Then with primordial fury, he snapped down on the arm of her assailant with the only weapon he had — his mouth.

Ivy felt like she was moving in slow motion, but she finally regained enough of her senses that she could act. Unbuckling her seatbelt, she tried to reach over Wes and grab hold of Nora. She clutched at Nora's ankle, and she pulled back with such force that she was afraid she was going to pull Nora's leg out of her socket.

She was aware of a great din, a medley of squealing brakes, screeching tires, and muffled curses. Then there was no more resistance and Loch's commanding tone over all else.

"Nora, you're fine. Ivy, he's gone. Wes, are you all right? Wes? Wes, can you answer me?"

"Wes!" Nora's cry was a wail of anguish. "Answer him! Answer him!"

It was Ivy who realized what was going on. "He can't!" she cried. "There's something in his mouth!"

"He's choking!" Nora gasped. She started prodding at Wes's lips, trying to force them open so she could feel for an obstruction. Wes only closed his lips tighter and shook his head vehemently. Loch had started to grab hold of Wes so he could hoist him up and begin the Heimlich maneuver, but he stopped when Ivy restrained him. "Something's wrong," she said. "He doesn't want you to."

Loch didn't let go of Wes, but he looked at Ivy, waiting for her to say something else. Nora was shaking, her trembling hands still on Wes's cheeks, but she, too, looked at Ivy inquiringly. Wes was staring fiercely at Ivy, as if willing her to understand.

"Oh, dear God," she said suddenly. "He wants us to save what's in his mouth."

Nora began to laugh hysterically. "I don't care about your teeth! Oh, Wes, you silly man."

"Take that cup from the door pocket," Loch said calmly. "He can spit into that."

Ivy quickly retrieved the cup and held it up to Wes's lips. With a huge splat, Wes spit the contents of his mouth into it. He made a grimace of disgust, and then said, "Water! I need water to rinse out my mouth!"

"We'll get you to a dentist," Ivy said, carefully holding the cup upright so its contents wouldn't spill. "He might be able to save your teeth."

"I've got all my teeth," Wes said, gargling and then spitting out several mouthfuls of water.

"Then what ...?" Suddenly Loch grabbed the cup from Ivy and said, "You didn't!"

"I did!" Wes said, suddenly laughing. "I did!"

"Did what?" Nora asked, her voice not as hysterical but still a bit maniacal. "What did you do?"

When Wes and Loch didn't answer right away, Nora turned to Ivy. "What did he do?" she asked. "Ivy, what did he do?"

"I think," Ivy said slowly, "that he took a bite out of him."

It took a moment for Nora to fully comprehend what Ivy said. Nora looked at Wes with disbelief. "You ..."

"Yep," Wes said, "Not a pound of flesh, but a good bite!"

Turning to Ivy he continued cheerfully. "It took you long enough to get me that cup! You don't know how hard it was not to swallow, though of course knowing it was someone else's blood in my mouth helped me fight against that natural need to swallow."

Loch swirled the contents of the cup and said in a so ordinarily conversational tone that one would think he habitually held a mixture of someone's blood and flesh in his hands, "We've got more than enough for DNA analysis." Then even Loch couldn't help himself. "Jesus, you really took a chunk out of him! I think there's even some of his sleeve in there!"

Nora spoke for the first time. She must have felt that Loch's last statement was a slur on Wes's actions. "My husband," she said in an admonishing tone to Loch, "is a carnivore, not a cannibal."

Loch was so abashed at Nora's choice of words and undeserved reprimand that he could only stare at her. His mouth opened and closed several times, as he didn't know exactly what to say or how to reassure her that he was not belittling Wes. After several attempts, he looked desperately at Ivy.

"What Loch meant to say, Nora," Ivy said, "is that your husband is a hero."

"Well, then, we're all fine," Nora said primly.

Ivy stood uneasily in the foyer of Loch's home. Loch closed and bolted the door behind them. "I've turned on the security system," he told her, noting her uneasiness. "We're safe. You can relax."

"It's so grandiose," Ivy said, lifting her feet up and down several times. "Just the cost of these tiles must be more than the worth of everything I own."

"They are marble," Loch said. "A gift from one of my clients. I prefer wood floors, but so it goes. I got this place for the location."

Ivy walked over to the wall filled with floor to ceiling glass. "It's so airy," she said, "and this terrace is amazing!" Shaking her head in wonder she said, "You could grow an orange grove on it!"

"Well, it works," she said, turning to face Loch. "It all works."

"Works? As in …?"

"As in, it all works on whomever you bring here. It's breathtaking. Very impressive."

"I bought it because it's the top floor," Loch said shortly. "I have control of the roof. I control access to all entry and exits. It's safe. You're safe."

"So not to impress, but it impresses. I'm feeling a bit daunted, and I haven't even begun to admire the artwork."

"A weakness."

"One that you indulge in," Ivy said, walking up to a large oil canvas that dominated a side wall. She examined the painting carefully, and then she turned and said, "This isn't a copy, is it?"

"No."

"Joan Miró's *The Farm*. Ernest Hemingway once owned it, but them I'm sure you know that, just as I'm certain that you know how Hemingway felt about it."

Loch nodded. He walked over to Ivy and stood by her side. "Hemingway said, '*It has in it all that you feel about Spain when you are there and all that you feel when you are away and cannot go there. No one else has been able to paint these two very opposing things.*'"

"Love," Ivy said softly.

"Excuse me?"

"It is how love should feel," Ivy said, her eyes still on the painting. "Whole together; something missing when apart."

Loch cleared his throat, but if he was going to say something, he was stopped by Ivy's suddenly clapping her hands together and saying briskly, "I need to shower. Then you can show me where I'm sleeping."

"With me."

Ivy raised one eyebrow and looked at Loch inquisitively.

"I hope," he quickly added on. "I hope."

Ivy was an early riser, but when she awakened, she was the only one in the bed. She quickly donned her clothes and made her way to the kitchen where she could hear movement and a clatter of dishes.

"I hope you like eggs," Loch said, using a spatula to flip a perfectly shaped omelet. "Impeccable timing. The toast is about to pop. Butter and jam are already on the table."

"Like I said before," Ivy said, licking her fingers after sating herself on all that Loch set before her, "It works. All of it. Everyone must be reluctant to leave. Everyone must be eager to come back." With a saucy grin she continued, "Two very opposing things."

"I wouldn't know."

"What do you mean?" Ivy asked, pushing her plate away from her.

"I don't bring people here."

Ivy was startled into motionlessness. "You mean …" her voice trailed off.

"You're the first."

Ivy looked around at the kitchen, as if seeing it for the first time. It was bright and airy, with clean lines and steel appliances. The granite counter tops were an ocean gray, the color softened by lines of soft black waving through it. The table they were sitting at was made of thick slabs of cherry. The age of the wood brought out the warm richness of its color. The total effect was masculine, but with gracious utilitarianism.

"Well," Ivy said. "Well," she said again, this time a small smile growing from the sides of her mouth. "Then this table needs to be baptized."

It took Loch less than a second to understand what she meant. As he swept the dishes from the table and he laid her down on its wooden surface, he murmured into her ear, "There's a counter that needs that, too."

Twenty-four

"Who is this?"

The tone was acrid, and the woman dressed in an original Chanel suit and a three-strand necklace of lustrous pearls lifted her head with a dismissive gesture.

"Be polite, Grandmother."

Loch's grandmother stared balefully at her grandson. She started to say something, but Ivy stepped up and offered her hand.

"You're making me feel I should curtsey," she said, "but the truth is I don't know how. I'm sure we won't agree on many things, but I'll agree with you on this one thing – he forgot to say please. A nasty habit I have observed far too many times for my liking. Still, I do so hope you'll take my hand."

Any notion of aristocratic superiority was knocked from Loch's grandmother's entire being as she stared at Ivy in stunned astonishment. Ivy took the elderly's woman silence as assent. Gently, but with firmness, Ivy took Loch's grandmother's hand in her own and shook it.

Loch was just as flabbergasted as his grandmother. Most people quaked when they met her, as the dowager's regal manner and acerbic tongue would cause even the most confident individuals to eye the door and long for escape. Yet here was Ivy. She was not even close to the social strata of his grandmother, but it was Ivy who had taken control of the situation. With conversational ease, she had acknowledged the class difference while deftly refusing to bow to it. Loch could only look on in admiration.

"You'll stay for tea."

"We'd love to," Ivy said, following the woman into a sunroom. A maid was already there, setting down a tray with a silver tea service.

"Allow me," Loch's grandmother said, pouring the tea into delicate porcelain cups. She handed Ivy the first cup and saucer she picked up. She served Loch next, and then took up her own. As one who strictly followed social protocols, Loch's grandmother was very aware that Ivy waited to take her first sip until after she, the hostess, had taken hers.

"Why are you here?"

Loch's grandmother set down her cup and waited for Loch to answer.

Loch's answer was terse and just as direct. "Ivy's safety. I need to know why you left Scotland."

"Ah."

"Ah? Just ah?"

"You're not going to ask about your name?"

"Does it have anything to do with Ivy?"

Loch's grandmother didn't answer. Instead, she eyed Ivy thoughtfully. "Now I know," she said, sitting back. "It's been bothering me since I first set eyes on you. I knew it would come to me."

"Know what?" Ivy queried.

"You should be more voluptuous, and of course your color is all wrong."

"Am I being insulted?" Ivy asked. She didn't sound hurt or wounded at all, only curious.

"So, she is."

"Yes," Loch's grandmother said, agreeing with Loch. "Definitely."

"I am what?" Ivy said, looking from Loch to this grandmother. "What am I?"

"I'm going to let my grandmother answer you," Loch said.

Ivy looked at Loch's grandmother inquisitively. Loch's grandmother spoke so quietly that her words could have been snowflakes gently falling on a field of snow. When they landed, though, the icy crystals burned.

"The woman in the painting."

Ivy, with face gone pale, carefully set down her teacup. She remained mute, but the look she then turned on Loch was piercing.

"I didn't ask her about the painting," Loch said firmly, meeting Ivy's perusal with a stare just as steady. "Or mention it before. I'm as surprised as you are."

Ivy nodded, accepting the truth of what Loch said. She then turned to Loch's grandmother. "One only has to enter in the words *celebrity doppelgangers* on the internet, and seemingly identical look a-likes pop up in abundance," she said. "My reminding both you and Loch of a figure in a painting means nothing. I'd put it in the same class of a stunt-double who has the same body type and stance.

"Vic Armstrong was Harrison Ford's stunt double for the first three Indiana Jones movies. He was so similar in build, height, coloring, and the way he moved that at times even the director Steven Spielberg mistook him for his star actor!

"Celebrities aside, the only question that begs to be answered here is why you left Scotland. If you don't want to answer, then please tell us what little needs to be told so that your privacy can be maintained, and I am assured that whomever is after me has nothing to do with the trip I made to Scotland and to Castle Douglas with your grandson."

"Did you know that by 1750 tea had become the favored drink of Britain's lower classes?"

Ivy was so shocked by Loch's grandmother's ignoring her plea and change of subject that it was difficult for her to keep the anger out of her voice. Her response to the dowager was curt – a single word.

"No."

Loch's grandmother sighed. She set down her own cup of tea as carefully as Ivy had, and just as carefully, she traced the gold filigreed pattern along the cup's dainty edge. It was only after her heavily ringed and gnarled digit had gone full circuit that she placed her hands in her lap and clasped them that she spoke. "I understand your frustration, but allow an old woman the privilege of waxing nostalgic."

Loch's grandmother took Ivy's silence as consent. "Tea, though the most quintessential drink of all of Britain, is a relative latecomer to British shores. Though it was drunk in China as far back as the third millennium BC, it wasn't until the mid-1550's that it was brought to Europe. Portuguese and Dutch traders were making regular shipments by 1610. It took half a century more before it began to be sold in coffee houses.

"It quickly became popular, much to the dismay of all the tavern owners, as it was cutting down on their sales of ale and gin. One would think that the decrease of spirit sales and a more sober population and workforce would please a government, but this wasn't the case.

"It always comes down to money. Taxes from alcohol sales provided the government with a steady stream of revenue. Not wanting to lose it and having become dependent upon it, the king passed several acts. Tea was taxed, sales in private homes were forbidden, and coffee house operators were forced to apply for special licenses. The acts also created a new industry."

"Smuggling," Loch said with a knowing grin. "I don't know if I would call that a new industry. I'm sure people have been smuggling contraband from the beginning of commerce."

"Smuggling *tea* into Britain became a new industry," Loch's grandmother said, shooting him an icy stare. "There was no need to smuggle it before, as there were no duties against it."

"You're absolutely right," Loch said. "Yes, tea smuggling was a new industry." Despite Loch's attempt to keep his tone properly respectful, his grandmother stared at him witheringly.

"I'll continue, then," she said, and she did.

"Dutch and Scandinavian ships would bring the tea to the British coast. They would never land. They would wait for the smugglers to come out to them, and they would load the tea into the smaller vessels. It wasn't unusual for the smugglers to be local fisherman. Why bother to bait a hook or throw out nets when contraband products made a much more profitable catch?"

Believing the question to be rhetorical, Ivy and Loch remained silent. They were right, as Loch's grandmother continued her narration.

"The tea was brought inland through underground passages and hidden paths. Special hiding places abounded, the best and safest one often being the local parish church."

"Yes, a church," said Loch's grandmother. She paused to take a sip of tea and then said, "That's where I enter the story."

Loch thought for a moment, and then he said, "Grandmother, you skipped several centuries. The height of British tea smuggling was in the mid-18th century – over 250 years ago! Your looks belie your age, but nevertheless, you can't be that old!"

"History is always part of the present," the dowager said severely.

"You're right," Ivy said. She repeated what Loch's grandmother had said. "History is always the present." Then she added on thoughtfully, "Thus Loch's name."

Loch's grandmother's eyes narrowed as she examined Ivy once again. "Very perceptive, my dear," she said. She took a sip of tea and continued with the saga.

"One particular priest in one particular parish gladly provided space to one of his flock. The tea was cached in several hidden nooks throughout the church. The priest never looked to see if they were empty or full, and when he heard strange noises in the middle of the night, he would not investigate. He never questioned, either, his always full tea canister. 'God blesses rich and poor alike,' he would always say whenever he served a parishioner a cup of tea and a biscuit. 'Royal and peasant are all equal in His eyes. Let us bless our Lord.'

"The fisherman had a daughter who was often the one who brought the tea from the water to the church. I do not know how she came by her information, but she came one night to warn the priest that the King's men had gotten word of the shipment. She needed to divest the grounds of all evidence immediately. The task was large, but she had to do it unaided, as she did not know who had tipped of the King's soldiers. The priest should leave. If the soldiers came while she was still moving the contraband, so be it.

"Both the fisherman's daughter and the priest knew what would happen to the girl if she was caught. A quick death would be a blessing.

"I was told by my own mother who was told by her mother, and so on back to when this began and on until our family dies out, that it was the girl who thought of hiding the tea in the priest's own bed. At this point in time, I don't think it matters whose idea it was. The only thing of importance to remember is that the priest stayed. He could have fled. Instead, he helped to remove the straw from his mattress and strew it on the ground, trampling it into the dirt as they did so it became gray and dirty and blended into the landscape. The newly filled tea ticking made for a plump mattress, but with the bed freshly made up, no one would be the wiser.

"This is incredible," Ivy said softly. "It happened so long ago, but I'm on pins and needles."

"So, it is worth looking into one's ancestry," Loch said, flashing Ivy a smile. "One wouldn't find out incredible things if one didn't."

"In this circumstance," Ivy conceded, "but it remains to be seen in mine."

Loch's grandmother had no idea exactly what Ivy or Loch were referring to, but she didn't hide her opinion. "It is always better to know," she said. "Then one can choose what one reveals and to whom."

Loch held his head in mock dismay. "That's being incredibly unfair and self-serving to say the least! You yourself should know, but you are the one who decides who else is told and what they are told? Doesn't everyone have the right to know? Shouldn't everyone be given all information?"

There was a long silence after Loch's outburst. Loch had objected to everything his grandmother had done to him. He had kept his feelings hidden, but with his last few words it was apparent that he had resented his grandmother's actions. He had essentially called her selfish.

"Did you know," Loch's grandmother said, finally breaking the silence with conversant ease, "that the British will never agree when it comes to milk and tea. Should one put the milk in the cup first and then pour in the tea, or should it be the other way 'round — the tea in first, and then one adds the milk?"

"Science wins out," Loch said brusquely. "There was a study done at Loughborough University that established that putting the milk in after the boiling water is incorrect. The milk heats unevenly when it is poured in, as opposed to when boiling water is poured on top of it. The taste of the milk is affected because the uneven heating of the milk causes the proteins in it to lose their structure and clump. This denaturing of the proteins also contributes to the skin one sometimes gets on top of the brew."

Ivy wanted Loch's grandmother to stop digressing and go back to her story about the tea-filled mattress, but she couldn't help herself. Loch sounded so sure of himself!

"Well, George Orwell wouldn't agree with you at all," she said. He said that the milk-first school can bring forward some fairly strong arguments, but that his own argument was unanswerable. His argument was that, by putting the tea in first and stirring as one pours, one can exactly regulate the amount of milk."

"I'm familiar with that comment," Loch's grandmother said. "Orwell wrote an entire essay about what makes a good cup of tea. Growing up I was never told about what one wanted. I was told about stains."

"Stains?" Ivy questioned.

"It has been said that the upper class started pouring the tea in first," Loch's grandmother answered. "This was proof that they had fine china, so fine in fact and of such high quality that they did not fear the hot liquid cracking or staining the cup."

Loch stood up. "You're wasting our time, Grandmother. I have no interest in listening to class distinctions. Any time I hear someone lauding themselves or someone's actions being excused because of their being a blue-blood, I just think of all the European royals who died from hemophilia. I love the irony that they were sure they were better born, but all their inbreeding did was insure that their offspring would bleed to death. Action is what counts. One should just be glad that one has milk, tea, and hands to pour."

Loch's grandmother let out a long sigh. "You are wiser than I ever was at your age, but your callow youth reveals itself in your impatience. Sit down, Loch. Sit down."

Loch remained standing, his face betraying nothing as he stared at his grandmother. He didn't sit until Ivy softly said his name. When he turned to look at her, she made a motion with her head toward the seat. Loch's face remained impassive, but he sat. Nothing about Loch's acquiescence had escaped the eye of his grandmother, but she didn't comment on what she had seen. Instead, she resumed her narrative as if there had never been an interruption.

"The soldiers came just when they had finished plumping the bed. The priest and the young woman heard the soldiers clumping down the aisle directly to the part of the nave where the tea had been stashed just minutes before. When the soldiers found the cache to be empty, they were furious. Taking their battle axes from their belts and their swords from their sheaths, they began to destroy the church.

"There was no unseen exit for the priest and the girl, and they knew it was only minutes before the soldiers would enter the priest's rooms and find them. The priest didn't hesitate. He knew if the girl was seen as a smuggler, she would be killed. If she was lucky, it would happen in the heat of the moment — a stroke of an axe or the plunging of a sword. More likely, her death would not be so easy. A gang rape and torture would come first.

"Clothes off and into bed!" the priest commanded. "Into my arms."

The girl knew it was the only hope of her being saved. If not a smuggler, a sexual tryst could be the only explanation for her presence. The girl hesitated, knowing that if it worked that the repercussions would not just be for her. The priest, too, would suffer.

"Strip!" the priest ordered again. "Or I'll do it for you."

The girl needed no more urging. She tore at her clothes, ripping holes where there were laces in her haste to discard them. No sooner was she in the bed, the duvet pulled up, and the priest on top her, his arms around her, when the door was flung open."

"'In the name of God!' the priest cried.

"'In the name of God!' the leader of the soldier's cried."

"In the name of God what does this have to do with me?" Loch thundered, unable to contain his outburst. "Grandmother, this all happened 250 years ago!"

"Everything," Loch's grandmother said. "It has everything to do with you."

Loch may not have understood, but Ivy did. "Because they made love," she said.

"Yes," Loch's grandmother said, nodding. "The ploy worked. The soldiers were still enough in awe of the church that they backed out of the room. They may have never witnessed some of the clergy's indiscretions in such close proximity before, but they certainly knew about them. There were reasons laws were made that the church officials had to turn their wealth over to the church. All their bastards would have depleted the church's holdings."

"Lust is a powerful force," Loch's grandmother continued. "One has two unclothed young people in bed and with adrenaline still pounding from a near bout with death, things happen."

"You are a direct descendent of their progeny," Loch's grandmother said, looking at Loch.

"So, you and I are descendants of a bastard," Loch said shrugging. "Who cares? William the Conqueror's detractors called him William the Bastard, but William's being the son of Robert I, Duke of Normandy and his mistress Herleva didn't stop William from invading in 1066 and changing the course of British history.

"It's like what I said early about the European royals so concerned with their lineage that they all bled to death. I don't care about class distinctions. Being legitimate or illegitimate has no bearing on one's worth. Shame on those in society who consider it of merit or not."

"You say that," Ivy murmured, "but you are a strong man — in mind and body. Others, for reasons we are not to judge, have a harder time dealing with it. Perhaps because of what they were told or treated as children, perhaps because their very existence was not acknowledged. Take, for example, the Catholic Church in Ireland. It wasn't until 2017 that thanks to Pope Francis detailed guidelines addressing the plight of children born to Catholic priests and the women who bear them were released. Think about that — the church had tried to keep these children under wraps for centuries. It is only now that priests are being told they should face up their responsibilities, the mother must be respected and involved in decision-making, and that the wellbeing of the child is paramount. Only now!"

"Growing up I was never told about what one wanted. I was told about stains."

"You said that before," Ivy said gently. She set down her cup and then looked thoughtfully at the old woman, her back straight and rigid, her legs slanted, ankle and knees together. Even in the confines of her own house, this strong matriarch maintained royal decorum with her own posture. No slouching, and definitely no crossing one leg over the over!

Impulsively, Ivy reached out and clasped one of the dowager's hands with her own. "Do you ever relax?" she asked. Perhaps it was a rude question, but the concern in Ivy's tone took away any of its unintended impertinence.

"The golf course," Loch's grandmother said.

"It's nice to whack things," Ivy said, laughing. "You should come watch the team I coach when they play a game. I only went out on a date with your grandson because he sponsored my team."

"He paid you to go out with him?" Loch's grandmother asked, arching an eyebrow.

"That's not exactly what happened," Loch said, exasperated. "Ivy you may not be concerned with your well-being, but I still am."

"He did pay you!" Loch's grandmother shook her head. "I'm at a loss of words."

"Apparently not," Loch said dryly.

"I'm afraid what I said or how I said it didn't make myself or your grandson come across too well," Ivy said hastily. "I think our first date fits more under the class of a blind date. My girlfriend Nora set it up. But Loch did pay for my entire team to go to Scotland."

"My grandson doesn't do anything blindly," Loch's grandmother said dryly, "but you are very politic with your words. You are kind. One is not born kind. It is a beauty one must acquire. It takes hard work and is rarely recognized."

In the silence that followed, Loch shot a thankful glance at Ivy. His look of appreciation did not escape the sharp eyes of his grandmother.

"So, shall we speak of Scotland, then," the dowager said with a sigh. "People were not kind to me there. I was told I was not fine. I was of the lowest quality. I was nothing but a stain on the family."

The pain the old woman's voice was so tangible that Loch leaned forward and said gently, "Grandmother, I am only asking for Ivy's sake."

"My mother was bipolar. That term was never used, but today, thanks to all the public awareness campaigns, I can clearly see that she suffered from manic-depressive illness. Today of course we can control it with drugs, but my mother never had that luxury. In my family, mental illness was something to be hidden. My mother never had the comfort of knowing what was wrong with her was the result of chemical imbalances in the brain. Just as she could not be blamed for her eye color, she could not be blamed for her highs and lows. She had no control over the amount or lack of neurotransmitters like noradrenaline, serotonin, or dopamine, that washed over her brain.

"She was in a manic state when she decided to recreate our family history. I have no idea who my father was, but, I do know my mother was not welcome in our village church …" Here the old woman's voice trailed off, the pain of her memories apparent. Loch started to get up from his chair to move closer to her, but he sat back down when his grandmother shook her head. The dowager took a sip of tea, her hands showing a slight tremble. When she carefully put the cup and saucer down, she sat up straighter, delicately recrossed her ankles and placed her clasped hands in her lap.

"My mother committed suicide when I was eleven. I'm sure it was a combination of being in one of her severely depressed states and the way she was constantly belittled by her family. I don't remember one kind word anyone ever said to her. All I remember is every relative telling her she was a disgrace and that I was nothing but a filthy bastard.

"Yet she loved me. Adored me. Fought for me. Told me I was a child of love. That of course was in the manic states. I never knew from day to day what side of my mother I was going to face. There were signs, of course, that I learned to recognize, but often it was a complete surprise. There were times when after staying awake for over four days she would finally 'crash,' as you young people would say. She would sleep without moving for over 30 hours, and then when she would wake, she would lie in bed unmoving. The stillness was worse than anything one can imagine. Every time I was sure she was dead. I would lie close to her and put my hand on her chest, fearful every time that there would be no movement.

"One day there wasn't. I knew that, as she sat in a pool of her own blood, her wrists sliced upward so as to insure a rapid bleeding out, but still I hoped. I listened, my feet making tracks in her blood, as I squatted beside her, my hands on her chest, my face touching her own."

"Grandmother …"

"Enough of that," the old woman said. Her lips remained firm and there was no sign of a tremble as she continued. "It is right and proper that one's name appears in the newspapers only three times. A birth announcement, a marriage announcement, and then the final words – one's obituary. Perhaps it was selfish of me, as you claim, but that is what I adhered to you when it came to sharing your family history. You may have thought it was maliciousness on my part but it was only to protect. What good does it you knowing the sordidness of your past?"

"But my name …"

"My mother loved the legend of the Lady of Loch Douglas. She told it to me over and over and over. In her manic state, she would drape herself in wet clothes and tell everyone that the ghost of the lady was speaking through her. She made me promise over and over that one day I would go to the castle and find my true love.

"My grandfather did not lament my mother's death. She was not allowed to be buried in the churchyard. No one expressed sorrow. Perhaps they were too afraid of my grandfather, but not one person offered me condolences. When she was buried, my grandfather looked at me and said, 'The worst is gone. Now it's just you we have to deal with.'

"I could hate him, I suppose, and for a long while I did, but now I rarely think of him. When I do, all I can think is what an ignorant, mean, and pathetic man.

"I ran away from home at the age of 14. No one came to look for me."

"You made your way to Castle Douglas," Ivy said softly.

"How did you know?" Loch's grandmother asked, staring at Ivy intently.

Ivy moved her shoulders in a slight half-shrug and said, "because I would have."

"But I thought you thought the past should be left alone," Loch said, looking at Ivy perplexedly.

"I wouldn't go for me," Ivy explained. "I'd go for my mother."

"You went to honor your mother, didn't you?" Ivy asked, turning from Loch to his grandmother. "You went for your mother."

"Yes, I did."

"You told me you came to the U.S. when you were just fifteen. So, after visiting Castle Douglas it must have been almost immediately after that you came here."

"I was given a free ticket."

"A free ticket? By whom?"

"Lord Douglas."

At the sound of that name, an image of the angry old man who had spat at them flashed across Ivy's mind. In an almost involuntary movement, she put up a hand and wiped her face.

"Am I named after the man who gave you the free ticket? People don't just hand out free tickets. Why did he give you a free ticket?" Loch's voice demanded answers.

"I was beautiful and wild. I fell in love with him. Of course, he wasn't a lord then, and he still isn't today. He was the son of the present Lord Douglas. That Lord is still holding onto the title, at least he was the last time I checked. He must be close to 100. I'm surprised there's still blood to run through his veins.

"But my love … we were so young. His name was Hamish, and he was only six months older than I was. So young and so very naïve. When his father found out about us he was furious. He had me brought to him. He knew everything about me, having hired a private detective. He told me that no crazy bastard's child would ever inherit the title, especially one whose mother could not be buried on hallowed ground."

"The irony of religion," Loch murmured, shaking his head. "Your father was a man of the cloth! How much holier could your blood get?"

"So, you took his ticket and left." Loch said.

"Not his ticket," his grandmother said. "The one from Hamish."

"What?" Ivy asked confused. "Your love sent you away?"

"He said I had to go away from my own protection. He said his father would never relent, and his wrath would destroy us. He told me it was best for me to go, and he would meet up with me when he could."

"And what happened next?" Loch asked.

"I came to New York and met your grandfather. It all ended well."

"So, my grandfather is the son of Lord Douglas?"

"No."

Loch literally threw up his hands. "For God's sake, then why in the hell am I named Loch Douglas?"

"I hold no anger toward my old love," Loch's grandmother said. "He broke my heart, but young hearts are meant to be broken. It wasn't true love. Remember how young we were? My heart holds no rancor because now I know it was nothing but youthful passion.

"It was a good thing Hamish didn't come. If he had, I wouldn't have met your grandfather. That man, dear Loch, is the love of my life. One can say perhaps that he wasn't my first love, but he was my second, and third, and fourth, and on until all the stars will have been counted. Of course, we've had our battles, our times when we both needed to be a little deaf, but I've spent more time with him than any other human being in the world. He is my morning, my afternoon, and he will be with me for the night."

"Oh," Ivy said, her eyes shining. "You're a romantic! And you're going to make me cry! Love stories always do."

"I told you I hold no rancor, and I don't now, but I did for many years. I swore that I would never return to Scotland, but that was mainly due to my own family, not the Douglas family.

"But when you were born, I realized that by shutting out my past, I had thrown away my mother. I was older, I knew more about mental illness, and I realized that she had done the best she could. More importantly, I realized that she loved me. So many children are born for a parent's gain or out of fear that no one will take care of them when they are older. I was born because my mother wanted me, even if the reason at the time was a bit skewed. She did the best she could. And she did that with no support from her own family."

"But you paid my mother a million dollars for naming rights!"

"Yes, I did. Note, dear grandson, that I didn't pay for your first two names to be Hamish Douglas. I chose Loch Douglas. Remember that my mother loved the lady of the loch. My mother would have loved your name.

"As for not telling you why, it was two-fold. First, I didn't want to bring up my family history. I realize now I was wrong, but at the time I thought it would be a burden to you. I thought it would hold you back.

"The truth is that we – myself and your grandfather – would have given your parents a million dollars when you were born regardless of what name they had chosen for you. They had gone to great trouble to conceive you, and insurance does not cover several rounds of infertility treatments. We were more than glad to pay their medical bills, but they never asked. Your father was determined to do everything on his own.

"Your mother made a joke of selling naming rights on some internet marketplace to help cover costs. I told her not to bother, as I would pay one million."

"And that's it? You just stopped a bidding war on EBAY?"

"Your mother was a wise woman. She knew your father well enough to know that this was perhaps the only possible way your father could accept the money and not feel emasculated. Relationships are complicated, and sometimes it is best not to do things directly. When you are married as long as I have been, you will realize that at times one needs to contort and twist in order to come out straight. Your mother was being pragmatic. She was thinking of school costs and a house with space, and all the other special activities that extra money can provide for one's child. Of course, one can have a good upbringing without those things, but why make it hard on oneself when one doesn't have to?

"The whole idea of my daughter-in-law, son, and grandson not getting any of our wealth until we are both deceased is a little morbid in my taste. Money can spoil one, but it can also provide opportunity. Your mother took the opportunity, and it all came out well."

There was silence for a moment and then Ivy, unable to contain a smile, said "Loch, I think your grandmother has just given you a compliment."

When Loch didn't say respond immediately, his grandmother said, "You have been just as stubborn about receiving money, and I do believe that you would have done well regardless of your upbringing. You have always been perspicacious. They say motivation is a key factor – even greater than IQ – when it comes to success, so I'm sure you would have been a rags-to-riches success story. Nevertheless, your being well-schooled in all educational and cultural ways has certainly helped you achieve your ends. It has also allowed you to enter a profession that you chose and enjoyed. You did not have to concentrate on immediate needs – as in, would there be sufficient food on the table. As for that, I wish all children had the opportunities your parents provided for you."

"I thank you and my parents for that," Loch said, "but you said your reasons were two-fold. You've only given me one."

"You miss nothing," Loch's grandmother said, allowing a small pleased smile to cross her face. Then, turning to Ivy, she said, "You said I was a romantic. I don't know if that is the right word."

"What I hoped," she said turning once again to Loch, was that one day your curiosity about your name would make you go to Scotland. You would visit Castle Douglas, hear the legend, and walk around the loch. I hoped you would come back and tell me that all was well there, and Hamish had found as much happiness as I had."

"Instead," Loch's grandmother said in, her voice having regained its normal severe and regal tone, "you proved to be an obstinate and pig-headed man."

"I'm not sure your grandmother is paying you a compliment now!" Ivy said, a giggle escaping.

"Tell me now, why Ivy is in danger."

Loch looked at his grandmother for a moment. He picked up his cup of tea. The brown liquid had gone cold, as they had talked so long, but he took a leisurely sip. Then, he set down the cup.

"It will cost you," he said, speaking slowly but very clearly. "One million dollars."

Twenty-five

"Colombian Salsa is also known as Cali-Style Salsa or Salsa Caleña. That's because the city of Cali has the most salsa schools and salsa teams in the world. You should see their footwork. It's got quick rapid steps and skipping motions. Really intricate and precise. I don't care what Coach says. We're going to see some world class dancing. I'm going to see some world class dancing even if it means me staying behind. I'll beg in the streets for my ticket home. This is a once in a lifetime opportunity that I thought I would never have. Talk about luck!"

"Dance, you do know you're in a wheelchair, and you're missing …"

"I know, I know," Dance said to all his teammates who were trying hard not to contain their laughter. If anyone else teased them or mentioned limits due to their disabilities, it rankled, but as a team, they were free to rib each other. They were a tight unit who understood what each had lost. As a team, they had learned what they had gained. They took care of their own.

"I know, but hallelujah, we're going to a dance floor! We're going to see them strut their stuff in the flesh. You just wait! You'll see what I mean! None of you are going to want to come back!"

"What dance floor, where?" Ivy asked, coming up to the crowd of men who were grinning and shaking their heads good-naturedly at Dance.

"In Colombia, Coach. Where else?" Torrance said with excitement. "Back when I could ride a motorcycle, I met up with a Colombian who had bought a bike stateside so he could cross the US. We rode together for about ten days before I had to turn back. My leave was up, and I had to burn rubber so as to avoid going AWOL. Sometimes I think about what would have happened if I had kept riding, but then it would have been some other dumb sucker in my place. Better not to think too hard, Coach, but Colombia!

"The streets are rocking with motorcycles. I may no longer have my Harley, but I can show anyone a thing of two when it comes to machines and speed. Life is grand, Coach, just grand!"

Ivy had no idea what was going on. She was terribly afraid that someone was playing a prank that had gotten out of hand. Did the men really think they were going to Colombia? She knew they had a wheelchair rugby team there. They had even hosted the Pan-American tournament several years ago. But Colombia, in South America? "I'm not sure …" she started to say, but as soon as she had started to speak, Wes had maneuvered around some other players and rolled up to her with lightning speed.

"Colombia, Coach. Marcella helped us arrange it all. The games are in some city called Pereira, but maybe," and here he raised his voice and looked over at Dance, "if we win, you'll arrange us a side trip to Cali."

"Yeah," shouted one of the men, "because I haven't worn my dancing shoes since I lost my feet!"

"I've got a foot!" another man yelled.

"But does it move? asked another, chortling.

Ivy started to say something, but once again Wes interrupted her, though this time he spoke in a low voice that was meant for her alone. "Trust me, Ivy. It's all for you. I'll explain later."

"Ivy, it's your body parts. They want them."

Ivy started to say something. She was sitting on one of the couches in Dalziel Traders office. Wes and Vinny had escorted her there after practice. The two men had told Ivy her questions would have to wait until everyone was present. As much as Ivy wanted to pound it out of the two of them, she knew Wes well enough to know he meant what he said. She could ask, demand, plead, and beg, but it would be to no avail. He would not reveal a thing until everyone was present. He wouldn't even tell her who "everyone" was!

"We're all here," Loch said, opening the door when they arrived. Ivy expected to see Loch and Marcella, but she was surprised at Nora's presence.

She shot a querying look at Wes, and he just shrugged. "When you're married, you'll understand," he said. "Informing Nora isn't telling anyone else. She's part of me."

It took a moment for Ivy to understand what Wes meant. When she understood, she felt something unexplainable throb in her heart. Would she ever love so completely that her very being was part of someone else?

Ivy had no time to continue on this sentimental line of pondering, for no sooner had she taken a seat when Nora had spoken.

It's your body parts. They want them.

Ivy opened her mouth to respond, but then it all seemed so surreal that she couldn't think what to say. If Nora had spoken in her familiar histrionic and melodramatic fashion, Ivy could dismiss

Nora's words as preposterous. It was Nora's calm and measured tone that was so unnerving.

Ivy closer her mouth, but then she opened it again. Still, nothing came out. Finally, she looked at Loch for confirmation.

"I'll let Marcella explain," Loch said. "I think she might be a bit more expansive when it comes to details. Though as for that," and here he looked as if he was almost trying not to laugh, "Nora does have a way of getting one's full and rapt attention."

Marcella began immediately. Her first words were much more politic than Nora's. "There is a chance that someone may be trying to find you. It might be because of a transplant need, but we're not sure. We wrote an algorithm that started matching you with everyone on some kind of transplant list. We didn't come up with anything, but then Vinny had the idea of going backward. Ignore the list, and take your bone marrow and try to match anyone who has ever volunteered to be part of the registry. "So, perhaps a volunteer rather than someone," and here Marcella looked at Nora with a gentle smile, "who needs a body part."

Nora said, "I wanted Ivy prepared for the worst. You don't know what a horrible family she has."

"I do," Loch said quietly.

Nora looked flustered for a moment. "You know about her family? She told *you*!" Nora continued in a bewildered tone, "But Ivy doesn't talk about her family to anyone. That's why I know they're so terrible. I don't even know about them."

Nora looked at Ivy with a wild gaze, and then suddenly her face changed. She sat forward in her chair and looked straight at Loch. In a fierce voice she said, "If you ever mistreat her, you'll have me to deal with."

"Nora, what are you talking about?" Wes interjected. "Loch's helping, Nora. He's keeping her safe."

"Then let me be clearer," Nora said, tossing her hair. "Loch, if you break my Ivy's heart, I'll …"

"Be sure to send him a dead fish," Ivy said laughing.

"Right," said Nora, "but an inedible one. A really inedible one!"

"I don't get it," Vinny said. "What is going on here?"

"We're just talking about love," Nora said.

"Ah," said Vinny, "I don't get the fish part, but I get the love part. Loch's been working on his words!" "Good on you!" he said, turning to Loch with a grin. "Good on you!"

"Ivy, you're blushing," Wes said in astonishment. "I didn't know you could!"

"I think it's time to get back to body parts," Ivy said.

"Yes, of course," Loch said. He couldn't help but smile tenderly at Ivy. When he realized that even Nora didn't know Ivy's history, his heart had felt as if it was going to burst right out of his chest. Ivy had trusted him! And from Nora's reaction, he was the only man or person Ivy ever had revealed her secrets to. He planned to tell Ivy tonight when they were in bed, perhaps when she was curled up in the nook of his arm after passion spent, how the knowledge made him feel.

"Listen up, then," Marcella said. "Let's try and stay on topic." Despite her admonishing tone, she allowed everyone to see the twinkle in her eyes. Then giving a little nod, she became all business.

"A test called a tissue typing test is the standard test to see if one is a match for a bone marrow transplant. This test is also referred to as histocompatibility or HLA typing. With all the DNA research going on, it's no surprise that a second test has been recently developed. This newer test is called high resolution DNA typing. The first test is the one that was done on Ivy's blood when she entered the registry.

"Optimal matches are HLA compatible. This means that the donor and recipient cells will recognize each other as the same, and the risk of rejection is far less.

"I'm going to sound a bit technical here for a moment, but please bear with. Each person has two sets of chromosomes containing HLA genes. One set is inherited from the father and the other set comes from the mother. Each set has four genes, so there is a total of eight genes.

"So how likely is that two people have the same eight genes in common? When it comes to the general public, the chances are very unlikely – about one in a million. When it comes to a parent being a complete match for a child, the percentage is far better, but it is still only one in two-hundred. Siblings have the greatest chance of being complete matches. When it comes to a brother or a sister, the probability shoots up to 25%, or one in four."

Marcella paused for a moment. Then looking directly at Ivy, she said, "We found one match."

"In Colombia," Ivy said quietly.

"Yes." This time it was Loch who spoke.

"I'm not sure I want to go," Ivy said slowly. "Isn't a bit like kicking a hornet's nest?"

It was Wes who broke the silence. "Ivy, think of what happened to us in the van. They almost took Nora! The hornet's nest has already been kicked."

"But I don't have to go," Ivy said quietly. "Loch, Marcella, this is your business. You find out information and the whereabouts of people all the time. You don't need me there. I know you can find out whatever it is that needs to be known without me."

Ivy looked around the room at everyone's face. Loch's was completely impassive, but she could tell everyone else was shocked or at least puzzled by her attitude.

"I have my family," she said quietly. "I have Nora and Wes. I don't want or need anymore."

"Oh Ivy," Nora said, patting her knee, "You're always quoting things from books and people I've never even heard of, but now it's my turn to say something to you. Robert Frost – do you know him?"

"Not personally," Ivy said. "You know he's been dead for over 50 years."

"No matter," Nora said, waving her hand dismissively in the air. What he wrote was this: *Home is the place where, when you have to go there, they have to take you in.*"

Ivy was completely baffled. If anything, Frost's words supported Ivy's reluctance to go to Colombia. She had made her own life. She had made her own home. She didn't want or need to be taken in anywhere!

"I'm not …" Ivy began.

"Let me finish," Nora said. "Colombia or anyone down there who so happens to share some genes does not make a home. Or a family. They're just genes. Genes. That's all.

"Wes and I are your family. We're the ones that have to take you in, just as you have to take us in. And maybe …" Nora shot a glance over at Loch, "one day someone else will be part of it, too. So, don't use the excuse of not wanting to find some creep of a person who just so happens to carry some of the same genes as you be your excuse not to go to Colombia."

Everyone stared at Nora in complete surprise. "Well," Nora said, sitting back in a huff, "Think about it. We share 96% of our DNA with chimpanzees, and 98.6 percent with bonobos."

"Bonobos?" asked Vinny.

"Bonobos," Wes said with a huge grin. "You know – those good-natured and happy chimp like animals that have sex all the time."

"Are you for real?" Vinny asked incredulously. "Those animals never came up in my biology class!"

"However," Marcella asked, trying to keep the amusement out of her voice, "did African simians and sex enter into the discussion about Ivy going to Colombia?"

"What Nora means," Ivy explained, not bothering to try and stifle her amusement the way Marcella had, "is that genes may make us related, but it doesn't mean we're family, let alone the same species."

Throwing up her hands, Ivy continued. "Nora, you won! I don't know what a debate team would think of you, but I'm going. I'll go to Colombia."

"Not for you," Vinny said, with the same teasing tone he usually reserved for the court. "You're not going for you. You're going for the team. You better not lose your edge, Coach. We're depending on you for a win!"

"Oh," Ivy replied, "I thought we were going to dance."

Twenty-six

Marcella had arranged it well. The team flew into Pereira and landed in the dark after catching a connecting flight from the capital city of Bogota. They woke up to a bustling and urbane metropolis situated in the foothills of the Andes. After being given tiny but powerful cups of fresh-pressed coffee, glasses of fresh squeezed juices, plates of scrambled eggs mixed full with chorizo sausage, and mounds of small fried dough balls called buñelos, the men were given a quick bus tour of the city before the driver headed out into the countryside.

The men were astounded at the steep mountain sides covered in coffee plants and bananas, but as they went further along, it was the road that began to take up all their attention. It had turned to a single-lane dirt track, and the jungle vegetation scraped against both sides. At times, those on the right side, were given views of a sheer drop into the raging water of the Rio Otún far below.

It wasn't the narrowness of the deeply rutted road or the steep drop to one side that astounded Ivy. It was the bike riders.

Mostly men, but some women, too. Usually in pairs, though some rode alone or in larger packs. They had good strong mountain bikes with wide tires and heavy treads. All were amazingly fit. With backs bent forward and eyes on the road, they didn't even glance at the bus as it brushed against them. "Nerves of steel," Ivy thought, as she noted their muscled calves in admiration. When Ivy saw one man descending tuck his elbows into his sides and pass the bus so close to the edge that dirt crumbled, she didn't realize until he was safely past that she had stopped breathing.

It took two hours to cover a mere 15 miles. At one point, a man on a horse, a string of three pack horses roped behind him, passed them. "I thought I was slow," remarked one of the men, "but seriously, I think I could make better time pushing my own wheelchair than this bus."

When the bus finally stopped, they were at the road's end. "You're going to have to be put on horses," Ivy said. "It's just a short way, but there is no other way to get you to where I want you to go."

"This I gotta see," Dance said laughing almost hysterically. "Coach, even if someone gets me up on a horse, how am I going to hang on? You can hang Lance and Sal over the sides and tie them down like dead men, but there's not enough of me to go over both sides of the horse, let alone one."

"Got it covered!" Ivy said with a grin. "No one's getting out of this!"

The men had already gotten a sense of how kind and gentle the Colombians were by the way the way they had been solicitously treated on the plane, at the hotel, and with the hired aides who had met them at the airport. But it wasn't until they were hoisted up into the arms of riders already seated and held firmly in their strong arms as they were tenderly placed on saddles cushioned with blankets that they came to realize how dignity was an integral part of the Colombian society.

"To think that all I knew about Colombia was that it was the home of that cocaine warlord Pablo Escobar," one of the men remarked. "What a sick and twisted image."

The men became silent as the horses made their way down the path. The steep jungle covered hills loomed on both sides, but the men could hear the rushing sound of water to their right. When they came to a bridge, all the horses stopped.

"Listen up," Ivy said, as the horses and their riders stood in a horseshoe shape around her so she could be heard. "We're here to see a duck."

"You're kidding me," Torrance said. "That's why we're here? I just saw toucans flying overhead. Until this day, I thought they were nothing but made up mega-billed birds to go on cereal boxes. Now that I've seen birds with the mother of all beaks, you want me to look for a fu…excuse me coach, a flying duck?"

Torrance began to laugh, and one by one the others joined in. "Coach, you're too much," Joseph said. "I've got tears running down my cheeks because I'm laughing so hard, and I can't even wipe them off because I'm not letting go of this pommel with the one hand I do have."

At that, the men started laughing even harder. The interpreter Marcella had arranged must have been translating every word because huge grins soon crossed the faces of their guides. The one riding with Joseph took the corner of his scarf and carefully began to wipe Joseph's face. This brought even more hoots of hilarity.

"Yes, a duck." Ivy said, raising a hand to calm everyone down. "Please note, Torrance, that it is not really a flying duck. Though it can take to the air, it does reluctantly, and only for short distances.

"Its name is the torrent duck. It is uncommon and hard to see. One reason being because of the dwindling population, and the other is because one has to travel about 5,000 feet up into the Andes to see it. It only lives on fast-flowing Andean rivers. It's very territorial, and it's a very powerful swimmer.

"It's hard to see on the water, but it's much easier to see when its perched on a rock. There's a nesting pair here. Look for it on the boulders in the middle of the river. The male has a black and white striped head and a bright red bill."

The guides moved their horses onto the bridge, lining up the horses in a parallel fashion so that the men could look directly on to the rushing water.

"Coach," one of the men said, "it's nothing but white water here. Any duck that jumped into that water would be swept away."

Just then one of the guides pointed. There, on a boulder surrounded by perilous white rushing water on all sides perched a small duck. As the men watched, it dove into the white froth. The men couldn't help but gasp. "No way can anything survive that water," one of the men said.

One of the guides said something to the translator, and then he spoke. "It is diving for food. It eats little animals. It swims with and against the current."

"There it is!" shouted Dance. "On that squarish boulder with the white marking further up. How in Hell did it get there?"

It was in Ivy's pregame pep talk that she told them why she had taken them to see the duck.

"Tonight, when you go out to play, think of that duck. White water raging, but it dove right in. It swam equally well with or against the current. Men, you can't fly, but you know about fighting the current. Tonight, I want you swimming. Diving up and down that court, I want you staking out your territory and then disappearing right before the eyes of your opponents."

They were going to win. Possibly. The score was once against tied, but Ivy could sense it. They were in their last eight-minute quarter, and though dripping with sweat, her players still seemed to have the energy they had when they first rolled onto the court. The clash and cacophony was as discordant as the beginning of Beethoven's Ninth Symphony, but just as Beethoven knew where to place each note so that it all ended in a glorious triumph, so the men seemed to know exactly where to roll to on the court. The Colombian team was an equal match, but at least for tonight, it was Ivy's team that was the concert in motion. Every time the other team scored and they fell behind, they fought back relentlessly. When they matched point for point and inched ahead, they gave it no rest. Down to each man, they were having the time of their lives.

Then a wheel broke. There had been a clash of metal as four chairs struck each other head on as the players tried to avoid the downed man and the steel circle bowling dangerously across the floor. At first Ivy couldn't tell what team's player had the broken chair and whose players had been catapulted to the ground. As soon as a Time Out was called, it became apparent. The Colombian team was down a chair. And it had belonged to one of its best players. His name was Juan Alvarez Morales, and he was classified as a 1.5. This meant he had a high level of impairment in his upper limbs, and it wasn't easy for him to pick up or pass the ball. For that reason, he was being predominately used as a blocker, though occasionally and always in some crucial moment when one was least expecting it, he would pick up the ball and execute a perfect play. As for his blocking, Vinny said it best. "That man is an overturned semi-truck at the height of commuter traffic."

There was a stunned silence as everyone realized what this meant. Juan Alvarez Morales was out. A substitute player would have to come in, as there was no way Juan's chair could be repaired before the game was over. Juan's departure would turn the tide of the game. Ivy's team would have an easy victory unless they made a major gaff.

Ivy had a sinking feeling in her stomach, but she knew what she had to do. "Dance," she said quietly, "Give him your chair."

Dance's jaw clenched, and his face paled. The other men looked just as shocked, but when one of them started to argue, Dance shushed him. "Coach rules," was all he said, and then without a word of protest, he put his head down and rolled across the court.

At first, no one except Ivy and his teammates knew what he was doing. Even when he got to the opposing side and maneuvered himself out of the wheelchair, people still didn't understand. It wasn't until Morales hoisted himself into Dance's chair and rolled back onto the floor that the crowd fully understood.

The stadium erupted as play resumed. People were on the feet screaming, clapping, and stomping until the end of the quarter, and they remained so as the game went into overtime. Ivy couldn't even hear her own voice as she shouted at her players. It was the longest most thrilling three minutes of her life.

The crowd was roaring so loud that the final buzzer could not be heard. It wasn't until one of the referee's grabbed the ball that the players realized the game was over.

One point. They had won by one point!

It was almost a riot. People were screaming, hugging, shouting, and raising victorious fists into the air. Family members who had somehow gotten the funds together to come were weeping copious tears. Joseph's father was sobbing. "I love you, I love you, I love you," he said over and over, his head bent on his only son's chest.

"Look at Dance!" Ivy heard someone shout. At first Ivy couldn't spot him because of the mass of people on the court, but then she realized she was looking in the wrong direction. All she needed to do was look up. Dance and Juan were being paraded high above everyone's head by a huge mass of Colombian fans. Dance's face was aglow with happiness. He may not have understood much Spanish, but he understood full well that when people were reaching out to touch him and yelling in voices filled with adulation "héroe" and "gran hombre" that he was being honored for what he had once believed he was no longer capable of being: a hero or a big man.

The crowd surged forward, and Ivy felt herself losing her footing. Just as she began to stumble, two strong arms caught her from behind. Even in the mass of people, she knew instantly who it was.

"Loch!" she cried. Then turning, she jumped into his arms, her legs wrapped around him. "You came! Did you see …"

"Yes!" said Loch, his eyes shining. "I wouldn't have missed it for anything. Ivy, it was one of the most incredible things I've ever seen in my life. I'm so proud of you! I'm so proud of the team!"

As Loch talked, he kept his tight hold on Ivy while pushing through to a spot where the crowd had begun to dissipate. "I don't want to put you down. Ever."

Laughing joyously, Ivy said, "Don't! Not until I've kissed you proper!"

Then trusting Loch to keep her from slipping, she put both her hands on the sides of his head and brought her lips to his. The sounds of the crowd became nothing. The warmth of Loch's lips powered over all else, and in that magical moment, as Loch and Ivy passed a bit of soul to the other, no one else, nothing else, existed.

The aftergame talk was brief. Ivy, standing on a bench, said simply. "It was a clean win. Not any of you or I wouldn't have wanted it to be any other way.

"You're off to Cali for three days. There will be sight-seeing during the days and dancing at night for those who want it. Torrance has asked to remain here for an extra day, and that has been arranged.

He's going to be showing the Colombian team some of the wizardry he's come up with when it comes to rolling chairs of steel.

"As for me, I'm going to say good-bye to you here. I'll be with …"

Ivy hesitated. Then very clearly, she finished her sentence, "my boyfriend."

Twenty-seven

"My boyfriend? Makes me sound awful young. I don't think I've been called that since I was a teenager."

"And you'd prefer what? My manfriend? My bodyguard?"

"How about husband?"

The words had come out without thought. For a split-second Loch couldn't believe that he had even uttered them. But, as he waited for Ivy to respond, he knew he had meant what he had said. He had never wanted to marry anyone before. It's not just that he could marry Ivy, it was more. Having been with her now, he couldn't imagine life without her.

They were in bed, the sheets tangled around them. After leaving the locker room, having escaped from final hugs and offers of congratulations, Loch had firmly taken Ivy's hand. Holding it tightly, he had whispered into her ear.

"You need to sleep with me now."

Ivy looked at him, her eyes still glowing from the victory. When she didn't answer immediately, Loch asked, "You have something else to do?"

Cocking her head, Ivy had given Loch an appraising look, the upward curling of her lips revealing the delight in Loch's question.

"Those are my words!" she said, breaking into a laugh.

"And I still can't believe if you asked me if I was being deliberately obtuse!" Loch said, pulling her into his arms and kissing the top of her head. "Obtuse! Trust me Ivy, no matter how dimwitted or thickheaded you think I might be, I will always want to sleep with you!"

"Okay then."

"Okay, what?"

"I'll sleep with you now!"

They had begun to disrobe the minute the elevator doors had closed before them. Ivy had unclasped Loch's belt buckle and had slid the leather strap out from Loch's pant loops. She let it drop to the floor as she began on his shirt buttons. Loch was just as active, unbuttoning all of the buttons on her shirt as well as unhooking the top of her skirt. He was beginning on unclasping her bra as the elevator door slid open.

Holding her blouse together with one hand and her skirt up with the other, Ivy pushed him away, all the while laughing about public indecency.

"You make me lose control," Loch had said.

"What if the maid is in the room?" Ivy teased Loch as they walked, almost ran, down the hall to their room.

"Doesn't matter. I can't wait," Loch replied, his voice tight.

Ivy was so shocked she stopped mid-step. "Loch!"

Loch didn't waste time responding. He simply picked Ivy up and carried her into the room that fortunately had already been cleaned.

Their lovemaking had been wild, almost animalistic. They had torn off each other's clothes, putting mouth to flesh as each item was discarded. Each nipped and teased the other, till both were demanding more. Giving and taking became seamless, and when they finally climaxed, unable to hold back any longer, they did it together, holding tight to each other until all shuddering and throbbing had subsided into calm.

It was sometime after, but while still in this tranquil sated state that Loch had said the words he had never before uttered in his life. "How about husband?"

"No."

The answer was completely unexpected. Loch was not prepared for the hurt he felt. He wasn't one for figurative language, preferring bare facts, but now he understood why people used it. He literally felt as if someone had pierced his heart with a sword of the coldest, hardest, sharpest ice. With each pulse, he could feel his blood leaking torturously out, flooding his body with excruciating pain. It took all self-control that he had not to ask again. Instead he remained silent, falling back into negotiation mode and waiting for more information so that he could assess and then react to the situation.

The silence was interminable. Suddenly Ivy pushed her hands against Loch's chest and sat up. "Here's the thing," she said.

Loch sat up too, and made motion to get out of the bed. Ivy pulled him back. "Here's the thing," she said. "Something's been set in motion. I don't know what or why or how, and no, I'm not blaming you. But something has been set in motion, and whatever it is I want it finished. I need it to be finished so if you ask me again, I might have a different answer."

"Might?" Loch said, studying her closely.

"That's the best I can give you right now."

Mutely, Loch once again began to get up. Once again Ivy pulled him back. "There's another thing."

Loch didn't reply, nor did he sit back, but he didn't leave the bed.

"The thing is that I don't know who I am. It didn't matter to me before. It was enough that I wasn't related to the Richards. But now, now I can't help but wonder if I'm tainted somehow. What if I'm always being chased? What if I put *your* life in danger? What kind of life is that?"

"Oh, Ivy," Loch said, his voice breaking. He had no more words. Instead he reached for her and laid her gently down on the bed. He began to lay tender, warm kisses on every part of her body, leaving a trail of seared flesh as he left the softness of her breasts and began to make his way down to her more intimate parts. When Ivy began to raise her arms so that she could hold him and respond in kind, he pushed her back and whispered into her ear, "Allow me."

"So where are we going exactly?" Ivy asked after she buckled herself in and Loch had done the same before turning the key in the ignition slot and putting the car in gear. "You do realize," Ivy said, giving Loch a slight nudge on the arm, "that so far we've had a very peripatetic relationship. New York, Scotland, Iceland, Colombia, and of course always going back to New York in between. What's going to happen to us if we have to stay in one place for very long, let alone the same continent?"

"Learn to keep better track of our possessions, I suppose."

Ivy put her hands to her face. "Oh, Loch," she said laughing, "when the doorman held up your belt and asked us if could possibly be yours as we were walking out, I thought I was going to die of embarrassment! You handled it so well."

"'Why, yes sir, I believe it is," Ivy said, imitating the way Loch spoke. "'I must have dropped it in the hall.'"

"I wasn't going to tell him that you were the one that lost track of it after you stripped it from me! A gentleman always takes responsibility!"

"A gentleman doesn't begin to disrobe a lady in an elevator," Ivy replied, primly.

"You've got me there," Loch said, shaking his head. Then he got serious.

"We're going to a cemetery."

Ivy sat for a moment in stunned silence. "I think," she said slowly, "that you should go into a little more detail.

"Fair enough. It's close. In a little town called Marsella just a little under 20 miles from here. Sounds a bit like Marcella's name, but it's spelled with an *s*, not a *c*. The cemetery's name is Cementerio Jesús María Estrada. It was built in 1928, and though it's fairly small when thinking of American terms, it's been declared part of Colombia's artistic heritage. It was designed by Julio Cesar Velez."

"Those are details, I'll admit, but it's not good enough. Why are we going there?"

"Your match is there."

"Alive or dead?"

"Alive."

Ivy sucked in her breathe and said testily, "Stop making me ask questions. I feel like you're making me play the game of Twenty Questions, and I'm now supposed to ask you if its choice of pronoun is he, she, or they. Just tell me what you know!"

"He's a male, and he is not expecting us. He goes to the cemetery every day with fresh flowers for his wife. She died a few years ago. He's 79 years old."

"Your grandmother's age?"

"Interestingly enough, yes."

"His name?"

Loch explained, "His first name is Jamie, but in Spanish, it is pronounced like the two words *hi* and *me*. His last name is Dorazo."

Ivy was silent for the remainder of the trip. She mulled over what she was told as Loch expertly maneuvered the car around the tight turns of the steep hillsides covered in coffee plants. She remained mute when Loch had parked the car in front of a beautiful white, brick wall with towers at each end. It wasn't until they exited the car and Loch pointed to a beautiful ornate gate in the center of the wall and said that they should enter there, that Ivy spoke.

"This can't be the cemetery. As far as I can tell, all that wall is doing is enclosing a steep hill. I don't know if a cow could even keep her footing on it."

Loch didn't argue. He simply took Ivy's hand and said, "Come."

"Oh," Ivy said, stopping suddenly as they passed through the gate. "It's breathtaking," she said, her words soft. "I've never seen such a place before. These terraces, and the graves resting inside the hill. All this greenery."

Ivy let go of Loch's hand and started slowly up the stone steps that ran down the middle of the terraces covered in plants. She paused every few steps, looking left and right every time she stopped.

"What an incredible use of space," she said. "And going up — it's like we're ascending into the heavens."

She passed a few more terraces, reading some of the names of those interred. "It's so peaceful," she said. "I've always said that I want all my organs used for the living, and if there was anything left, just cremate me and spread my ashes somewhere beautiful. But this. I understand why someone would want to be buried here. It would bring solace to those who are still living."

"Which is why he comes."

"Yes," Ivy said, looking up to the top of the stairs which ended in a circular dome supported by ornate stone columns. A large white statue of the Virgin Mary stood toward the back, and matching curved marble benches were to either side of her. Ivy saw a man sitting on the bench to her left. He was quietly reading and appeared oblivious to their presence.

Ivy walked up to him with measured steps. She didn't say anything, but she stood before him. She waited, unmoving, while the man continued to read. He didn't look up until he turned the page.

At first, he stared blankly, but then his face paled. The book dropped from his hand.

"A one in 200 match or one in a million?" Ivy asked quietly.

The man didn't answer, but he began to wave his hands in front of his face, clearly distraught. Ivy took a step back. With back straight, she said, "I don't care which one it is. You have no rights to me. All I want to know is are you the one putting me in danger?"

"Isla," he said, tears streaming down his cheeks. "Isla, can it be you?"

He reached out his hands, but Ivy took yet another step back so as to remain safely out of his reach.

"Ivy," Ivy said. "My name is Ivy." She stared at the man who was clearly losing what little composure he had remaining. "You're a little old to be my biological father," she said coldly.

"An unexpected blessing," the man said, looking up at Ivy. "An unexpected blessing. That's what you were."

"Clearly," Ivy said, dryly.

"Let me show you your mother's grave," the man said. He stood up and moved to the part of the rotunda with the opening to the stairs. A spasm of pain crossed his face as Ivy quickly moved to the side so as to avoid him and keep her distance.

"No," she said emphatically. "I'm not interested. If you can't tell me if you are the reason I'm in danger, then I'm leaving."

"Ivy," Loch said, "I think …"

"No," Ivy said fiercely. "You don't get to think anything. You don't get to judge me, either. Your circumstances and upbringing were completely different. This man is nothing to me. He has never been part of my life. I would have passed him by in the street and never known the difference."

"He is nothing to me," she said again.

The man had taken a few steps down, but at Ivy's words he turned around. "I'll accept that," he said, softly. "It is enough that I got to see your face. It is good to know that you are strong and willful. Very important traits that are too often underrated and unappreciated."

The man took a step up. He no longer showed any sign of emotional distress. Just as Ivy had straightened her spine, so had the man his. Looking steadfastly at her, he said, "You have come a long way. If you would sit, I can tell you a story. Its veracity is yours to doubt or accept, and what you do with it, is yours for the taking."

He nodded toward the benches in the rotunda. "If you could sit," he said.

The man didn't move. He stood motionless, waiting for Ivy to make her decision. A flock of parrots flew over, their screeching raucous.

"Blue-headed parrots," the man said.

"But you didn't look up," Ivy said. "How do you know?"

"Deduction and familiarity. They're common here, and that particular flock flies over about this time every day. They're flying to a clay lick."

Ivy looked up at the sky, but the flock had already disappeared.

"When people come here they think they've seen something really special when they see parrots or toucans. Makes sense because they're all so brightly colored, and of course, with the toucans, their bills are just a huge announcement that one is far from home. Still, if I had to pick one bird to see here, I'd go for a duck. It's not really a flyer, and it's not that big, but it's amazing what it can do in the water. It's called the … "

"Torrent duck," Ivy said, finishing the man's sentence. She took a deep breath and said, "You have things to say. I'll listen for a bit."

"I was too old for your mother. I told her that over and over, but she was the most stubborn and beautiful and amazing woman to have ever walked on this earth. She took my breath away the very first time I saw her, and even in the last days of her sickness, she was still the most beautiful and willful creature God ever put on this Earth.

"At first I thought she was only interested in me so for financial security. I was tempted to find that a sufficient reason to wed, but I couldn't. She was too beautiful and good, and I wanted her to love someone with all her being. I could not take that away from her.

"She, of course, was of a different mind. She told me I could feed my money to the black vultures that abound here for all she cared. She said I had been born too early and she too late, but all that meant was that we had to seize the time we had left. We could not waste a day."

The man looked up at Ivy. "I had to bow to her. You do not know her strength."

Loch was tempted to say that he had seen Ivy exhibit the same stubborn will several times, but he thought better of it. Instead, he simply picked up Ivy's hand, kissed it, and then still clasping it, placed it on his thigh.

"I did not think I could father children. I know that there are old men who leave babies with a string of younger wives, but I thought I was sterile. I had numerous relationships before I met your mother, and with the callowness of youth, I never bothered with birth control. None of my girlfriends ever conceived, even with the ones I had been with long enough who felt it was time to have a baby.

"No one could have loved you more than your mother. She loved you even before you were born."

"And yet you gave me up for …" Ivy started to say.

"You were taken," the man said quietly. "You were not given."

Ivy's intake of breath was audible. She was silent, and then she asked, "Why should I believe you? Your love story wasn't mine, or my life."

There was no anger or bitterness in Ivy's voice when she asked these questions. Her tone was matter of fact.

The man did not answer, choosing instead to continue with his monologue. "My father was nothing short of a tyrant. He was always hostile and I returned his feelings in kind. My very first girlfriend described us as two pit bulls fighting over sausages that had been tied to each other's collars.

"My father hated that girlfriend. Thought she was an abomination, but then he thought that of most people. I sent her away to keep her safe, thinking one day I would meet up with her, but once she was gone, I realized it was for the better. I was too young. Incapable of behaving responsibly.

"College, graduate school, staying away from home as much as I could. I worked as a petroleum engineer throughout southeast Asia and in almost every country here in South America. Your mother was an American. Blond, brown-eyed, just like you. She was from Indiana. Graduated from Purdue University with an engineering degree — saw it as her ticket out of what she called the meanly religious flatlands. We met on her first assignment. I was thinking of retirement, but after seeing her, I wasn't going anywhere.

"We worked in the field side by side until she was pregnant with you. We had you for two days." For the first time the man's voice broke. He passed a hand in front of his eyes, and Ivy saw two tears trickle down his cheeks.

"It was my fault."

Ivy didn't offer any comfort, but she leaned forward, showing she was listening carefully. She held Loch's hand tightly, and her knuckles grew white.

"Cali and Medellin were where the drug lords were centered. Pablo Escobar Gaviria was at his height. They had so much cash – American dollars – that they were wrapping it up in huge mattress-sized plastic bags and burying piles of them out in the jungle.

"I came across one of the processing stations on one of my exploratory forays into the jungle. They didn't kill me, but I wish they had. I promised I would keep quiet, as all I cared about was oil. They let me go, though at that time I didn't know why or how. I guessed that it would bring too much attention to them if a European engineer disappeared, and honestly, a lot of the foreign petroleum companies cared very little about what was going on in the drug world. All they wanted was rights to the oil. If entire swaths of the countryside were out of bounds for the police, then it was far easier for roads to be built into supposedly protected jungles for indigenous peoples and other green spaces. The truth is that all I wanted was to just get back to Rachel."

"Your mother's name was Rachel," the man said softly. The pain in his voice apparent, he continued.

"I never told her what happened until the day Escobar's men came and took you. They said it was to keep my silence. When I talked, you would be killed."

"Your mother never gave up hope. We knew we couldn't look for you directly. If they knew, you could be killed in retaliation. Your mother was the one who thought of changing our names and moving here to this little town after 'disappearing.' Easy enough here with enough money to get new identification papers, and no one ever came to investigate. As I said, I hadn't had contact with my father for years, and Rachel's family had condemned her long ago for leaving their church. She was also the one who put us on the bone marrow registry."

"But the name was removed …" Ivy said slowly.

"I did that," the man said looking directly at Ivy. "I did it after Rachel died. Rachel was the one who never accepted your death. As for me, I could not bear the pain of hope."

"If your mother were alive," the man said, a small, rueful smile crossing his face, "she would be laughing now, telling me I told you so."

"How did she die?"

"Liver cancer."

"What was your name before?"

"Hamish Douglas."

Ivy was so shocked that she actually trembled. She stood up very slowly, resting her hand on Loch's shoulder who remained sitting. At that point, there were so many things she could have said or done. Instead, her only utterance was a simple command.

"Take me to my mother's grave."

Twenty-eight

"He saw me in you."

The three of them – Ivy, Loch, and Hamish – were sitting on Hamish's terrace. They had been served an array of fresh fruits and juices, as well as little cups of strong coffee by the woman who worked for Hamish. After Hamish had shown Ivy photographs of Rachel, as well as the few he had of Ivy before she was kidnapped, he had sat back and said quietly, "I didn't keep you safe before. I will never forgive myself for that. You said you came here because you're in danger. What must I do to keep you safe?"

It was Loch who explained the situation. He seemed to know what words to use so that the story was told succinctly, but with enough detail so that the chronology was clear.

"He saw me in you," Hamish repeated. "My father, Lord Douglas. You have your mother's coloring, but your body and features, though of course feminine and much more beautiful, are mine. Even if I had not been missing a daughter, I would have known you were of the Douglas clan.

"As I said before, I haven't seen my father in a long time – over 50 years now. It's a wonder to me that he's still alive, but the Douglas's are known for their longevity. Though with him, I think he's just too bitter and filled with spite to die.

"One thing my father was inordinately proud of was his common sense. He never believed any of the claimed sightings of ghosts or any apparitions, but he knew they provided good fodder for the tourists that he needed to come, as their fees helped pay for the upkeep of the castle and grounds.

"Seeing you would have been quite the shock. He had to deny your existence. If he accepted it, it would be a sure sign of senility. The Lord Douglas might accept tourists into his home as a necessary evil, but losing his mind, never!"

Ivy was silent, pondering Hamish's explanation. "But his reaction was so vile," she said doubtfully.

"It doesn't help that you're a bit like that painting that he keeps above his bed," Hamish responded. "After all, doppelgangers are often seen as harbingers of bad luck."

"Could you repeat what you just said," Ivy asked.

"That doppelgangers are seen as harbingers of bad luck? Look-alikes of a living person are often portrayed as a paranormal phenomenon, but then, you're not really a double of that painting. The resemblance is strong enough, though, that my father could find it unsettling. A little too eerie to digest if one is already feeling vulnerable when it comes to one's mental state."

Ivy looked at Loch, but she didn't say a word. Loch looked at Ivy, and then he did something neither Ivy nor Hamish expected. Loch put his head back, and he laughed, loudly, and whole-heartedly.

At first Ivy just watched, but the sound was so unabashedly merry, that Ivy couldn't help but join in. After all the emotions that had been churning inside of her all day, it was a relief to hold nothing in. She laughed until tears began to seep from the edges of her eyes.

"What a welcome sound," Hamish said, unable to keep from smiling, "but quite honestly I don't understand what is funny."

"I blamed Loch for this entire mess," Ivy explained, wiping the tears from her cheeks. "I blamed him because he said I looked like the woman in the painting. Now you're telling me that I'm not related at all."

"Sheer coincidence," Hamish replied without hesitation. "Sheer coincidence."

"He says I'm a Lady now." Ivy nudged Loch playfully in the side.

"You always were."

"No, I wasn't," Ivy laughed. "You know that very well."

"Lady Douglas, I respectfully disagree."

"Seriously, Loch? If you recall, I was furious at you. I treated you atrociously."

"Quite wrathful," Loch said cheerfully, as he pulled Ivy up higher on his chest. "But, a lady nevertheless. And as it ends up, rightfully so."

"Rightfully a lady or rightfully wrathful?"

"Both," Loch answered, "as the proper title of a daughter or granddaughter of a Lord is Lady, and I was wrong about the painting."

"I accept your apology."

"I haven't apologized!"

"Actions speak louder than words."

"Oh, so you like …"

"Yes, all that you did to me."

"I could do more."

Ivy nodded in contented agreement, but as Loch's hands began to rove freely over her body, she whispered into his ear, "and I'll do things to apologize for my spiteful anger."

Loch was going to protest that she had done nothing wrong, but then she began to nibble on his earlobe and move her hands downward. For all his effort, Loch could not concentrate on the words or remember what it was exactly he meant to say.

Ivy awoke to the smell of fresh pressed coffee. She sat up in bed and took the cup from Loch. He was already dressed. Despite tucking a stray tendril of Ivy's hair behind her ear, he got straight to business.

"Hamish texted me from the airport. He's already on his way to Scotland. Even though he is sure that the answer is no, he is going to Castle Douglas to make sure there is no connection between his father and your assailants."

Loch hesitated for a moment and then said, "He's a good man, Ivy. He's going to Scotland for you. "He's not going to rest until he knows you are safe."

"Can you imagine," Ivy said, "going home after staying away for 50 years? I wonder how he will feel."

"You can ask him," Loch said. "He's giving you space, but you should have seen his face when you gave him that hug good-bye. He's not going to let you out of his life, even if you don't allow him in."

Ivy abruptly changed the subject. "So that's being cleared up, but …"

"I'll get to that. Vinny, Marcella, Wes, we're all working on it, but first I want to say something."

Ivy made a slight grimace and asked, "Am I going to like it?"

"It's part of what makes you a Lady."

Ivy looked puzzled, but before she could say anything, Loch put his fingers to her lips.

"When Hamish asked you about your upbringing, all you told him was that you were adopted into an American family. Then when Hamish expressed relief that you had been taken care of, you didn't say anything to make him think otherwise. You just told him America is a rich country."

Ivy shrugged. "The past is over. He has suffered enough."

Ivy saw something in Loch's eyes, but she wasn't sure what it was. She looked at Loch inquiringly.

"You're a Lady, Ivy," he said with finality. "Born and self-made. Let's leave it at that."

"It's of no matter," Ivy said as she got out of bed. "What matters," she said saucily as she turned her head and looked at Loch before entering the bathroom for her morning ablutions, "is whether the Lady's knight in shining armor can help protect her!"

"Where to now?" Ivy asked as she appeared dressed and ready to go.

"Back to New York City for you."

Ivy stood completely still. "And you?" she asked slowly.

"I'm going to Brazil – Sao Paulo."

"I can't go with you?" Ivy looked at Loch with narrowed eyes.

Loch shook his head. "Ivy," he said tilting up her chin so she had to look at him. "I'm already on my way back."

But he wasn't. It had been a week, and Ivy was furious. With eyes blazing she stood in the office of Dalziel Traders demanding that Marcella tell her where exactly Loch was.

When Marcella didn't answer, Ivy leaned over the table. "Tell him, then, that I'll be in Sao Paulo."

"Ivy, you need to stay here."

"Marcella, unless you tell me what's going on, I'm disappearing. And that will be without my bodyguard. Either I'm part of this, or I'm not."

Marcella sat back in her chair. "He went from Brazil to Uzbekistan," she said slowly.

"Uzbekistan?" Ivy said, wrinkling her nose. "One of only two doubly landlocked countries in the world. I learned that by watching Jeopardy, and that about sums up all I know. Why Uzbekistan?"

"He's been sparing in his details, but …"

"But what?"

"He keeps having me track the sale of paintings."

"Paintings?"

"All done by famous and fairly famous artists."

Ivy thought for a moment. Then she said without question, "But all the artists are dead."

"Yes!" Marcella answered. "How did you know?"

"Han van Meegeren came to mind."

When Marcella looked inquisitively at Ivy, Ivy explained. "van Meegeren painted some fake Vermeers. One of his tricks was some complicated system of baking his paintings so they appeared aged. Over the years, he was able to pass off millions of dollars worth of art. His forgeries hung on the walls of world class museums.

"He was caught for having sold a painting to a Nazi during World War II. That was an act of treason, punishable by death. He confessed to the forgery in order to save his life, but no one believed him!"

"This is unbelievable," Marcella said. "Did they kill him?"

"No," Ivy answered, but he had to paint a 'new' Vermeer at his trial to prove that he hadn't sold the Nazi a priceless original. I think he ended up only spending a year in prison, but you have to understand that the museums and collectors that had purchased his forgeries were very upset. Their reputations were damaged, and they were out millions of dollars.

"He's not the only forger who has rocked the art world. Just a few years ago, they were able to trace at least 25 forgeries to some obscure French collector-turned-dealer named Giulano Ruffini. The Louvre in Paris actually started a fund-raising campaign to purchase one of the fakes that came through him! They called the painting a 'National Treasure!'

"There were a bunch of fake Joan Miró, Pablo Picasso, and Henri Matisse drawings uncovered in Spain, and then there was the Knoedler forgery ring right here in New York. They specialized in the abstract expressionists, like Jackson Pollock and Mark Rothko.

"Art forgeries are big bucks, and the thing is that once one pays an astronomical amount for a painting and has had it authenticated by one's experts, as well as the experts at auctions hours like Sotheby's, one really doesn't want it exposed as a fake."

"So, one single forgery, once discovered, could really have a domino effect," Marcella said, thoughtfully.

"Just imagine," Ivy said, "If one had proof that the Mona Lisa was a recent copy! The true painting stolen some years ago, and the Louvre kept it a secret! About six million people go every year to view that painting. No one would want to lose that crowd. Think of the revenue it brings in! And the prestige."

"What does prestige matter when I've got my love?"

Ivy turned to look at Vinny, but not before seeing Marcella's cheeks turn a rosy tinge.

Vinny rolled his chair up to Ivy. "Have you heard?" he asked. "Or did she tell you?"

Marcella came around to give Vinny a kiss on his cheek. "I haven't had a chance to tell her," she said. "We've been discussing other things."

"I'm getting a bionic arm!" Vinny couldn't contain himself. The words came bursting out of his mouth. "I'm going to be able to open a drawer by just thinking 'grab, drawer, pull'! Ivy, I'm going to be two-handed again!"

Vinny's excitement was palpable.

"Oh," she said, tears coming to her eyes. She bent down and kissed Vinny on the cheek and then hugged him as hard as she could. "You've always been man enough for me."

"But he's mine," Marcella said. "We're getting married!"

Ivy was not going to let her questions about Loch drop, but she wasn't going to allow anything to take away from Vinny's moment.

"I thought you didn't believe in mixing business with pleasure," Ivy teased Marcella as she stood and gave her a huge hug, too.

"Business is done and over with," Vinny said. "It's all copacetic."

"Over? You're not working for Loch anymore?"

"Where'd you get that idea? I'm now full-time."

"Business is over …" Ivy said, her voice trailing off.

"Coach, are you losing your edge?" Vinny answered. "Your case is all done. Loch's just tying up the details."

"Is this true?" Ivy asked, looking directly at Marcella.

Marcella said, "Basically, yes."

"And the details are what?"

"I'm not sure exactly," Marcella replied, "but you shouldn't go to Uzbekistan. Loch is going to be coming home very soon, and he will explain everything."

"Uzbekistan," Vinny said. "Did you know that's one of the only two double land-locked countries in the world? The other one is

Liechtenstein. Liechtenstein is surrounded by two landlocked countries – Switzerland and Austria, but Uzbekistan is surrounded by five. All of which, I am sure you begging to know, are countries that end with 'stan.'"

"So, what are the five?" Marcella asked. "I can think of Afghanistan and Tajikistan, but for the rest I'm drawing a blank."

"Kazakhstan," Ivy said, "that's the third." Then she and Marcella looked at Vinny, waiting from him to tell them the names of the remaining two.

"There's only so much a man can know," Vinny said.

When Ivy and Marcella burst out laughing, they were told that they could google it if they were really interested.

"I'll ask you next time I see you," Ivy said to Vinny.

"Where are you going?" Marcella asked quickly.

"Not to worry. I won't be going to Sao Paulo or Uzbekistan or any *stan* country for that matter. If Loch really is just tying up details, then I think I'll go ahead and put my name back on the list at work. I might be able to pick up a few deliveries today."

"I really think it better …"

"Marcella, I'll be fine. And please tell that bodyguard that she can go home. It's a little creepy knowing that someone is following you everywhere you go."

"You do know, Ivy, how hard it was to find her? Loch insisted that we get one who was at the level of a competitive bike rider. They're not a dime a dozen."

"You mean I could have been riding all this past week?" Ivy said, trying to hide the ire she felt. She had stayed off her bike out of consideration for the guard. She hadn't wanted her to get in trouble for not being able to do her job!

"That's it, then," she said. "I'm leaving."

She kissed both Marcella and Vinny while offering her congratulations again and headed for the door.

Twenty-nine

Ivy had been teased mercilessly when she showed up in the control room about losing her top courier status due to all the time she had been away, but Ivy knew it all good-natured. "I'll get it back," she had told all the other riders as she sipped some of the horribly bitter black coffee that was there for the taking but always seemed to be the second to last cup in the pot.

When Ivy took her first call, she found it almost indescribable how good it felt to be back on her bicycle. She felt herself "relax" for the first time in too long, as she had to clear her head of all else and concentrate solely on road conditions and potential hazards. Despite the insouciance she had showed about any potential harm that could come to her, she had been unnerved. The fact that she had allowed Loch to hire a bodyguard for her upon their return from Colombia was proof of that. Her only condition had been that the bodyguard had remained largely unseen. Life now, as she put her body down to decrease wind resistance and maximize her speed, had at least come back to a degree of normalcy.

Ivy had just completed her third drop when her two-way radio cackled and phone rang simultaneously. "Ivy," she said into the radio, opting for work first.

"Special request came in for you. Word must have gotten around pretty quick that you're back. Do you want it? It's close. No rush. You could have two flats and still make it in time."

"Yes!" Ivy said, laughing. "I'll take it!"

Although she had a good idea of where she was going, Ivy entered the address into her phone in order to view some potential routes. Google maps was showing that traffic was blocked on one street, but Ivy figured she could hop onto the sidewalk and cut several minutes off her time. Feeling no rush, she checked her email.

There were two unread messages from Hamish Douglas. Ivy still hadn't gotten comfortable calling him her father, but she had read every one of his emails. He had been sending her daily messages since their meeting. Some had been only a line or two, but others had described a memory, a thought, or a discussion about a particular book or piece of music. Despite her reserve, Ivy had to admit that she enjoyed receiving them. He was a good writer, and his comments about what was going on around him were proving him to be a keen observer with an insightful wit. She hadn't responded to all of them, but she had sent a brief note saying that she was enjoying reading them. And although she didn't say when or where, she had said that she looked forward to seeing him again.

The first message was brief but succinct:

The weak cannot forgive. Both your grandfather and I are very strong men. You were the impetus to make us stronger. We both are in your debt.

The second message was even shorter:

P.S. He did think you were a familial ghost. When you come, you will be met ONLY with a loving hug by all.

As Ivy regained her seat and began to pedal, she couldn't help smiling. She so wanted to share the messages with Loch! The entire

Scotland trip had not turned out at all like anyone had expected, but it had turned out well – very well – nevertheless.

The address was at the end of a dead-end alley. As Ivy sped down it, she shivered involuntarily as she entered its shadow. The buildings on both sides appeared derelict, and they were both high enough that they effectively blocked any sunlight from entering. Ivy didn't feel any fear due to the building's facades, as many old factories in New York had interiors that had been turned into amazing and vibrant spaces. What she didn't like was the gloom.

There was no place to lock her bike, but Ivy, familiar with that situation, pushed it through the metal door when it buzzed open. Once inside, she took off one of the wheels and then locked the remaining wheel to the bike frame with two different kinds of locks. Ivy knew her bike could still be stolen, but two different locks and the lack of a wheel did a lot to making a bike very unattractive to anyone with nefarious intent.

Although the pick-up was on the seventh and top floor, Ivy decided to forego the elevator. Wheel in hand, she entered the stairwell and began to race up the metal stairs. Before Wes's accident, he had told Ivy about a race called the Empire State Building Run-up. The competition took place once a year in the iconic tower, and the top runners raced up the 86 flights – 1,576 stairs – in less than ten minutes. Wes had told Ivy that they would do it together, and at that time, Ivy had started the practice of using the stairs or taking the elevator to ten flights below the delivery floor and then running up the remainder in way of preparation. Although there was no mention of the race after Wes became wheelchair bound, Ivy had kept up her practice of only partial use of the elevator when she felt the yen.

It was rare that Ivy met anyone in a stairwell, but when she did, she had never found cause for alarm. She heard voices coming down when she reached the fifth landing, and seeing a couple who looked to be in their early twenties, she simply smiled and continued on her way.

"Doesn't it make you angry?"

Ivy had gone a few steps up before she realized that the question was directed at her. "Excuse me?" she said, turning mid-stride.

"Those jerks on the top floor — filling up the elevator with all their crap so no one else can use it. They've been going up and down all day, and when we complained, they just ignored us."

"Top floor — that's where I'm headed," Ivy said. "I'm doing a pick-up."

"Just make sure you get paid ahead of time," the taller of the pair said. "They're closing up shop."

"Thanks for the tip," Ivy said. "Business is always hard."

"Especially art," the second person answered. "Now that is one volatile market."

Something registered in the back of Ivy's mind. An image of Marcella at her desk telling her that Loch was asking her to track the sale of paintings flashed before her eyes. And what was it that the dispatcher had told her? That her name had been specifically asked for with this delivery.

Yet Marcella said that Loch was on his way home, and Vinny hadn't objected when she had said she was going to try and get in a couple of delivery runs. Ivy felt a stab of uneasiness, and for a brief moment she thought of calling in for back-up. She wouldn't even have to say why. Bikes were always breaking, and though most messengers carried around some tools and could fix or at least jerry-rig most anything faster than any mechanic in a bike shop, there were many times when messengers just had to call it a day. No one could ever know exactly what part was going to be needed or what damage a bike would suffer.

"Paintings?" Ivy asked, trying to keep her voice casual and devoid of concern.

"Yeah, and by what they were driving, they did pretty well."

"Or were," laughed the taller person as they continued down the stairs.

Ivy watched them for a moment, and then gazed uncertainly up the remaining flight of stairs. "Don't be ridiculous," she said firmly to herself. "You're feeling spooked, but there's no such thing as ghosts. Even Lord Douglas knows that now!"

Jaw set, Ivy climbed up the final steps and stepped out into the hallway, being careful to shut the door very quietly behind her. Looking around, she saw only two doors. One was to the elevator, and it was on the same wall and to the immediate left of the door she had just exited. The other door was directly across the elevator, and it was open.

Very quietly, Ivy walked to one side of it and looked in. The expanse seemed to stretch forever, as there were only evenly spaced round pillars to provide constructional support rather than walls. Paint splotches covered the floor, pillars, tables, and legs of easels. It looked like an artist's loft, but there weren't any paintings.

"She's here!"

Ivy turned to the voice, and saw a man and a woman spreading what appeared to be a large, heavy canvas on the floor at the edge of the far wall.

"Come here, please," the woman said, beckoning to Ivy.

As Ivy approached, the woman turned and said something to the man that Ivy couldn't hear. It was when the woman turned and Ivy saw her profile that Ivy knew who she was. She was the woman who had followed her that day after she had crashed her bike when someone tried to run her over. Ivy was sure of it!

Just as Ivy could sense sometimes when she was on her bike that she needed to turn or that someone was coming up behind her,

Ivy knew that something was greatly amiss. She had to run, and she had to do it now.

Without saying a word, she simply turned and bolted toward the door. If she was wrong, then so be it. She would suffer the wrath of the lost clients and her boss, but she could live with that. If she was right, then she could not escape fast enough.

Ivy heard a shout as she began to run, and then she heard the sound of heavy feet pounding after her. That was when she knew had been right to bolt. Over the years, she had had many strange delivery calls, but no one had ever chased after her! A wave of panic flashed over her as she thought of the canvas. Was it for her? Were they going to wrap her in it?

Her fear only increased her adrenaline, and she sped through the door into the hallway, seized the handle to the stairwell door, flung it open, and began to leap down the stairs, two at a time. When she turned the corner at the landing, she took a quick look up. She only saw the man following her, and she guessed that the woman was taking the elevator.

Ivy could hear the man gaining, the thud of his heavy boots pounding on every stair. Ivy was hampered by her messenger bag and her wheel, but she didn't want to drop them. Her phone and radio were in the bag, and getting them out now would take too long. And the wheel? It was no longer a wheel. It was a weapon. Ivy would turn and thrust it hard into the man's Adam's apple if he got any closer. Or at least she hoped to.

Ivy was panting by the time she reached the main floor, but the man had slowed enough that she had sufficient time to open the door. Grappling at the handle, she flung it open and there, facing her, with what could only be described as an expression of evil, was the woman. Ivy didn't hesitate for even a fraction of a second. She kept on running, full force, and instead of using the wheel against the man, she used it on the woman. Holding it in front of her, Ivy rammed the woman with it. She had meant to hit her in the neck, but she got her directly on the nose. The woman let out a scream of pain, and for a moment seemed bewildered at all the blood that began spurting from her nose and pouring down her face.

Ivy continued to run. She reached the exit door, but out of the corner her eye as she was pulling it open, she saw that the man had exited the stairwell and was racing toward her. Ivy knew that he had seen what she had done to the woman, and he would be prepared to protect his face and neck from the wheel. So, Ivy did what he wasn't expecting.

She bent and heaved the wheel as if it were a frisbee. She let it fly right into his shins. It hit him on his left leg as he was striding forward, and then as it fell to the ground, his right foot stepped on it, causing him to lose his balance. As he tumbled ungainly to the floor, he let out a string of profanity.

Her heart pounding so hard that Ivy could feel it hitting the sides of her chest, Ivy flung open the door and ran outside. Her intent was to dart up the alley as fast as she could.

She couldn't. The alley was blocked.

Thirty

"There's something Vinny wanted me to tell you."

Ivy's mind reeled. It took her a second to understand what she was seeing. Wes was sitting in his wheelchair, just a few feet from the door. His van was blocking the alley, and Ivy could see Nora sitting in the driver's seat. She was speaking into a phone that she was holding up to her ear with her right hand, while the left hand was out the window, waving someone or something forward.

As Wes spoke, a bike rider shot through the narrow gap between Wes's van and the building. Two more came sidling through, and then Ivy heard the sound of sirens.

"Behind me!"

Wes snapped the words as the door began to open. Ivy didn't hesitate. No gazelle with an entire pride of lions after her could have leaped as quickly as she did.

When the man and woman burst out, blood still pouring out of the woman's nose and covering her chest and hands, they looked as startled as Ivy had.

"They're taking pictures!" the man cried, immediately covering his face as he pushed the woman back inside. That's when Ivy noticed that everyone, including Wes, had their cell phones out and were taking videos.

As the door closed behind the attackers, Ivy felt her entire body begin to shake. As yet another bike rider came from behind the van, Ivy squatted down next to Wes in his chair, hugged her legs, and looked at him. She couldn't speak, as her entire body had begun to tremble, but she waited for Wes to explain how he and everyone else came to be there.

"Kyrgyzstan and Turkmenistan."

Ivy stared at Wes incomprehensibly. She didn't understand anything he had said. The syllables might have as well been in some alien or futuristic language.

"Kyrgyzstan and Turkmenistan," Wes said again, his eyes lighting up with mischievous laughter. "That's what Vinny wanted me to tell you."

When Ivy still blankly stared at him, Wes said, "The two remaining *stan* countries – the ones that surround Uzbekistan. Vinny remembered, and he said you would want to know."

"It would be quite hard to live without that knowledge," Ivy said.

"That's why Loch wanted you to know as soon as possible."

Loch! Ivy's heart had finally begun to regain its normal rhythm, but Ivy felt her pulse quicken with the sound of his name.

"Is he here?" Ivy asked.

Wes knew that he was one of the people Ivy was closest to in the entire world. Yet when she had asked her question, Wes knew that his position had changed. There was something in her voice that Wes recognized. Wes was okay with it. He had Nora. Now he knew Ivy had Loch.

"He's the one who sent us. He'll be here any minute, I'm sure. The way he was raging on the phone, there was nothing else we could do but get over here. He would have killed us if we hadn't."

"I think," Wes said, as several police cars came racing down the alley, "that there isn't anyone Loch hasn't called."

Ivy didn't care about the police officers who came hurtling past Wes's van. She didn't care about all the bike riders that seemed to keep pouring forth. What she cared about was that the door to the building she had fled from, in fear for her life, was opening.

When she saw the worried look of the man who exited, his jaw set as if in steel, she let out a cry and rushed forward.

"Loch!"

She had only time to utter the one syllable of his name before she was lifted into the air and swept into his arms. "Ivy, Ivy, Ivy," he said over and over again, as he held her close.

Her legs wrapped around him, Ivy was half laughing, half crying, as all her questions came out garbled together. "How did you know? Where did you come from? How did you get here? Where are those …"

"Oh, my love, I'll explain it to you all, but first …,"

Easily continuing to support her with just one hand, Loch cupped the back of her head with his other hand and bent his lips to her own. The kiss was a drink of nectar. It was a message of love, of want, and of desire. It was an exchange of souls.

"I have a gift for you. Do you want it now?"

Ivy looked at Loch and laughed. "Aren't you supposed to wait until after the ceremony?"

"There's nothing traditional about anything here," Loch said, as he grabbed Ivy's hand and brought it to his lips.

"That's right," Ivy said primly, as she withdrew her hand. "You weren't supposed to see me in my wedding dress until the ceremony, and I'm sure you weren't supposed to see me putting it on!"

"Someone had to zip it up!"

"Ah, and since you were the one who unzipped it, you would know best how to zip it up."

"I like it."

Ivy cocked her head and looked at Loch curiously. "Like what?" she asked.

"How we're getting married."

Ivy's eyes danced as she snuggled against Loch, savoring the feel of his chest behind the softness of his white linen shirt. "You said you would leave it all up to me, as you were completely wrong!"

"You're making me sound awful, but as long as I have you, then you can say anything you want about me."

"To think," Ivy said, "that it had nothing to do with Scotland or that picture above the bed. It was all due to that painting I saw in your office!"

"All due to a simple pineapple," murmured Loch. "A lowly bromeliad that set off the downfall of one of the most successful forgery/money laundering operations in the world."

"Who knows how long they could have continued if they hadn't gone after you," Loch said musingly. "I don't think I would have looked into it. Why would I have? I was able to return the painting, and at the time, that was sufficient."

Ivy couldn't help but give a little shiver as she remembered how she had been hunted. "Out of all the things people have called me," she said, "I've never been considered an art expert."

"How words can make a difference," Loch agreed. "Robert is a brilliant financial manager, and in truth, his ego helps make him as good as he is. When he was dealing with returning the painting, he didn't want to admit that it was – what was it he called you – a *simple little messenger girl* who authenticated it as a forgery. He thought calling you an art expert provided more merit. He had no idea what chain of events his giving you that title would set off. He is truly sorry, Ivy."

"Yes, he's told me so," said Ivy, "and I don't blame him for anything. Why should I when all that matters is that I have you?"

"I like hearing that," Loch said. "Should we make it official?"

"I guess we could go out," Ivy said.

"Make our grand entrance?"

"Not so grand as when you came out that building!" Ivy said, still feeling astonishment at the remembrance.

"I knew you had to be in there," Loch said tightly, his muscles tightening at the thought of what might have happened to Ivy.

"So, you just jumped from the roof of another building and through a window …" Ivy said, shaking her head.

"It's not impressive. I went through an open window."

"Oh, well then," laughed Ivy.

"Oh, Ivy, if something had happened to you …" Loch couldn't stop himself from grabbing Ivy and holding her tightly in his arms.

"I'm safe," Ivy said, laughing, as she pushed him away. "And now we should really go get married. Nora's going to be in a dither until it's over, and you know how she wants everything to go just so. She's taking this best groomsman thing pretty seriously."

Loch said, "I still can't believe that she's my groomsman and not your bridesmaid."

"You're unhappy with your groomsman? I just thought since I was Wes's, she should be yours."

"No, no! I told you I was happy with all your decisions, and I mean it. I love that Nora is my groomsman. I love that you're wearing a red dress."

"I wanted intimacy," Ivy said softly. "And I wanted my loved ones. You, Wes, Nora. Hamish because one day I will regret if he wasn't here, and your grandmother and parents because they are part of you. Perhaps I'm being selfish with such a small gathering, but it's what I wanted on this day."

"You forgot to mention your flower girl."

Ivy looked confused. "I don't have one. Nora's our wedding party. I didn't want anyone else. I told you – my team, my workmates, your friends, your grandmother and parent's friends – they can all come to the party we're holding later. Lots of great food and dancing. No presents. No hassle. A Merriment Bash."

"A Merriment Bash. Yes, I agreed to that, but …"

Ivy's face paled. "You know I wanted intimacy," she said quietly. "Please don't tell me that this has turned into a huge public affair …"

"Let's go."

Ivy smoothed her hands down the sleeveless sheath that fitted exquisitely over the curves of her body. Her voice troubled, she said, "Tell me …"

Loch didn't tell her anything. All he said was, "Trust me, Ivy. Trust me."

At first Ivy had no idea who the young woman standing by Wes and holding Nora's hand was. All she knew was that she had never seen a person look happier. The young woman may have had the body of a young lady, but she was more like a young puppy, trying not to wiggle and burst out of her skin. Ivy slowed her step, looking first at the young woman and then back again at Loch.

And then it hit her. Ivy stopped walking and looked at Loch in surprise. "How did you …" she started to say, and then she couldn't say anything else because the young woman with Down's syndrome raised her voice.

"I told everyone you're my angel. That's what my mom calls you. I'm Tricia, Ivy, and you're my angel who kept me safe. And today I'm your flower girl. There are no bad people here today, Ivy. Only good people."

Languidly, Ivy curled up against Loch in the huge bed. She rested her head against him while she trailed her fingers down his chest with one hand. "We really should get up," she said softly. "Not all of a honeymoon should be spent in bed."

"Why?" asked Loch, gently stroking all the places he could reach without moving from his supine position or disturbing Ivy. "You've made time immortal."

Ivy was silent for a moment, and then she said, "Say that again."

"What?"

"You know," she said raising herself so that she lay directly on top of him, her chin resting just below his collarbone so she could look up at him. "That thing about time."

The words were spoken gently but with all of Loch's being. "You've made time immortal."

Ivy's gaze was soft, and though she felt something well up and spread throughout her entire body, she had no words to say. All she did was turn her head to the side and let her cheek rest on Loch's chest. She knew when she felt his heart beat beneath her own, that she was home.

Epilogue

It was the day before their honeymoon was over. Loch had gone for a run, and Ivy was in the back stacks of a used book store. She had wandered in to get out of the rain, but the serendipitous miss-match of titles and subjects had kept her moving deeper into the store's piles of serious tomes, dated works, and pulp fiction. She had decided that she would return to the more lighted areas of the store when she happened to see a small ink drawing. It was resting flat, on a waist-high pile of books.

Ivy picked it up and carried it over to a little alcove with a window so she could examine it more closely. What she saw delighted her so much that she immediately decided to buy it for Loch. It was a bucolic scene of an Italian peasant who had stopped working in a hay field so as to eat his lunch of bread, cheese, and tomatoes that he had spread beside him on his striped woolen scarf. His weariness was apparent as he sat, his legs outstretched before him, but his face was turned up, as if he were looking to the heavens to thank God for all of his bounty.

"This isn't a copy. It's an original woodcut," Loch said with delight when Ivy gave it to him. Look at the detail just in the man's arms."

"I know," Ivy said. "Scarred, but strong. The artist must have had an incredible knowledge of anatomy."

"I read once that Leonardo da Vinci performed dissections on bodies he had dug up in secret. All so he could understand how the human body worked and how to draw it."

"That may be so, but this drawing has nothing to do with da Vinci."

"How do you know that? It's obviously Italian. It wouldn't be the first masterpiece to show up in unexpected places. Some guy in Indiana once covered a hole in the wall with a painting he had bought along with some old furniture for all of 30 dollars. Then, some years later, he's playing some board game where you try to outbid the other players for artwork. One of the cards in the game was of a painting by the American artist Martin Johnson Heade. The guy thought it looked a bit like his painting, so he asked around. His painting was worth more than 30 dollars. Much more! The guy ended up selling it in 1999 to the Museum of Fine Arts in Houston for 1.25 million dollars."

"That may be, but this one isn't worth any more than what I paid for it. I just liked it, and I thought you would like it too."

"Are you sure it isn't from da Vinci's time?"

Ivy looked at Loch incredulously. His eyes were twinkling, but still, she wasn't sure if he was serious or not. She didn't know until he laughed and pulled her to him.

"That tomato," he said. "It's that tomato in the painting. It keeps getting in the way."

About the Author

Ruth Foster started this book in Indiana, but she finished it while spending seven amazing months in Colombia. Seeing the torrent duck was a highlight, but nothing can compare to the people she met there who so generously and warmly opened up their hearts.

Made in the USA
San Bernardino, CA
05 November 2018